EIGHT PEOPLE. E

THE BOARD ROOM

NEW YORK TIMES #1 BESTSELLER TONY LEE WRITING AS

JACK GATLAND

Hooded Man MEDIA

INSPIRATION ★ PRODUCTION ★ PUBLICATION

Published by Hooded Man Media.

Cover design by L1 graphics

First Edition: February 2023

PRAISE FOR JACK GATLAND

'This is one of those books that will keep you up past your bedtime, as each chapter lures you into reading just one more.'

'This book was excellent! A great plot which kept you guessing until the end.'

'Couldn't put it down, fast paced with twists and turns.'

'The story was captivating, good plot, twists you never saw and really likeable characters. Can't wait for the next one!'

'I got sucked into this book from the very first page, thoroughly enjoyed it, can't wait for the next one.'

'Totally addictive. Thoroughly recommend.'

'Moves at a fast pace and carries you along with it.'

'Just couldn't put this book down, from the first page to the last one it kept you wondering what would happen next.'

There's a new Detective Inspector in town...

Before The Boardroom, there was DI Declan Walsh!

An EXCLUSIVE PREQUEL, completely free to anyone who joins the Jack Gatland Reader's Club!

Join at www.subscribepage.com/jackgatland

Also by Jack Gatland

THE LIONHEART CURSE

STANDALONE BOOKS

THE BOARDROOM

AS TONY LEE

DODGE & TWIST

For Mum, who inspired me to write.

For Tracy, who inspires me to write.

CONTENTS

T-MINUS TWENTY

DEVIN MACINTOSH WAS IN THE MOOD FOR A CELEBRATION.

The champagne was on ice; the lights turned down low, the room-service oysters now at room temperature and, if he was a little honest, not up to the par he'd expected from the hotel.

The Madison Hotel was as "five star" as you could get, and to rent a suite, even for a Sunday night, was more than most of the staff at the hotel earned in a month.

Devin called it "pin money".

To be brutally frank, though, Devin wouldn't spend so much on such a frivolity; he wasn't one for bells and whistles. Sure, he enjoyed a steak dinner like the next guy, but he was just as happy chomping down on a Burger King bacon double cheese with onion rings – as long as he didn't have to sit in the bloody restaurant, that was.

Those places stank of poverty.

And Devin Macintosh hated poverty.

This wasn't some kind of irrational hatred; this was because one time – many years earlier – Devin had been one of those poor, penniless bastards, scraping a living in any way he could, regardless of the legality of the situation. In fact, it was why, many years later, Wrentham Industries poached him from their closest rival with a rather impressive benefits package, including his own box at Madison Square Garden, and the use of a couple of executive suites at the Madison Hotel.

As he'd said, Devin wouldn't spend on such a frivolity. He expected someone else to cover the cost for him.

Lying on the bed, the satin sheets crumpled, Devin ran a hand through his hair. For a man in his late forties he looked good for his age; at least a good five or ten years younger. This was partly because of his exercise regime, and also because of the hair plugs he'd gotten around five years earlier, when he'd seen his family's genetic disposition for balding had knocked upon his own door.

His wife had called it a vanity exercise and a waste of money, saying he didn't need to do such a thing, that he was "still attractive without hair". But he'd called her a hypocrite, pointing out she'd happily let him pay for her new breasts, and the conversation drew to a close.

Still, they both got what they wanted.

But, for all his complaints about costs, Devin had his fancies. His underwear, currently the only thing he was wearing right now, was worth more than the average suit of his corporate team, and his watch, currently on the sideboard next to his expensive, top-of-the-range phone cost six figures.

But neither of them were as beautiful as the woman laying breathless on the bed next to him. In her late thirties, her own expensive and incredibly flimsy lace underwear had been half removed already, occurring during their first play fight, her incredible breasts free from restraint and quite frankly, in Devin's opinion, spectacular, no matter how much money they cost.

Rising, Devin leaned across those spectacular breasts, grabbing one of the two champagne flutes on the side table. Downing it, he toasted her.

'Happy anniversary,' he said, and was about to speak again, to say something more, maybe even about love, or something equally sappy when the woman grinned, leant closer, and bit him hard on the arm.

'Ow! You bitch!' he hissed, snapping back as she laughed at his response. 'Dammit Gina! Don't leave marks! I exercise with the Board tomorrow morning! How will I explain teeth marks to Miles or the others when we're on the treadmill?'

'Tell him you have a very healthy sex life, while your CEO's cock is covered in cobwebs.' Gina lounged now against the bed, her hands gripping the silk sheets, inviting him to retaliate against her.

To retaliate *on* her.

'You should punish me,' she said, in an apologetic "little girl" voice. 'Punish me, Daddy.'

Devin smiled in response, tossing the now-empty champagne flute across the room as he rose on his knees, towering over her as they—

The phone on the sideboard *pinged*.

'Leave it,' Gina ordered.

'It could be important,' Devin's attention was now split between the gorgeous, half-naked woman in front of him, and the glowing screen of his phone, just that little too far away to see what the message was.

'*I'm* important,' Gina snarled, and gone was the apologetic little girl. 'If it's life-threatening, they'll send you an email. Or they'll call your PA and she can call you.'

'It's Sunday. She's not at work.'

'She's your PA. She's *always* at work, even when she's home.'

The phone *pinged* a second time. Not a reminder for the message, but a new, second message.

'I swear to god, Devin,' Gina hissed. 'You touch that goddamned phone and I'll punish you.'

'Be serious,' Devin replied, the fun now drained from the situation, rolling across the bed and grabbing the phone. Gina tried to stop him halfway, but he slipped past her, grabbing the phone and holding it high, out of her reach as he looked up at the messages displayed on the screen.

9-1-1 BOARDROOM

9-1-1 BOARDROOM

'Crap,' Devin slumped down, showing Gina the messages. 'I've been called in.'

Gina snatched the phone from him, staring down at the last message, as if hoping that by doing this, she'd somehow change the text on the screen.

'It's all in capitals,' she said, furrowing her brow. 'It's never in capitals when they send this.'

'I know.'

'This probably doesn't mean anything good,' Gina looked up at Devin now. 'Are you in trouble?'

'Why the hell would you think I'm the one in trouble?' Devin now hissed, straightening, as he faced Gina. 'There's nine of us on the Board. Why can't one of them be the one in trouble?'

'Because you're a sneaky, backstabbing shit, and you've always been half a step ahead of everyone else and a firing squad?' Gina suggested. 'Tell them you're sick. Tell them it's a Sunday night and God said you could have the day off.'

'Not with that code,' Devin shook his head, already walking over to his trousers and pulling them on. 'You don't get that unless someone's shit the bed on a massive scale.'

'So, let the person who shit the bed clean it up,' Gina replied.

'*I'm* the one who usually cleans it up!' Devin exploded.

'It's what they pay me an extortionate amount of money to do! This isn't a debate or a negotiation, Gina! I've got to go in!'

He stared at the ceiling, considering the other members of the Board.

'Bloody Victoria will go, and she's at her kid's recital tonight.'

'Yeah, but she hates her kids,' Gina pouted. 'You can't go! It's our anniversary!'

Devin, currently pulling on his dress shirt, paused, nodding.

'It's not fair, and I get it,' he said, now sitting on the bed placing a hand on Gina's arm. 'And it's really not how I wanted to spend the night with you. But I have to do this. It's why I get the perks I get. It's why I get …'

He waved a hand around the suite.

'… this.'

Gina said nothing, but her confrontational body language was softening as she glared at Devin.

'This is shit,' she said.

'I totally agree,' Devin leant in, kissing Gina lightly on the lips. 'It'll only take an hour or so. Wait here, crack open another bottle. Go wild on room service. Try to beat the amount we spent here two years back.'

Gina frowned at this as Devin rose, tucking his shirt into his trouser band.

'Do you actually pay for the room service?' she asked suspiciously. 'Out of your own pocket?'

'Fuck no!' Devin laughed, now texting his driver to get off his ass and meet him out front. 'Do you think I'd suggest it if you were spending *my* money?'

Gina folded her arms now, still angry at what was happening.

'I'm not happy about this, Devin,' she said as he pulled on

his socks. 'There might be ... consequences ... when you come back.'

Devin slipped his shoes on and, grabbing his jacket and tie, he blew Gina a dramatic kiss.

'Promises, promises,' he mocked.

'I'm serious!' Gina shouted at Devin as he walked to the door of the hotel suite. But by then he'd already gone, the memories of the beautiful, topless woman in the lacy under-wear now replaced with concern about what was so bad, that someone had to send the DEFCON text.

He knew it wouldn't be good.

The driver was waiting for him outside the hotel as he stormed out, still doing up his stupidly expensive tie as he nodded at him.

'Got your message,' the driver said, without any hint of sarcasm towards the tone of the message, as he opened the door. He waited for Devin to enter before closing the door behind him, walking around to the driver's side, and taking off his own cap as he entered.

Now looking over his shoulder, the driver smiled.

'Home or work, sir?' he asked.

'Why the fuck would I be going home?' Devin snapped, looking at his watch as he did so. The time read 7:02. 'Take me to the office. And knock that stupid fucking smile off your face.'

He'd had the driver, a young, irritatingly handsome Albanian for at least three months now, and as he berated him, Devin realised he'd never once asked what his goddamned name was. He had a very brief moment of concern, a wonder whether he should ask the driver now, but this was wiped away quickly by the simple fact he didn't really care.

Now admonished, the driver turned back to the road, and Devin pressed a button to his side, relaxing as the privacy window rose between them.

Devin hated having to make polite conversation with the drivers. He hated to make any conversation, to be honest. Again, the issues of his past, of having to converse with lower classes rose its head, and Devin reached across the limo seat for the small drinks cabinet, held within a side compartment. He poured himself a whisky, downing it in one hit, and wiped his mouth with his hand before pouring out another glass.

Looking out the window, watching Manhattan pass by, he sighed.

'Fuck.'

Pulling out his phone, he stared at the repeated message one more time.

9-1-1 BOARDROOM

What the hell had happened? Was it a takeover? Maybe Miko Tanasha, that backstabbing bitch, was finally making her play. Either way, he'd lied to Gina; this would not take an hour. Just getting the contrary bastards to sit at the table was going to take half of that.

Sighing audibly, Devin dialled a number on his phone, holding it to his ear and waiting for it to connect, watching the privacy screen intently, as if expecting it to drop at any moment.

After a couple of seconds, the call was answered.

'Hey, it's me,' Devin smiled as he spoke into the phone. He didn't feel like smiling, but he'd been told once by Jason Barnett, director of sales, that if you smiled when you spoke down a phone, you sounded friendlier. Personally, Devin thought it was bullshit, and he thought Jason was nothing more than a mercy hire, but he was happy to try it at that point. 'I've been called into a Board meeting.'

There was a pause as Devin listened to the voice on the other end of the line.

'It's the message,' he said. 'The bad one, and you know what that means. I could be there all night.'

Another pause, another conversation from the other end of the phone.

'I know, but there's nothing I can do,' Devin rubbed at the bridge of his nose as he replied, trying to keep his voice calm, to not shout. 'It's gonna be a late one, so kiss the boys for me and I'll see you when I get home.'

He looked back at the privacy wall; it was up, but the glass was opaque, and he could see the driver's eyes through the rear-view mirror, watching him, maybe even judging him for the conversation he was having right now with his wife, at home, with his children, unaware of any anniversary tonight.

'I love you too,' he said, looking out of the window, unable to allow the driver to see his eyes as he lied, disconnecting the moment he said this, holding the phone in his lap.

He'd fire the driver tomorrow, he decided, as he poured himself another whisky, settling back into his seat. The nosey bastard was too interested in what his betters were doing. Or, rather, *who* they were doing.

And that simply wasn't the way they did things around here.

You had to *gain* the power first, before you started black-mailing.

The office was dark, and he liked it that way. He could have put the lights on and seen better what he was doing in the office, but he didn't need to. The light from the chrome and glass building opposite was enough for him, bleeding through the windows, casting shadows across the room, hitting the rifle on the floor.

He crouched now; the window was floor-to-ceiling glass, tempered and strong, but not strong enough to resist the glass cutter he placed against it, making a rough circle before using a suction cup to bring the now detached piece of glass back into the office.

The last thing he wanted was for it to fall the other way, crashing to the pavement a dozen floors below him.

Someone might call the police, and that would not do.

They weren't in his plan until later.

Now with a hole in the window around a foot off the ground, he climbed down onto the carpet tiles of the office and, laying prone, he took the rifle, placed the muzzle through the opening, only an inch or so out into the night air, but enough to provide a clear shot. The rough circle was large enough to aim his sight through, too, focusing on the lit-up boardroom on the other side of the street, as he unclicked the arms of his stand and readied the rifle, aiming it at the window.

This done, he started on the second part of his plan, pulling a roll of duct tape out of his duffle, and preparing a space beside the sniper rifle.

The night hadn't even started yet, and he was already excited about what was about to happen.

For tonight, *justice* came to Wrentham Industries.

T-MINUS FIFTEEN

THE LIMO PULLED TO A STOP OUTSIDE THE MAIN ENTRANCE TO Wrentham Industries at seven-fifteen pm. For the journey, through midtown and in the middle of theatre traffic, to only take that long was actually good, but Devin wasn't going to let the driver know this, instead stepping out of the car the moment the door was open and slamming the now empty whisky tumbler into the driver's hand.

'You should have been faster,' he hissed.

'I couldn't have been any faster,' the driver replied with a surly 'sir,' added after a second's delay. 'The only way we could have been quicker was if I jumped every red light—'

'Next time, jump the red lights,' Devin snapped back, emphasising each syllable with a tap of his index finger on the driver's chest. 'Your delay of even a minute could have cost the firm billions.'

'I'll try to remember that for next time, sir,' the driver replied, stone-faced. Devin almost laughed. He was starting to like the driver. He could even see a future for the man – if he wasn't firing him first thing Monday morning, anyway.

'Do you want me to wait for you?' the driver asked, still staring dead ahead, not even trying to catch Devin's eye.

'No, you're done for the night,' Devin yawned. 'I'll get an Uber back to the hotel when we're done. It'll be faster than you can do it.'

'Very good, sir,' the driver replied and, irritated by this, Devin waved his hand dismissively.

'Just piss off, yeah?' he said, turning away from the car and already starting towards the door. 'You're making the building look lower class.'

As the driver, silently fuming, strutted back to the driver's seat, Devin smiled. He didn't have to be such a dick to the guy, but if you didn't use the power, what good was having it? That great power and great responsibility bullshit was the stuff of superhero comics, and those arrogant, spandex-wearing fags weren't real.

Another car pulled up at the side before he reached the door, and Devin turned to face it as the driver, almost identical in looks, size and uniform as his soon-to-be-fired one, walked around hurriedly and opened the door. Devin wondered whether there was a particular company that only hired chauffeurs that looked like that, but then stopped with a grimace as he realised who was getting out of the car, and therefore would share an elevator with him.

Victoria Harvey was a grade-A, diamond-carat bitch. In her late thirties, but constantly claiming she was five years younger, she was fit as hell – Devin had to give that to her – and currently wore an expensive mink jacket, with an extortionately expensive handbag under the arm.

She seemed to have a better relationship with her driver than Devin did, as shown by the slight but visible finger trace along the driver's arm as she told him to wait for her.

They're probably screwing, Devin thought to himself as he

faked a smile for the cheap seats. *And if not already, they will be later.*

Walking up to Devin, Victoria didn't even acknowledge the fact he'd held the door open for her, waltzing through and into the lobby as if she expected him to do such a selfless act.

Devin *hated* Victoria.

As they fell into step, walking across the lobby and nodding at the security guard behind the counter in that way people do when they really don't expect to be stopped, Victoria looked over at Devin.

'You smell of fucking,' she said. 'Can't be your wife, it's not her birthday.'

'Always a pleasure,' Devin ignored the jibe as he motioned for the guard at the elevator to call for the carriage.

'Do you know what the hell this is about?' Victoria continued. 'Bloody cloak and dagger bullshit always gives me ulcers.'

Devin raised an eyebrow at this.

'Wait, you didn't call it?' he asked. 'I assumed this was as dramatically drama queen as you can get, so it had to be you or the Asian.'

Victoria sniffed as they entered the executive elevator, the guard leaning in to press the button for them, because *God forbid* they should have to lower themselves to such an act.

'I was at my daughter's recital,' she muttered irritably. 'Had to leave three songs in. Are they called songs? I don't know. All I know is someone had better have died for this, because I'm missing important moments in her life.'

'They usually do die when we get calls like this,' Devin puffed out his cheeks as he watched the number slowly climb upwards. 'I've only had the 9-1-1 once since I arrived. And that was when Ryan whatshisname jumped out the window.'

'God, I forgot about that, the stupid bastard,' Victoria

tutted. 'Still, you should be careful, Macintosh. You almost sound like you give a shit.'

'Just stating a fact,' Devin flashed an incredibly insecure smile. 'How was the recital?'

'Fucking abysmal,' Victoria moaned. 'You'd think with the amount of money I was paying, she could play a vaguely recognisable tune. If I hadn't been there when she was born, I'd wonder if she was actually mine.'

'So, with you here, is she with her father right now?'

'Why the hell would I do that?' Victoria stared at Devin with the expression of someone staring at the most stupid man in the room. Which, in her mind, she probably was. 'He's not been around for months. Living in Barbados, I think. No, she's with the au pair. Hopefully, they'll both be asleep by the time I arrive home.'

Reaching into the inside pocket of her mink coat, Victoria pulled out a small, silver pill box. Opening it up, she took out one of the pink pills from within between a finger and thumb, popping it into her mouth.

'Ah, the usual pre-meeting ritual,' Devin smiled. 'Sharing your sweets?'

'Acid reflux,' Victoria replied as she closed the box up. 'Been suffering for a little while now. Probably the stress of being near you, and the other pricks I'm going to have to suffer tonight.'

'Or, it's because you take a tablet every time you enter the elevator,' Devin winked. 'Maybe you're overdosing on your … acid reflux … tablets.'

Victoria said nothing, simply flipping Devin the finger.

'Well, as long as it doesn't turn into a really painful, maybe even *cancerous* ulcer,' Devin said with mock sincerity. 'That would be terrible.'

The doors opened onto the twenty-third floor, and with a

wave of his hand, Devin offered Victoria the option of leaving the car first.

'Fuck no,' she said, motioning for him to take the lead. 'If the shit's hitting the fan, I'm not the first one walking in. You're junior to me. You can be the meat shield.'

Laughing, Devin walked out into an empty, open-plan corridor, the workers on this floor long gone. Only a single cleaner still worked at this hour, a man in his thirties, brown hair under a red baseball cap, headphones on over the top, his face half-hidden as he cleaned the marble floor beside the doors.

Victoria wasn't watching the cleaner as closely as Devin was, however, and bumped into him, her silver box falling to the floor, clattering over to the man as he quickly picked it up, and, rubbing his sleeve on the wet side, where it had fallen on the mopped floor, he passed the box back over to her.

Victoria didn't thank the man, instead snatching the box back and, this time, adding it into the inside pocket it'd originally come from.

'Piss off and do that later,' Devin snapped at him, backing away a little as he walked past the man, resisting the urge to pull out some antibacterial hand gel.

The man grumbled, and then walked into the elevator before it closed, pulling his mop and bucket behind him.

Watching him, Victoria was amused by this.

'Worried you might catch "poor" if you stood too close?' she mocked as they continued down the narrow corridor that led to the boardroom. 'Prick.'

'I wasn't the one who had him wiping his dirty arm all over my property,' Devin muttered.

Victoria went to reply to this, maybe even recover her box from the pocket and wipe it down herself for good measure, but stopped as a sudden thought came to mind.

'What if they're already making alliances?' she hissed,

trying to look through the glass walls of the boardroom as they approached. The angle wasn't good for spying, but she could see Miles Fenton in the doorway. The CEO of the company was fat, balding, red-faced from years of neglect, and was currently checking his watch. 'We should team up. Strength in numbers.'

'Yeah, right up till you stab me in the balls, Brutus,' Devin shook his head. 'I'll take my chances alone, thanks. Besides, I think it's Miko.'

'You do?' Victoria almost clawed at his arm, to pull him back to ask more, but Devin had already walked into the boardroom, and it forced her to follow suit.

The boardroom itself was swish and futuristic. One side, facing into the office, was opaque glass, blocking the view into the office space, giving secrecy – and the main reason Victoria hadn't been able to count the deals happening inside. The other side of the boardroom was a wall of full-length glass windows, looking out into Manhattan. It would have been an incredible view, if it wasn't for the fact that fifty yards away another building, a half-lit floor matching the level of this room, stood, a black monolith in the night, and blocking any postcard panorama.

Devin hated the location here. It meant his office, up on the top floor, could only see half of Manhattan. And, annoyingly, nobody else wanted to help him get the other buildings destroyed, even when he'd drunkenly mentioned he knew men with demolition experience, and was happy to "Fight Club" the whole damn city to get an unobstructed view.

The room itself was nothing more than a boardroom table, with twelve seats at it. In the middle of the table was a conference call phone, a remote next to it, and this remote controlled the massive flat-screen television on the wall at the end. This was mainly used for presentations and suchlike, or when one of the Board couldn't be bothered to attend and "Zoomed" in from their homes, or even, on one occasion when he was so hung over, from his office two floors up – as Devin simply couldn't muster the strength to walk to the elevator.

Apart from that, the room was quite sparse. Against the opposite wall was a mahogany side cabinet, where the bottles of water were placed, and the bottles of scotch were hidden in the deep filled drawers. Devin paused as he realised each drawer now had a small brass number on it – probably some other bullshit HR idea for productivity, decided by Miles while fucked on Ketamine.

Devin was sure Miles took that. Or something similar. After all, it wasn't as if Miles didn't know someone who could get it for him in this very room. Because nobody could be as mind-numbingly boring as Miles Fenton and *not* be on horse tranquillisers.

On top of the cabinet were a coffee machine and a microwave, and Devin made his way straight towards it. He had a feeling this was going to be a long one, and he needed caffeine.

'You're late,' Miles chided both of the new arrivals.

'Piss off, Miles,' Victoria snapped, also ignoring him as she walked past. 'You're only here on time because you've got nothing else to do.'

It was definitely not the sort of language expected at a boardroom meeting, and Miles looked abashed at the insult, but said nothing as Victoria turned her attention to the rest of the room.

'And that goes for you brown nosers too,' she said, pulling off her mink jacket and slumping it onto the back of a chair, its back to the window, effectively claiming the space before anyone else could.

There were six other people in the boardroom, either sitting already at the desk or standing, talking in hushed whispers to each other, probably considering the same short-term alliances that Victoria had, or texting angrily on their phones, annoyed to be called out.

First, there was Jason Barnett. In his late thirties, and in fact only a year older than Victoria, he was Wrentham Industries' fast-talking sales director – immaculately dressed in a sharp suit and a trendy tie, his hair on point, with a style screaming loudly he was desperately trying to stay in his twenties and looking almost as if he'd been waiting for the call, or hadn't actually gone home yet. Which, even though it was a Sunday, was probably the case. He seemed to live in the office.

Next to him was Tamira May, director of finances. She had just turned forty, as she'd had a really shitty party recently, where she spent the whole night getting more and more shit-faced while telling everyone she was fine, and life *began* at forty, all that self-help bullshit people told themselves when hitting a milestone year, before collapsing after doing some MDMA, better known as *Ecstasy* in its tablet form, and telling everyone her life was over. As far as Victoria was concerned, though, it wasn't her age that was stopping her from getting laid; it was the fact she was a mixture of angry Mom and stern accounting governess in her outward appearance; harsh and cold, wearing simple clothing that belayed her status and position in the company.

If Victoria was honest, Tamira was probably the one person here she was intimidated by, and not because she looked like an extra from the *Addams Family*.

Now with a coffee in hand, Devin also looked over the group, his eye instantly drawn towards a stunningly attractive Asian woman by the wall. Director of communications Miko Tanasha was one of the older members of the Board, only a year or two younger than Devin, but she still looked in her twenties, the bitch. A Japanese woman with steel in her eyes, she wore a simple yet expensive suit, and was watching everyone surreptitiously while pretending to examine her phone.

Devin wanted more than anything to take her there and then, on the table, but even if she wanted to – and he knew she definitely didn't – he already had Gina.

Oh, yeah. And his wife.

Beside Miko, however, was the complete opposite. Director of HR Hayley Moran, plump, bubbly and with a fondness for pastels puffed nervously on a Vape, pulling her cardigan close around her as she stared out of the window, looking out across the city – or at least as much as she could see, with a thousand-yard stare, her mind far away.

Devin tapped the top of his mouth with his tongue as he watched her, considering what he was seeing, and deciding it was a nervous, guilty woman.

Was HR Hayley the reason they were all here?

There was a loud, bellowing laugh from the other side of the boardroom table, and Devin looked across to see Eddie Purcell, an early fifties gangster of a man; in particular a man built like a brick shithouse and who looked like trouble no matter how expensive his suit was. His gold jewellery and signet rings rattled as he shook with laughter at something Miles said, but the moment the decrepit CEO turned around, Eddie's face became one of bitter anger, a stare that was literally burning through the back of Miles Fenton's skull.

The Wrentham Industries Board was here. All that was missing was Corey Gregson, director of legal affairs, but he was nearly always late.

There was, however, someone new in the room. Someone Devin didn't know. A young, scared-looking woman with long, mousey-blonde hair and horned-rimmed glasses, no older than her mid-twenties, sitting at the table with the look of a woman who really didn't know why the hell she was there.

'Hello,' he said, walking over and sitting down. 'Who are you?'

'She's Donna,' Hayley replied for her, sitting down across the table, away from Devin as she called across it. 'She's from the secretarial bay. To note the minutes.'

'Where's Trisha?' Tamira asked, looking at Miles. 'It's corporate policy to have your PA take the notes. There's too much sensitive stuff in these meetings for a simpleton from the secretarial pool to be involved.'

'Trisha's on vacation this week,' Miles replied. 'Don't worry, we had an email saying she'd signed off on Donna as note-taker in her absence.'

Tamira nodded at this, and the others, seeing people now sitting, made their own way over.

'Well, sit there and shut up,' Devin growled at Donna, while keeping his smile plastered on. 'Two ears, one mouth, yeah?'

'And if anything we say off the record turns up online?' Miles added, sitting at the head of the table. 'I'll personally end you.'

'She's just doing her job. No need for you both to be dicks about it,' Hayley snapped irritably as Donna reddened, as if horrified to find herself the subject of attention.

'Yeah, she's stuck here with you,' Jason joined in now. 'Give her a break.'

He finished this by giving a friendly wink at Donna, sitting back and looking at Miles, a smug expression on his face.

Devin forced the smile off his own face. The two of them were as bad as each other.

The young bull and the wounded old bastard.

Shame neither of them would end up on top. Not while he was around.

'If I wanted your opinion, Jason, I'd look for it in the gutter,' Miles muttered, and was about to continue when Jason rose angrily to his feet, the chair clattering to the floor behind him.

'Now listen here, you dusty old prick—'

'Guys!'

The word wasn't shouted, but it was spoken with such force that everyone stopped, even Jason, turning to look at Eddie, sitting beside the television.

'Can we just sort out why we're here and get on with it?' he asked, almost patronisingly. 'I dunno about you, but I got better things to do tonight. And I hate wearing a tie on a Sunday.'

'You didn't have to wear a suit ...' Jason began, but stopped. Of course, Eddie had to wear a suit.

They were on the Wrentham Industries Board.

There was a consensus of nods, before Victoria, frowning, spoke.

'Where's Gregson?'

'No show so far,' Eddie shrugged. 'Which is annoying, considering he was the one who sent the message.'

'You sure he did it?'

'I'm director of security,' Eddie smiled darkly. 'I *know* he did it.'

'He's probably pissed up in a bar. Again.' It was Tamira who added that, and as the two of them discussed the uselessness of Corey Gregson, Jason took this opportunity to look over at Victoria across the table.

'How was Lucy's recital?'

'Fuck off, Jason. Like you give a shit.'

Reddening, Jason backed off.

'Right then,' Miles eventually spoke. 'Let's get this Board meeting started while we wait for Gregson.'

He watched them through his night-vision sniper scope, stroking the barrel of his rifle as he watched them sit at the table, still arguing. They were probably wondering where Corey Gregson was, unaware that he was sadly unable to join them tonight.

Or ever, even.

They had no idea he was watching them.

They had no idea what he was about to do to them.

He smiled, pulling the bolt back, clicking the bullet into the rifle's chamber and smiling wider as the *ka-chuk* echoed around the empty office room.

It sounded good. *Righteous.*

Soon, there would be blood. Soon, there would be danger.

Soon, there would be *justice.*

And soon it would be time to start both the clock – and the game.

T-MINUS TEN

'Can someone call Gregson and find out where he is?' Eddie lounged against his chair, relaxed and for the moment looking like he was in charge of the meeting.

'What, you're unable to do it?' Devin mocked, pulling out his smartphone and showing it to the older man, Corey's currently empty seat between them. 'This is a phone. You type numbers into it and magical fairies make someone talk to you on the other end. Maybe you should take some rings off those sausage fingers of yours and give it a go?'

He looked over to Donna, leaning past Victoria to speak to her, still waiting to transcribe.

'I want it put on record that Eddie Purcell doesn't understand how a telephone works,' he insisted.

Donna looked nervously around and then picked up the pen.

'You write that down and I will fucking end you,' Eddie snarled at her. 'You know what I do here. You really don't want to make that mistake.'

As the secretary halted from writing, Eddie glowered at Devin.

'I didn't say I couldn't do it, you smug little prick,' he growled.

'No, you just acted like you shouldn't,' Victoria snapped from the end of the table. 'That you're better than us.'

There was a consensus to this, as the other members of the Board made mumbles of agreement. In response, Eddie flipped them all the finger, the showy signet ring on his finger glinting in the light.

'Jesus,' he eventually slumped back into his chair, the anger dissipating. 'I only said to make a phone call.'

Miles looked to Donna to his left.

'Please?' he asked, as Donna rose from her seat, leaning across and tapping the phone in the centre of the table.

'Call Corey Gregson,' she said, although there was definitely a nervous tremor in her tone. There was a beep as the phone followed the voice command, and through the room's speakers, the sound of a phone ringing could be heard.

'See?' Eddie muttered sullenly. 'Wasn't that bloody hard, was it?

On the television screen the display lit up. The details on record for Corey Gregson were now there for all to see: contact details including an image of him, date of birth, address, even likes and dislikes, all prepared for a potential video call.

There was a click, and then a voice spoke.

'Hello?'

Devin frowned. Corey Gregson was a Texas native through and through, and was super proud of his dumb, "yee-haw" accent. This voice, however, was clipped, definitely the East Coast. *A new assistant, perhaps?*

'Gregson!' Not noting the change in accent, Miles half rose from his chair as he shouted at the phone in the centre of the table. 'Where the hell are you? We've all turned up because of your blasted message!'

There was a long pause, and then the voice on the other end chuckled.

'Oh, I'm sorry,' it carried on. 'But I'm afraid Mister Gregson can't come to the phone right now … on the account of him being *dead*.'

'Yeah, whatever, dickhead. Keep taking those meds,' Jason now raised his voice as he spoke into the phone, before looking around the room. 'The prick's high. He's called us all in for a fucking wheeze.'

'That's not Gregson,' Devin whispered, an icy chill now travelling down his spine. He even looked around at the window behind him, as if expecting the breeze to have come from some open window.

'Bullshit,' Miles looked over at Devin. 'Of course, it is. We—'

'Called his cell phone number?' Devin shook his head. 'Gregson has a shitty accent, but it's still an accent. Unless he's pretending to be someone else, it *is* someone else.'

There was a moment's silence around the table as the others took this in, the scratching of Donna's pen against paper as she took these minutes the only sound.

'Bullshit,' Tamira shook her head. 'You're the one on drugs.'

She turned back to the phone on the desk, leaning closer as she spoke into it.

'Gregson? Is this you, or is—'

'Oh, I'm afraid Mister Macintosh is perfectly correct,' the voice spoke. 'I'm the voice of God. And I'm watching you.'

Jason, sick of this, rose to his feet in anger.

'Fuck this bullshit!' he shouted in impatient rage, looking around the table. 'I didn't come here to be screwed around tonight—'

'Shut up, Jason,' Victoria muttered. 'You were probably the only one of us actually still here already. For all we know, this is you playing around.'

Ignoring her, Jason turned his attention to the phone.

'You're sick, Gregson. If you called this meeting just to screw around—'

'Sit down, Mister Barnett,' the voice on the other end spoke.

Jason, paling, straightened, looking around the room.

'Nobody said I was standing,' he whispered, turning his attention back to the phone. 'How the hell did you know I was standing?'

'The same way I know that Mrs Harvey spends too much on fur, and that Mister Purcell is one cream cake from a heart attack,' the voice explained matter-of-factly.

At this, Victoria and Eddie glanced at each other in surprise.

'That's not an answer,' Victoria stated, loud enough for the phone to pick up. 'And it's *Ms*, not Mrs.'

'You're right, that's remiss of me, in both instances,' the voice continued, still relaxed, the clipped tones almost playful as it spoke. 'Let me explain myself more fully. Currently, I'm watching you all from across the street, through a Nightforce NXS sniper scope.'

Jason, still standing and facing the window, looked out into the city. The lights of the room turned the entire wall-window into an effective mirror, but the backs of the chairs were dark, and allowed him to see past the reflection.

'Bullshit,' he said. 'We'd see you.'

'Why would I want you to be able to do that?' the voice asked, confused. 'I don't want you to see me. If I wanted that, I'd be there in the room with you.'

There was a chuckle.

'Although I suppose I am, in a way.'

'Fucking games—' Jason growled, looking to move from the table, but the next lines from the mysterious stranger halted him.

'If you don't believe me, Mister Barnett, just look down.'

Jason didn't want to, but he slowly looked down at his chest, already seeing the horrified expressions from both Victoria and Donna, staring at him from across the table. And, when he looked down, he saw a little red dot of light, slightly wavering as it focused on his tie pin.

'I don't need the laser sight to kill you,' the voice continued. 'But I'm hoping you'll take this message as your only warning. *Sit down.*'

Without another word, Jason sat down, and the moment he did so, the little red light disappeared.

'Oh, this is marvellous,' Victoria sighed, leaning back into the chair. 'Well worth the trip. Stuck in a room held by a fucking nut bar.'

'Victoria!' Miko shook her head, her eyes wide, and Devin knew what she was trying to say.

Don't piss off the insane man with the sniper rifle.

Carefully, and with her voice forced to stay calm and considered, Miko leant closer to the phone.

'Look, I'm sure we can sort something out here,' she smiled reassuringly out at the window, knowing whoever was watching would see that. 'Tell us, what is it you want tonight?'

'A goddamned psychiatrist,' Eddie grumbled, raising his hands in surrender as Miko glared across the table at him. 'Tell me I'm wrong.'

The voice didn't answer her, but the television screen at the end of the room lit up, showing the image of an oil refinery on it. But the image was that of a disaster, a news report footage, the sound muted of the refinery burning at night, flames and smoke spewing into the air.

'Shit,' Miles whispered. 'He's got access to the system.'

'What do you mean?' Jason looked over at him, frowning. Miles, looking exasperated at the younger man, pointed at the screen.

'He turned on the fucking TV!' he half-shouted. 'What the hell do you think I mean? Christ, Jason!'

'Have you finished?' the voice spoke through the speakers. 'Yes? Good. So, as you can see, this is a photo from two years ago. Mercy, Arizona. The Protex Oil Refinery disaster. Remember it?'

Devin remembered it well; he'd been part of the team cleaning up the mess after it happened. And by "cleaning", he didn't mean turning up with a mop and some solvents – he meant silencing anyone who spoke out about this, usually with a healthy cash payout, or a threat to destroy their lives in court.

'Of course, we remember this,' Miles spoke for the Board. 'It was a terrible accident.'

'Accident?' the voice seemed surprised at the answer.

'Of course!' Miles replied, looking out of the window, as if trying to lock eyes with a mad killer watching him from an empty office window. 'What else could it be but terrible?'

'Terrible is an understatement, Mister Fenton.' Devin could sense a harsher tone in the voice now. Whoever this was, the answer Miles had given had angered him, and that probably wasn't a good idea, as the voice continued. 'Three hundred workers died, and over a hundred surrounding homes were destroyed as part of the accompanying blaze.'

'So, go shoot someone at Protex,' Tamira piped up now, folding her arms as she interrupted. 'This wasn't anything to do with us.'

'Are you sure about that?' the voice mocked, and on the screen images appeared: photos taken candidly, and unknown to the subjects within the photos. Images of members of the Board walking out of buildings, shaking hands with business-men, looking around, expecting someone to be watching. Devin saw one appear on the screen of him and a PR firm hired to keep this quiet – a firm that had been given a strict and pretty brutal NDA to keep silent about the work – sitting at a table in a cafe, the person Devin was meeting, whose name he couldn't even remember, signing a document. Another image, appearing a moment later, showed the document being passed across to him.

And he wasn't the only one in the photos – Victoria was seen cosying up with the Protex CEO, Miles was seen arguing with a known journalist named Stephanie Blake, and Eddie – violent Eddie – was seen holding some kind of protestor against a wall, his fist pulled back to punch him hard in the face.

'Fuck me,' Tamira, not seen in the photos, but understanding of what they were, whispered. 'It's show and tell time for Wrentham Industries.'

'You took photos of us?' Victoria, furious at seeing herself on the screen, shouted at the phone. 'What the hell?'

She looked at Donna, still writing.

'Stop noting this,' she said, leaning past Devin and pulling the notebook from the terrified secretary. 'Read the room! This doesn't get out!'

'It already has,' Devin said.

The photos disappeared, replaced with one image: a scan of a contract page.

'Five years before the fire, Wrentham Industries became the sole provider of Protex Oil Refinery's infrastructure,' the voice continued. 'Four years ago, Wrentham Industries, as part of a presidential decree, were forced to upgrade the pipe cladding around the refinery, protecting the pipes from the corrosive properties of the refinery substances, as well as the electrical systems within.'

'And we did that!' Tamira hammered a fist onto the table, the sudden noise and action making Hayley, two seats down from her, leap back with a yelp. 'We did everything those jobsworth inspectors told us to!'

'For the cheapest price. Your contractors undercut each

other, desperate for the work – and you sat back and forced them lower.'

Devin glanced at Miles as the voice spoke.

How does he know this, he mouthed silently, his eyes wide. Miles pursed his lips and tapped at a single word he'd typed onto his phone.

Gregson

Devin leant back. It had to be Corey Gregson. The stupid bastard had let his conscience go wild, and was now working with whoever this maniac was to soothe his own soul. The selfish goddamned bastard.

'We followed the White House's guidelines,' Tamira was still arguing with the mysterious voice. 'We did what they told us to do, and you can't have a go at us for that.'

'A new White House,' the voice retaliated. 'One that gave global businesses an easier ride.'

'So, vote differently next time!'

'Will you stop prodding the goddamned bear!' Miko hissed down the table.

Tamira, angry and sullen, sat back, her arms folded again.

'Fuck this guy,' she hissed. 'He's probably not even there. Some teenager with a laser pointer, tugging off in an empty office as he watches us shit ourselves.'

Jason, remembering his own brush with the laser pointer now, leant forward.

'It doesn't matter who gave us the guidelines,' he argued, his voice calm. This was a negotiation now, and these sorts of situations were his bread and butter. 'Do you have a name? What should we call you?'

'Call me … Justice,' the voice of the man, now known as *Justice,* replied. 'For that's what I offer.'

'Okay, cool, Justice,' Jason smiled at the window. 'I can

work with that. We did what we were told for the best possible price. It's simple business, and perfectly legal.'

'It might be legal, but it's morally criminal, and you know it,' Justice responded. 'The materials were substandard. The contractors were unqualified, and many of them used illegal immigrants, off-salary to keep wage costs down. They also, on your company's orders, cut back on fire drills and safety checks.'

'How the fuck does he know this?' Victoria muttered, mainly to herself and too soft for the phone. But Devin heard it and, as she glanced at him, he saw fear in her eyes. But not fear of being killed, no …

It was fear of being discovered.

'You created a death trap,' the voice of Justice continued, but now Devin turned to face the window.

'Bullshit. This is all circumstantial conspiracy crap,' he raised his voice as he argued the statement. 'We vetted everything on quality, not cost—'

'Do not treat me like a fool, Mister Macintosh!' Justice interrupted, his voice now raising in anger for the first time in the conversation. 'This Board signed off on every decision. And when the original contractors decided on a more expensive, safer alternative, this Board deliberately removed and replaced them, so as not to pay the difference!'

On hearing this, though, Miko, her eyes wide, looked across the table at Devin.

'Wait,' she whispered. 'Is that true?'

'He's twisting the facts. Fake news,' Devin responded, looking around to face her as he spoke. This didn't calm her, however.

'Is he twisting the facts?' she now asked Miles.

'Senate held an enquiry. We were cleared,' Miles replied coldly, the last part aimed out of the window.

'By people you paid off,' Justice responded.

'Prove that in a court of law, *you son of a bitch!*' Miles yelled, Jason leaning over and stopping him from rising, as he spat his words out at the window.

There was a long moment of silence after this. Justice was either deciding his next words, or he was waiting to see what the Board would do.

In the end, it was Donna, the secretary, who spoke.

'I shouldn't be here.'

Placing her pen on the table, she rose from the chair.

'You're all terrible people, I shouldn't be …' she began, her voice trailing off as she glanced out of the window.

'Sit down,' Miles ordered.

'No, no … I need to go. You all need to be here. I don't.'

Still standing, Donna looked at the phone in the middle of the table.

'I have a dog. She needs to be fed. I should be leaving.'

'I'm sorry, but if you leave the room at any point, I will be forced to kill you,' Justice replied, almost apologetically.

Ignoring this, and still shaking her head, Donna now backed away from the table, away from the Board.

'Sit the hell down, woman!' Tamira snapped, but this only seemed to speed Donna up as she carried on, backing away towards the entrance to the boardroom. 'You'll get us all killed!'

'This isn't fair!' Donna cried out at the window now. 'I'm not one of them! I didn't do this!'

'Please, get back in your seat,' Miles was half-rising again as Donna reached the door, still facing into the room.

'No, I think that I'm just gonna leave now,' she said, a faint, resigned smile on her face. And, turning to face the door, she opened it, the corridor in front of her.

And on her back, the red dot of a laser sight appeared.

'No! Don't—' Jason jumped up, shouting, but it was too late.

Donna took another step, walking out of the boardroom, but as she did so, the window behind her shattered as a bullet, fired from a sniper rifle across the street, smashed through it, continuing on and slamming into her back, exploding out in a blossoming spray of blood. She was blown forward by the force of the bullet striking her, landing in a heap in the corridor, blood from the open hole now pooling on her back, her eyes glassy and wide open in death as she lay face-down on the floor.

'I told her,' Justice said as the wind from outside whistled through the now open and shattered window. 'Now maybe you'll believe me.'

T-MINUS FIVE

'Fuck!' Eddie rose from his chair running across the room towards the door.

'Eddie! Sit the hell down!' Hayley pleaded. 'He'll kill you, too!'

Eddie, now at the doorway, stared down at the body of Donna, the unknown secretary from the pool, who'd had the bad fortune to be called up here tonight. She was lying on the floor where she'd fallen, dead; her back a mass of blood—

'You *chickenshit bastard!*' he screamed, looking around to face the window again. 'She was nothing to do with us! You killed a poor, innocent girl for nothing!'

'It wasn't nothing,' the voice of Justice spoke through the phone's speakers, his voice as calm as he ever was, as if the act of murdering an unarmed woman meant nothing to him. 'She didn't follow the rules. I needed to make a statement. She was the statement.'

'She wasn't a fucking statement, you madman!' Eddie was walking towards the window, furious, his knuckles clenched in anger. 'She was scared! We're all scared! You didn't have to shoot her!'

'Close the door and lock it.'

The order was calm and assured and came through the speaker. Instead, however, Eddie stood still, staring through the broken window, across the street at the building in front of him.

'Piss off.'

Hayley stood up, moving towards the door.

'Sit down, Miss Moran,' Justice continued. 'I asked Mister Purcell here to do it.'

'And Mister Purcell says eat his dick,' Eddie snarled. 'Can you hear that? Or should I shout a little louder?'

'For Christ's sake, Eddie, she was just a secretary,' Miles muttered. 'Just shut the bloody door.'

He paused as a realisation struck him.

'You weren't screwing her, were you?'

At this, Eddie turned in fury, about to march towards the CEO – now backing into his chair, aware he'd stepped over the line – but Eddie stopped as the red dot of the laser sight appeared on his chest.

'Nuh-uh-uh,' Justice spoke, and his tone almost gave the impression of a man waggling his finger. 'You hurt each other only when I *tell you* to hurt each other.'

'You'd better consider telling me to do it sooner rather than later,' Eddie growled, still staring at Miles. 'And no, I wasn't screwing her. I didn't even know her.'

'Then shut up whining and close the door,' Victoria grumbled. 'If anything, it's creating a wind tunnel and I'm bloody cold.'

'So put your expensive coat on, you callous bitch,' Eddie snapped as he walked to the door, taking one last, saddened look at the dead secretary on the floor, her eyes staring off, before closing it.

'And lock it.'

Eddie made a point of exaggerating the moves of locking the door – the windows facing into the office still turned opaque, blocking any view into the building from the boardroom.

This done, he now turned to the broken window and held both middle fingers in the air.

'Mission complete, motherfucker.'

There was the soft sound of laughter through the speaker. Justice was chuckling at this act of defiance. And, now deflating slightly, Eddie walked back to the chair he'd risen from, picking it up, placing it back into position and sullenly sitting on it once more.

There was a long moment of silence as Devin, watching both Eddie and Miles, wondered if Justice had disconnected. He was about to speak, to ask if Justice was still there, when Miko straightened in her seat.

'I shouldn't be here, either,' she muttered. 'I wasn't on the Board when this happened. It's before my time. Haskell's—'

'Neil Haskell crashed into a pickup truck two years ago,' Tamira said. 'I don't think he's turning up for this.'

'Either way, he was in my job when this happened,' Miko protested. 'I shouldn't be grandfathered into your screwups.'

'Well, you're on the Board now, so shut the hell up,' Victoria, pulling her mink coat back on, snapped across the table.

At this, however, Miko leant back in her seat, an amused expression on her face.

'Jesus, Vicky,' she laughed. 'What's this? Growing a spine for a change? What if I don't shut up, eh? You going to make me?'

She put up her fists in a mock boxing pose, waggling them at her rival across the table.

'You think I can't?' Victoria half rose in anger. 'Call me Vicky again. I fucking dare you.'

'Ladies!' Jason was the first to shout now, hands held up to defuse the situation. 'This is what he wants – for us all to fight. Don't give in to him.'

Sitting back on the chair, Victoria leant back, glaring at Miko as she grudgingly accepted the comment.

'This isn't over,' she said, eyes still locked on Miko's own. 'I'll finish you later.'

Miko's gaze didn't flinch as she glared back.

'Count on it, bitch.'

The boardroom was silent again, and Devin leant closer to the phone.

'Are you still th—'

'On the side cabinet, there's a microwave,' Justice spoke once more, and the shock of the voice returning made Devin sit back in surprise, as Hayley made a soft yelping noise across the desk.

'So, what, you're in the mood for a snack?' Eddie couldn't help himself, and turned from the boardroom table, once more watching out of the window. 'Want us to heat you something up, you sick—'

'Eddie,' Tamira hissed and, muttering under his breath, Eddie turned back, glaring at the others.

'You might all want to suck his dick, but I want out,' he said, likely meaning to whisper the statement, but coming out as a grumbling snarl.

'Then shut the hell up,' Devin snapped. 'Let's just get through this. See what he wants, do what he needs, and then get out.'

'Well said, Mister Macintosh. So good of you to volunteer.'

The voice was still amused as Justice spoke through the speakers, and Devin couldn't help the brief twitch he gave at the sound of his name, already checking down at his chest in case there was a laser sight showing on it.

'Volunteer? What did I volunteer for?' he asked suspiciously.

'Everyone, I would very much like you to now take your cell phones out and place them on the table in front of you,' the voice said. 'Don't play games, I know what you have on you. I know everything.'

'Yeah, yeah, you're the voice of God,' Tamira was already reaching into her bag to find hers.

'What about the girl?' Hayley whispered, looking back at the locked door. 'Should we … I mean, maybe someone should go and get her phone too?'

Eddie shook his head, making a "sucking cock" motion with his hand as he stared at Hayley, his disdain for her clear.

'If you continue to be an absolute ass, Mister Purcell, I will be forced to shoot you in the skull,' the voice of Justice snapped, and for the first time, the anger behind the words could be heard. Eddie heard it too and instantly stopped.

'Fine,' he muttered, pulling out his smartphone and slamming it onto the table. 'We ordering a pizza or something?'

'What about the girl?' Hayley, now returned to staring at the door, repeated.

'Oh, I'm afraid she's very dead right now,' Justice replied, his voice lighter once more. 'Best that you forget about her. You need to concentrate on the living, Miss Moran.'

There was a pause, and Hayley went to argue.

'Phone. Now.'

Hayley swallowed and nodded, reaching into her coat to pull her phone out. And, one by one, the others did the same.

As she fumbled in the bag, however, Tamira managed to quickly send a text out.

TO: DOPEY BITCH

911 board hostage sniper

'Mrs May, are you texting someone?' the voice of Justice asked, and Tamira jerked her head up quickly.

'No, I've just got a lot of shit in here,' she said, pulling the phone out, holding it up. 'See?'

'Don't lie to me,' Justice replied. 'The bag lit up. You opened your phone. What were you doing?'

The other members of the Board now looked at Tamira with the expressions of people knowing they were about to see a car crash, or worse.

Tamira looked at the phone, and pressed a finger onto the screen, allowing it to light back up.

'I'm just looking at my daughter,' she said, turning it to face the window, the image of a young girl smiling out at the sniper. 'It might be the last time I get to do so. You got a problem with that?'

'If that was what you were doing, then no,' Justice replied. 'But if you texted someone, I *will* find out. And then I will go to their home and I will gut them. Slowly. Is that what you were doing?'

Tamira swallowed.

'It was just a photo,' she lied.

'Is it on the cloud?'

Tamira hadn't expected the question and looked around, confused.

'What?'

'The photo. Is it backed up on the cloud?'

'I think so,' Tamira looked down at the smartphone, in case it could tell her the answer. 'Why?'

'Because you're about to lose it, if it isn't,' Justice explained. 'Mister Macintosh, if you would be so kind, please gather the phones, walk over to the side cabinet, and then place the phones in the microwave.'

'Now wait a minute,' Miles replied angrily, grabbing his phone back up. 'I don't—'

'There will be no waiting, Mister Fenton,' Justice interrupted, and Devin gathered the phones together, reaching across the table to do so. 'I think the people of Mercy have been waiting long enough, don't you?'

Grudgingly, Miles passed Devin the phone, and with them in his arms, Devin walked across to the side cabinet, opening the microwave door and tossing them all into the compartment, before closing the door.

'Now what?' he asked. 'Want them on defrost?'

'Don't make me say things twice, Mister Macintosh. I said all the phones.'

Once more, the relaxed tone was gone, replaced by a bitter anger.

'I've done that,' Devin argued, holding his hands in the air. 'See? All gone.'

'I must be mistaken then,' Justice replied. 'Let's test that theory. Please reach into the microwave, pull out your own phone and show it to me right now.'

Devin turned, facing the microphone, his stomach flip-flopping.

'You can't, can you,' Justice mocked. 'And why is that?'

'Because it's in my pocket,' Devin breathed apologetically.

'Louder and into the microphone, please,' Justice ordered.

Reluctantly, Devin turned and faced the table.

'I said it's in my pocket,' he repeated, louder this time.

'Oh, good, I'm not mistaken then,' Justice said. 'And just for future reference, Mister Macintosh, I suggest you don't treat me like an idiot again, or I'll shoot both your kneecaps out.'

Chastised, Devin placed his own phone into the microwave.

'You're such a prick, Devin,' Tamira muttered, loud enough for him to hear. And for a change, he realised she could be right.

'Now what?' he asked.

'Thirty seconds at high power will do it.'

'Do what?' Miles asked as Devin set the timer and walked back to his chair.

'What the hell do you think he's doing?' he snapped as he sat down. 'He's wiping the phones with the microwave's emissions.'

The microwave was crackling now as the energy passing through the electrical items inside began creating sparks between them.

'If that explodes and hurts me in any goddamn way, my lawyers will destroy you,' Hayley muttered, backing away on her chair as she spoke.

'I eagerly await their call,' Justice chuckled, his good nature returned. And, with a *ping*, the microwave turned off, leaving the boardroom relieved, if not still nervous.

'Your phones are now dead. Your exit is locked, and you've seen what I'll do if you attempt to unlock the door,' Justice continued. 'You are now under my control. Do you understand?'

'Yeah, we understand,' Miko snapped back. 'Just get on with it.'

'As practical as ever, Miss Tanasha. I appreciate that,' Justice replied. 'So, as I have your full attention now, let's discuss what's going to happen.'

'Let me guess. This is the ransom part, right?'

It was Victoria who spoke the words, but she wasn't the first person to think about it. Devin had assumed it was about money from the start, but his expectations had been altered the moment the secretary had been blown to pieces – people who want money rarely kill for pleasure.

Zealots and madmen, however, that was a different story.

'Ransom?' Justice seemed almost surprised by the suggestion.

'Yeah. You're not doing this for shits and giggles,' Eddie

muttered, this time not turning to face the window. 'Just give us your demands and fuck off.'

There was another pause, and Devin wondered if Justice had gone to find the sheet of paper with the ransom demands on but, after a few seconds, he started speaking again.

'As I have already pointed out, Wrentham Industries are to blame for hundreds of deaths in Mercy.'

'So, this is for them, right? Some kind of billion-dollar care package?' Miles forced a smile as he looked at the window. 'I'm sure we can discuss that.'

'Can we?' Justice asked. 'As of right now, nobody has ever taken blame for this, and dozens of families have no closure, or financial recompense for your – well, let's call it your cash-incentivised fuckup.'

'Well, then we can totally have that discussion,' Miles nodded vigorously.

'How wonderful! I'm so glad.'

Justice was in full flow now, and Devin felt there was a *but* coming down the line.

He was right.

'But as the old saying goes, "the buck stops here". And by here, I mean with you.'

There were a few seconds of silence, as the members of the Board did their best to understand what was being said here.

Eddie, however, started to slow-clap his hands at this.

'Impressive speech. Inspiring,' he stated sarcastically. 'You should do those self-help seminars.'

'Thank you. I try.'

'But you forgot one part,' Eddie turned to glower out of the window. 'You forgot to get to the bit where you tell us *what the fuck you actually want.*'

Hayley almost rose from the table, but it was a reaction to Eddie, an anger built from the fact that she was stuck here with him. In response, Eddie looked at her with a "what?" expression on his face.

'My demands. Yes.' Justice now sounded like he was weighing his words carefully now. 'How about these for demands? The Board of Wrentham must, and *will,* accept responsibility for the events leading up to the atrocities at Mercy.'

'No way!' Jason protested.

'We're not going to agree to that!' Miko joined in, siding with him. 'That's insane!'

'Oh, I don't expect you all to fall on your swords right now. After all, as Miss Tanasha said, she wasn't even here when you agreed to the route you decided to take,' Justice replied, the voice echoing through the speakers as if he was moving locations.

'So, I can go?' Miko asked optimistically.

'No,' Justice said, and there was almost a hint of sadness in his voice as he spoke.

'Then what?' Devin asked.

'Democracy,' Justice explained. 'The voting of a Board, just like you've done countless times before. But this time, it ends in someone's sacrifice. You have two hours to make your choice, or all of you die.'

DOPEY BITCH

Penny Martin hadn't expected to deal with any work issues on a Sunday night, and so she had left her office cell phone on the side table in the apartment's hallway since she had arrived home at eleven pm the previous Friday.

Penny had worked for Wrentham for over five years now, having started there after graduating college. She'd majored in English Literature, however, planning to become some kind of successful author, writing the "great American novel" everyone always spoke of completing, but instead, finding the newspapers and magazines starting to collapse and move to a digital platform, and seeing publishing houses nail down on what they accepted and didn't, Penny had quickly realised her dreams were just that.

And, after the fourteenth rejection of her magnum opus *"Aaron Burr and Alexander Hamilton, and their effect on historical literature's greatest rivalries,"* she decided that having money to eat and pay rent was a far better option than consistently living on writer's tears, so found the first job she could find, which happened to be in Wrentham's Corporate secretarial bay.

She hadn't trained as a secretary but she was quick to pick

it up, and her years of writing gave her a style of phrase and a speed of learning that soon got her noticed, and moving through the ranks, she eventually moved into the PA, or *personal assistant* dock, where she'd assist several of the bigger names on a daily basis. One of these had been Tamira May, who wasn't only one of the high-rollers, but was actually director of finance for the whole company, and one of the Board itself. At the start, Penny had been one of several PAs working for Tamira, but as the others all quit the firm, and nobody else wanted to work for such a bitch of a boss, Tamira May's reputation made sure that for the last year, Penny had been her only PA.

It was tough; Penny was doing the work of three people daily but, at the same time, Penny was aware this was her way up the ladder. Not only was she very visible as May's main point of contact, she'd spent the last three years learning every deep, dark, dirty secret about her boss, as well as several of the others on that level. And this meant she would, at one point soon, be in a position to demand her own seat at the table, or at least a far better executive position where she, too, could work her way to the top.

She was in her late twenties now, and Tamira was forty, so Penny was very aware she had to work fast if she wanted to be a company director, and by default the youngest Board member in Wrentham history.

That said, her family and friends couldn't understand why she wanted this. After all, for most of her life, she'd wanted a creative job, something as far from the nine-to-five roles as you could get, and Wrentham had not exactly had the most glowing of press relationships recently, with companies they'd invested in doing more damage to the country than doing good. None of it could be brought back to Wrentham's door, however, and Penny would *tell* people that every time the conversation came up. There had been investigations, especially with the recent Mercy incidents, and Tamira had held a meeting for everyone under her, informing them of all the findings, showing Wrentham to be in the clear.

Actually, it had been Penny reading a message out. But it was the same. Tamira's words from Penny's lips.

Although Penny had *written* them, too.

But Penny also knew the truth; she'd seen enough emails and messages thrown around, WhatsApp threads Tamira was part of that Penny moderated on her behalf, all talking about kickbacks and Government employees looking the other direction. She'd weighed up whether this was too much for her, whether she felt right lying to people about the company she worked for, but in the end she'd realised she was more the Aaron Burr than George Washington in this situation. As the musical *Hamilton* said, she wanted to be in "the room where it happened," and that was a conversation coming up very soon.

If she was honest, Tamira May wasn't that tough a woman to PA for; several of the others treated their PAs far worse, with one spending days every Christmas hunting for the perfect gifts for their boss's presents, only to find in return they'd been given a pack of crappy chocolates – usually the pack they'd bought for someone unimportant earlier that same month. Tamira didn't care about the niceties of things like Christmas, and so Penny didn't need to look for presents, as Tamira simply didn't give them out, saying to Penny to "get something taxable and sign off on it" for her own present.

Penny had given Tamira a present, once. It had been a very expensive bottle of whisky, almost four hundred bucks in cost, as a thank you for the faith Tamira had given in her abilities. The next week she'd seen it on a head of division's desk, and learned Tamira had passed it to him the very next day for "good work".

The "good work" she'd been talking about was work *Penny* had done on his behalf.

Penny never gave her another present. And, to be honest, Tamira never seemed bothered, as Penny had sat in her chair, worked at her desk, and waited for an opportunity to excel.

But not on weekends. Tamira May owned her body and mind from Monday to Friday, but weekends were her own.

And on this particular Sunday Penny Martin was sitting on her sofa, in sweatpants and joggers, her blonde hair pulled into a ponytail as she binged her way through some *Netflix* docuseries, while her boyfriend Mark put together a late dinner, which was likely to be frozen pizza and garlic bread. It was his "signature dish," after all.

Mark, a human Ken doll with zero fat on any part of his body, walked out of the kitchen, his tight t-shirt soaked.

'What the hell happened?' Penny asked, looking at him.

'Your freezer needed defrosting,' he explained, pulling at his t-shirt. 'And ice melts.'

Wincing at the wetness, he pulled the shirt over his head, now topless, as he watched the television from behind Penny's sofa. Penny refused to look back at him. She knew this was a ploy, that the moment she saw his tanned body and rock-hard abs she'd end up forgetting all about the television, or the rich people currently tearing each other apart on the show she was watching – his body was one of the main things she liked about him – and so she snuggled into the sofa, digging in against his advances.

His next advance, therefore, was to kiss the top of her head and start massaging her shoulders through the hoodie. She couldn't lie, this was an epic choice to make, as she'd been tense all week, and with a low groan, she melted into his hands.

'Mmm, keep going.'

'You're so tense,' Mark said, working down her shoulders. 'You need a break, Pen.'

'Miss May doesn't like people who take breaks. It shows

"weakness and a lack of fortitude" in them,' Penny purred as Mark now leant over, kissing the side of her neck as he slid his hands down her arms.

'Miss May is a prissy bitch who needs to get laid,' he replied.

At this, however, Penny pulled away from Mark, turning to face him with a mask of utter horror on her face.

'I wouldn't wish that on my biggest enemy,' she shook her head.

Mark frowned, knotting his eyebrows together, unsure of where this was going.

'Why?'

Penny smiled.

'I think she kills them after she mates,' she finished, as the pair of them laughed.

'Talking of May, her bat phone beeped while I was in the kitchen just now,' he said. 'I wasn't going to say anything, as I know you have your "no work rule" and all that.'

Now it was Penny's turn to frown in mild concern.

'What, just now?'

'A few minutes ago. Why?'

Penny went to rise.

'She never texts me on weekends,' she replied cautiously. 'Something's happened.'

'Leave it,' Mark held a hand up to stop her. 'Come on, I shouldn't have said anything.'

'You know I can't,' Penny was already walking to the door to the hallway. 'She's my boss.'

'Not on weekends,' Mark protested, following her. 'It's gone seven. You're home. Fuck her. She can wait until the show you're watching finishes, at least.'

'There's three more episodes.'

'Then she can wait three more episodes!'

Penny faltered, looking back at the television for a moment.

'I'll just check, make sure it's nothing major,' she said, her voice unsure as she spoke. Mark went to reply, but it was too late, as Penny had walked to the table and picked the phone up, turning its screen on.

She stared at the message on the screen, her lips thinning, her eyes narrowing in confusion.

'Shit …'

'You okay?' Mark came closer now. 'Is she okay? Not that I care or anything, but is she?'

Penny looked up, showing the message.

'I don't think so,' she said.

911 board hostage sniper

Mark read the message slowly, and then a second time.

'What does that mean?'

'I was hoping you could tell me,' Penny replied, already dialling a number into the phone, holding it to her ear as she waited for it to connect. 'It's like she's picked three random words and strung them together.'

'Sounds like she's high on something,'

'If only,' Penny smiled.

'Let me guess. Drugs lead to weakness and a lack of fortitude …' Mark's eyes widened with remembrance as he trailed off. 'Wait a moment, wasn't she out of her box on MDMA a week or so back? Her fortieth or something? Maybe it's a drug problem. Maybe you can use this to get rid of her.'

He frowned again as Penny disconnected the call.

'No answer?'

'It's going straight to voicemail.' Penny was trying the number a second time.

'So, leave her a message.'

'She never checks her voicemails,' Penny replied.

'How does she know if someone's called her?' Mark asked

and then laughed. 'Come on, Pen. Tell me you don't check her goddamned voicemails for her, too?'

Penny disconnected the call a second time, staring down at the phone.

'I should call the police,' she said, but stopped as Mark placed a hand on her wrist.

'Think about what you're saying here,' he shook his head. 'You're calling the cops on what could be just a prank text? A misplaced one meant for someone else. A fucked-on-MDMA fantasy post which, when they smash in her door and drag her off for drug use, she will not be happy for you to have alerted them?'

Penny had opened another app on her phone, now showing a map of Manhattan.

'What now?' Mark sighed.

'I have her cellphone on my "find my phone" app,' Penny explained as she scrolled into the map. 'It's so I know when she's coming into the office, or if she's somewhere else.'

'You're stalking your boss.'

'I'm being a fucking PA, Mark,' Penny snapped back. 'She's not showing up, but her phone was last picked up on the network about five minutes ago at the Wrentham building.'

'So, she's in the office.'

'On a Sunday night, at seven pm,' Penny shook her head. 'She sent this message a minute before the phone turned off. Something's very wrong.'

'Or she's playing silly buggers,' Mark sighed, turning towards the kitchen. 'Fine. Go wild. I'll leave you to it.'

'Don't be like that!' Penny exclaimed after him. 'She's my boss. I should at least flag this.'

'I know,' Mark smiled back at her. 'I was going to put some coffee on, while you call the cops. I think this is going to be a long night, and you'll need all the caffeine you can get.'

As Mark walked back to the kitchen, pulling his damp t-shirt back on as he did so, Penny stared at the message one last time.

911 board hostage sniper

Then, taking a deep breath and praying to anyone listening that this wasn't Tamira May screwing around, she dialled 9-1-1 on the keypad, and waited for the response.

'Police, please,' she said once the phone was answered. 'Hello? I'm … I'm not sure what I'm reporting, but it might be important.'

She looked out of her apartment window, across the city, towards where, if you removed all the various buildings between them, you'd see the Wrentham Industries building, and Tamira May.

'I think my boss is in terrible danger,' she continued.

120:00

THERE WAS A VERY UNCOMFORTABLE MOMENT, AS THE MEMBERS OF the Wrentham Industries Board now looked at each other. For the first time since they arrived, they knew not all of them were going to make it out.

'Explain what you mean by that,' Victoria demanded. 'You can't say shit like that and walk off. What does "someone's sacrifice" even mean? How do we take a vote on it? Why would we all die?'

'It's very simple,' Justice's voice was icy now as he replied. 'All you need to do, as a democratic company boardroom, is decide which one of you here will be the one that personally takes the blame for everything.'

'For Mercy?'

'For *everything*.'

Devin looked around the table again. Not only did they now know they weren't all getting out, they also had to vote on which poor bastard became the scapegoat.

'That's a death sentence,' Victoria whispered, her face ashen. 'Whoever takes that is committing career suicide.'

'Literal suicide, even,' Tamira added ominously.

Hayley had been sitting there, shaking her head, and now she shook more vigorously, almost rising from the chair.

'No, no, no …' her voice grew as she looked up. 'You can't be serious! None of us are going to do that!'

Eddie raised a hand.

'If it gets me out of here? I'll scapegoat you in a second,' he smiled. 'Who else votes for Hayley to be hung by the pitchfork brigade?'

'Shut up, Eddie, you're not helping,' Miles said, and Devin noted he wasn't as shocked as he had been earlier, and was, now he was more aware of what was going on, seemingly more professional.

Devin was impressed. *Maybe he was a good CEO, after all.*

'So, what's the deal?' Miles carried on, leaning closer to the phone. 'We sit up here and take a vote? Sure. Why not? I've nothing better to do tonight, even if the others do. My wife's out with friends, so she won't even know I'm gone until tomorrow.'

'A vote must be taken, yes,' Justice agreed.

'And what if we don't unanimously decide?' Devin added. 'What if we can't decide at all? When do we run out of time?'

'You're already running out of time,' Justice replied, and the simple statement sent more shards of ice down Devin's spine. 'I started the two-hour timer almost three minutes ago. Now you're a hair's breadth under two hours until the deadline.'

There was a pause as Justice let that sink in.

'A hundred and seventeen minutes now, to decide who keeps their salaries, their extortionate bonuses, even their lives, so to speak, and who sings the corporate hymn, stands in front of the waiting press and takes a bullet for Wrentham.'

'Waiting press?' Victoria looked around the room, as if

expecting to see them in the corners. 'And where are they right now?'

'Don't worry about the small things. Concentrate on your survival.'

The Board all spoke at once now, as each member wanted to make sure everyone else knew why they needed to survive.

However, after a few seconds, Devin spoke.

'Guys.'

Nobody listened to him though, and Eddie fidgeted, a sure sign he was about to do something reckless, and possibly suicidal, considering the circumstances.

'*Guys!*'

The boardroom fell into silence now, as everyone around the table stared angrily at Devin, having now risen to his feet.

'If you're about to sell your own case for survival here, you've sadly read the room wrong,' Jason muttered.

'We don't need to vote,' Devin smiled. 'We don't need to play his stupid game! The scapegoat's right here!'

'Where?' Miles asked, looking around the table at the others now watching him in return.

In answer, Devin stood staring down at him.

'You,' he said.

Miles rose to face Devin now, his face reddening.

'Now you look here,' he replied icily. 'You might think you're shit hot and all that, but I'm the CEO of the Board, and if you think—'

'Exactly!' Devin interrupted, snapping his fingers. 'You're the CEO! All roads lead to the top. Captain of the ship and all that!'

He pointed at Miles, who was no longer reddening – in fact, he was paling significantly.

'The buck. Stops. *There.*'

'At no point did I say I'd sign up for anything like this!' Miles protested.

'Go on, Miles. Go find your sword and fall on the damn thing,' Tamira smiled now, her eyes glittering as she saw a chance for survival. 'We'll hold a massive party when you're gone. Sorry, I mean a massive memorial. In your honour.'

She looked around the room.

'Too soon?'

'I'll bring cake,' Eddie looked over at Miles. 'I'll even hold the sword as you run onto it.'

'Piss off!'

'Look at it like this,' Eddie continued, now enjoying this. 'You're the oldest here, you're the one at the top, you were always going to be replaced, and it was never going to be willingly. Pretty much everyone in this room wants your job, and it was always going to be a hostile removal. This way, you get to do something good for a change.'

'And how do you see that?' Miles was getting flustered now.

'You get to go out in a blaze of glory, as you get your—' Eddie ran his finger across his throat, making a *krrrkkk* noise, '—retirement package.'

Miles looked horrified at Eddie, as Hayley nodded.

'As HR, it makes the most sense,' she said. 'Think of it like an old lion being put out to pasture.'

'Lions don't get put out to pasture!'

'I don't think she's talking holiday homes,' Eddie closed an eye, pointing a finger gun at the CEO and pretending to fire. 'I think she's talking about taking you around the back and "blam." Job done, "Old Yella" style.'

Miles looked in desperation around the boardroom, and then locked onto Miko, focusing his attention on her now.

'Miko's the newest member!' he exclaimed, pointing wildly at her. 'Surely it's more sensible to make this decision based on the adage "last in, first out," yes?'

'Fuck you, old man!' Miko rose to face Miles now, her fists clenched, her expression one of righteous fury. 'I've already said I wasn't here back then! Why the hell should I take the blame for your screw-ups?'

'You might not have been here when it happened, but you knew about it when you joined,' Jason muttered. 'That makes you worse than all of us.'

'And how do you work that one out?'

Jason shrugged.

'All of us here. We were in the room when it happened,' he replied. 'We were stuck with the situation, in real time, as it unfolded around us. You, however, you came in after it all came out, which means that you not only knew the problems, but you didn't give a shit about them.'

'It's like *Speed* with Keanu Reeves,' Eddie smiled. 'The one where the bus can't go under fifty miles an hour or it explodes? Well, we were all stuck on that goddamned bus, but Miko here? She willingly jumped on in Act Two.'

'Wait, are you saying Miko is Keanu Reeves here?' Hayley frowned.

'Does she look like fucking Keanu Reeves?' Eddie turned to her, his eyes widening in incredulity at the comment.

'But he got into the bus after it went over fifty,' Hayley argued.

'*It's just a film, Hayley!*' Tamira exploded. 'It's not even a good allegory!'

'Still makes the point,' Eddie sat back in his chair. 'She willingly came on board after this all happened. We should vote her out.'

'Piss off, Eddie,' Miko growled in anger. 'I know where your bodies are buried, too, don't you forget that.'

'Oh, no, hold that thought, I need to tremble in my boots for a moment,' Eddie mocked.

'Hold on,' Victoria said, looking around, frowning. 'Hold on.'

'What now?' Devin sighed, sitting down. 'I gave you a solution already.'

Victoria leant closer to the phone now.

'What happens if we don't, or can't, decide within the next couple of hours?' she asked cautiously. 'You said we all die. How?'

'Ah, I'm glad someone had the sense to ask,' the voice of Justice echoed through the room's speakers again. 'I had a PowerPoint made for this very question. If you could all look at the screen?'

Slowly, the members of the Board all turned to look at the television at the end of the table, where the image of an underground garage appeared.

'That's downstairs, isn't it?' Jason straightened, staring closer at the image. 'Yeah, look, in the corner, that's my Porsche.'

'What, the hideous yellow thing?' Eddie shook his head. 'All money, no class.'

'You shouldn't be admiring Mister Barnett's car,' Justice spoke again as the photo changed to that of one of the parking garage's support pillars. 'You should look at these.'

On the screen the people around the table could now see some kind of package wrapped around the concrete pillar with a mixture of clingfilm wrap and duct tape. It was in blocks, and it was grey, with a small stick poking out of it.

'Oh, shit,' Jason realised what it was. 'My car.'

'In answer to Ms Harvey's question, as to what happens if you don't decide by the time the countdown ends?' Justice spoke again, relaxed and almost jovial in his tone. 'Well, then the twelve C4 explosive devices I have attached to the support structure throughout your lovely, shiny building will detonate, destroying everything – including you.'

The screen flicked through several images as Justice spoke, each one a photo of a different support pillar, blocks of C4 taped to the sides, each with the same type of detonator sticking out of the top.

Then, the image changed to a child's drawing, in crayon, of the building exploding, the upper floors on fire with the Board leaping out of windows waving their arms as they fell to their deaths.

'I know, it's a bit melodramatic, but you need to know the stakes,' Justice continued. 'You will make a decision here, or else you will all die.'

'Can we move?' Tamira asked into the phone. 'Or are we stuck at this bloody table?'

'Oh, you can move around the room as much as you want,' Justice replied. 'However, if you go near the side cabinet for more than a glass of water, try to open the door, or even lean out of the broken window to gain attention, I *will* shoot you.'

'So, basically, we can straighten our legs, but that's about it until the fucking building explodes,' Tamira said, rising and pacing around the room. 'Good to know. Thanks for that.'

'At least we know why he's not in the building, and why he's over there,' Miles stated knowledgably.

'That's what you took from this?' Devin stared at Miles. 'That being in an exploding building might not be something this maniac enjoys?'

'It's information,' Miles spoke softly, tapping his nose. 'And that's key.'

'Christ,' Devin slumped back in the chair. 'How the hell did you stay in power for so long? You're a goddamned cretin.'

Miles was about to reply to this, straightening in his chair for another argument, or possibly even a more physical response, when Justice interrupted, speaking once more through the speakers.

'Make your cases as individuals, as a group, it doesn't

matter,' he explained. 'You can nominate, accuse, whatever it takes. But in just over a hundred and twelve minutes from now, at nine-thirty pm tonight, one of you will exit this building through the front doors and take the blame for Mercy, in front of the world's press, while the others get to stay up here, safe, while they work out how to spin this mess to save their careers.'

'You're enjoying this, aren't you?' Victoria snapped at the phone.

'Oh, very much so,' Justice chuckled. 'It's not often the little man sees the big man suffer.'

'Is that what you are, then?' Victoria replied. 'A little man?'

'Victoria, don't,' Devin shook his head. 'All we need to do is decide who takes the fall. Then we can all leave.'

'If it's so important to you, then you can take the fall,' Victoria snapped. 'I'm missing my daughter's recital for this.'

'Are you sad about that?' Justice asked, and Victoria winced – she'd forgotten he could hear everything.

'Of course, I'm sad,' she said. 'What kind of mother do you think I am?'

'I think you're *this* type of woman,' Justice said, and there was a slight click in the speaker's audio before two fresh voices spoke.

'I was at my daughter's recital. Had to leave three songs in. Are they called songs? I don't know. All I know is someone had better have died for this, because I'm missing important moments in her life.'

Victoria looked in horror at Devin as their conversation in the elevator played.

'They usually do die when we get calls like this. I've only had the 9-1-1 once since I arrived. And that was when Ryan whatshisname jumped out the window.'

'God, I forgot about that, the stupid bastard. Still, you should be careful, Macintosh. You almost sound like you give a shit.'

'Just stating a fact. How was the recital?'

'Fucking abysmal. You'd think with the amount of money I was paying, she could play a vaguely recognisable tune. If I hadn't been there when she was born, I'd wonder if she was actually mine.'

'So, with you here, is she with her father right now?'

'Why the hell would I do that? He's not been around for months. Living in Barbados, I think. No, she's with the au pair. Hopefully, they'll both be asleep by the time I arrive home.'

There was a second, faint click before the conversation stopped.

'Ryan Whatshisname,' Eddie snarled, staring daggers at Devin now. 'It was Ryan Blake, and he was one of my best friends, you heartless shit.'

'Did you love him?' Victoria asked.

'Like a brother.'

'Then maybe you should consider why you didn't stop him jumping out of a fucking window, and keep your opinions to yourself,' Victoria angrily snapped back, before looking at the phone, and by default, Justice.

'You bugged us?'

'Your security is very easy to hack,' Justice replied, as annoyingly calm as he had been before. 'And you'd be surprised with what I've been finding on you all.'

'Don't listen to him,' Hayley folded her arms. 'He's a sick bastard, and this is all his game. I refuse to play it. I'm not doing this.'

'Yeah, me neither,' Jason looked across at Hayley, nodding in support before looking back at the others. 'I'm not throwing any of you to the wolves.'

'Christ, it's a Hallmark moment,' Devin shook his head.

'I happen to be a fan of Hallmark movies, Mister Macintosh,' Justice interrupted. 'And I think these have been lovely sentiments spoken by Miss Moran and Mister Barnett. Such corporate loyalty shown.'

Justice's voice darkened as he continued.

'If only the other members of the Board felt the same way as they do,' he finished. 'Let's see what they really think, shall we?'

110:54

Slowly, and with no small amount of confusion, Jason stared around the boardroom table.

'What's that supposed to mean?' he asked.

In response, the television at the end of the table turned on once more, and they all could now see CCTV footage of Miko Tanasha, taken from a secret camera in the corner of her office, currently on the phone as she paced around the room in anger.

'You son of a bitch, Trent! You told me they'd take the meeting!' "television" Miko snapped into the phone as she looked up at her door, making sure nobody could hear her. Seeing nobody there, she turned away from the door, but was still picked up by the camera in the corner as she continued. *'You said – yes, you goddamned did! I did what you told me to, and I swallowed every fucking drop! Get me that meeting!'*

Before anything else could be shown, however, the television clicked back off.

There was a long, awkward moment of complete silence as everyone in the room took in what they'd just seen. The person who'd been in the video, Miko Tanasha, straightened, forcing every fibre in her body to stay calm, giving her an almost robotic stiffness, as she slowly and quietly turned to face Miles.

'You had cameras in my office.'

It was a statement more than a question, and voiced slightly higher than a whisper, completely emotionless – but this was more because of her forcibly willing herself to keep the emotions at bay, rather than an ice coldness. And Devin could understand why – of all the conversations she probably had in her office, unaware she was being watched, or recorded, even, *that* had likely been the most embarrassing. Especially if the "swallowed every drop" line was literal.

'Of course I bloody did,' Miles sat up in his chair, trying to look down at Miko while he explained himself. 'I'd received reports you were looking to leave us, that you were offering secrets in return for a good acceptance package.'

'And who did you hear this from?' Miko insisted. 'Were you spying on me, you ancient old pervert? Did you have cameras in the toilet, too?'

'Of course not!' Miles looked shocked at the suggestion. 'That would be intrusive.'

'And putting cameras in my goddamned office isn't?'

'It was a friend at the club,' Miles admitted, changing the subject from toilets.

'Which club?' Devin couldn't help himself. 'The one in the city, or the "gladiator" sauna in Greenwich Village?'

Miles spun to face him now, his face almost purple with rage.

'I will end your shitty little career, you parasitic little sycophant—'

'That was a personal call!' Miko rose now, returning the attention to her as she faced down Miles, tears in her eyes. 'Personal!'

'Have you put cameras in all our offices?' Eddie asked, his voice scarily calm.

Noting the tone, Miles turned from Devin now, the argument forgotten.

'Of course not,' he said to Eddie. 'I only—'

'Only did the girls offices?' Victoria chimed in now. 'Or only do the ones you know can't kick the shit out of you when they find out?'

'That doesn't include the girls, then,' Tamira muttered, standing by the television. 'Because every woman in this room, with maybe the exception of Hayley, could do that.'

'You had no right,' Miko sat back down, arms folded, chin on her chest as she stared sullenly at the table. 'No right.'

'Oh, but I think they had every right, didn't they?' Justice returned now, the voice echoing through the room. 'You were looking to get out, after all. Whether Mister Fenton gained the information over a gentlemen's club meal, or while prostate-examining a twink in a hot tub, the answer stays the same.'

The television lit up once more, and now showed a new contact sheet, similar to the one shown when they'd first looked to call Corey Gregson, but this sheet showed a man in his early forties, athletic, his short hair peppered with grey, his eyes blue, his suit very much off the peg at *Brooks Brothers*. As the people looking up at it read the details, Justice began narrating.

'Trent Nemeth,' he explained. 'Head of Resources for *Alliance and Western Insurance*. The best opportunity you had to get you a job interview there.'

He chuckled.

'And apparently, a man you performed oral sex on to ensure the opportunity.'

'You bastard.'

'Now, now, don't blame me, Miss Tanasha, I think Mister Fenton is fully deserving of your ire. But let's be honest, and cards on the table, you were looking to leave, after all.'

Miko looked around the table slowly, taking in the expressions of everyone there, watching her, judging her ...

And then she laughed.

Her body language shifted, relaxed a little, even. As if the act of being found out had given her some relief in the situation.

'So, I wanted to get off the sinking ship,' she shrugged. 'You know I'm not the only one.'

'You're the only one who'd suck cock to do it,' Devin replied, but then looked over at Eddie. 'Well, that we know of, anyway.'

For a change, Eddie didn't rise to anger, instead simply flipping Devin the finger.

'He's hot,' Tamira said, looking at the photo on the screen. 'I'd have done it. Hell, I'd have done him without the job offer. You go, girl.'

'Doesn't matter, I didn't get the meeting, anyway,' Miko rested her head on the back of the chair, looking up at the ceiling now as she expelled a deep breath. 'Nobody wants Wrentham rejects right now. The company's tanking bad and we all know it. Shares have been free-falling faster than ...'

She looked at Eddie, smiling as she did so.

'Faster than Ryan Blake does on a Wednesday.'

Although Eddie had taken the insult from Devin with a simple finger gesture in response, at this he jumped up, his chair clattering to the window as he almost dived across the table, his hands reaching out for Miko who, laughing, pulled away. It was Devin who moved first, grabbing and pulling Eddie back to his side of the table.

'Get your hands off me!' Eddie snapped, tearing away, straightening his tie as he regained his composure. 'She's going out the window. Maybe not right now, but mark my words, before the night is over, she's gonna fly.'

He looked back at Miko, whose expression of triumph had now understandably dissipated.

'You know why they didn't want you?' he snapped. 'Because you sucked Trent's cock for an interview. That's desperation, right there. And nobody wants a desperate, two-faced traitor in their midst.'

'No, we're toxic,' Jason admitted, still sitting calmly in his chair. 'We see it every day in sales. We talk to companies all the time, and the first thing they ask is about our problems. If it's not Mercy, it's one of the other countless mistakes we've made.'

He looked over at Victoria.

'Make all the jokes you want about me staying here when you all go home, but it's the only time I can do my job without having to speak to someone whose assistance, money or services we need, while they utterly fucking hate us.'

He looked at Miles now.

'You know what they all suggest?' he asked. 'And I'm not making a generalisation, I mean every damned one of them. They all say the best thing we could do to get a new start would be to appoint a new CEO and get rid of the dead weight.'

He leant closer, his fear of Miles Fenton now gone.

'In case you weren't aware,' he said. 'You're the dead weight. They all think you should be given a prison sentence for what we did at Mercy. That you're the one that deliberately held back on upgrades--'

'What else did you offer?' Eddie's voice cut across Jason, still watching Miko as he spoke.

Miko looked over at him with a glare that could melt buildings.

'What do you mean, offer?' she asked, her voice one step away from full on anger.

Eddie pursed his lips, shrugging.

'You sucked a man off to get a meeting,' he said, nodding at the image, still on the screen. 'Regardless of whether playtime Tammy over there would want a go on the ride too, what did you offer if they actually hired you? You must have promised them *something*.'

All eyes now turned back to Miko, who shuffled uncomfortably under the scrutiny.

'She probably offered to take turns on all of them,' Victoria sneered, a cruel smile playing at the edge of her lips. 'One after the other. Or maybe all at once, who knows?'

'Oh, piss off,' Miko looked over at Victoria now. 'Like you haven't wiped cum off your precious mink to gain a deal or two.'

'You're wrong,' Victoria shook her head as she stroked her coat, rubbing her cheek against the lapel.

'Am I?' Miko asked, her expression showing she didn't believe this for one second.

'Yes,' Victoria placed her elbows on the table, resting her head upon her hands as she smiled winningly at Miko. 'I always take the mink off first.'

'You do? Well, that explains why your driver's always helping you back into it,' Miko retorted.

There were a couple of chuckles at this, and for a second, it felt like the situation had been slightly more defused than it was earlier. But then the laughter faded, as the solemnity of the situation and the pressure of what awaited them all returned to the forefront of their minds.

'What did you offer them, Miko?' It was Hayley who asked this time. 'He's right, isn't he? He might be a knuckle-dragging Neanderthal at the best of times, but he's correct here. You offered them something big if they took you in. What was it?'

Miko pushed her chair away from the table, rising from it as she walked to the side cabinet. Taking a carafe of water, she poured a glass of it, draining it in one go before taking a deep breath and letting it out.

'Advanced reports for next quarter,' she said, facing the wall, unable to look any of them in the eye as she confessed.

'You *what?*' Devin was stunned at the admission.

'Once a whore, always a whore,' Victoria added, getting in another strike while her opponent was injured and defenceless. And Miko, stiffening at the comment, said nothing, still staring at the wall, ashamed of what she'd done. Or, more likely, ashamed she'd been stupid enough to be caught.

'You promised the advanced reports for the next quarter, or you sent them?' Miles asked, turning to face her back.

'What does it matter?' Miko asked sadly.

Miles waved around the table as he replied, as if expecting everyone there to side with him as he spoke.

'It matters a fucking lot!' he exclaimed. '*Alliance and Western* can gut us on the NASDAQ if they have that! If they know about any major client acquisitions we're aiming for, they could take them from us! Force us to collapse!'

'Good!' Miko shouted back in response as she returned her attention to the table. 'Maybe we should collapse!'

'There she is,' Victoria hissed as she leant back, enjoying the humiliation. 'The woman who feels she shouldn't be here, that she wasn't part of the Board, proving once and for all she was *never* part of it. All she wanted to do was destroy the Board, each and every one of us.'

'Bullshit!' Miko looked back at her now. 'I've been to bat for you so many times! Just because we hate each other doesn't mean we've not worked well together! Just because I think this company is toxic and that Fenton's a waste of oxygen, doesn't mean I don't respect all of you!'

'You respect us now?' Eddie leant back, unzipping his pants. 'Come over here and show me how much you respect me. And I want you to swallow the lot, as I hear that's your thing.'

'Eddie!' Devin snapped. 'Women present.'

'Yeah, you're right,' Eddie looked abashed as he zipped his pants back up. 'Sorry, Jason.'

'You don't respect us at all,' Miles said, and he almost seemed hurt as he spoke.

'No, she doesn't respect *you*,' Tamira reminded him. 'She said she respects *us*, not *you*. Should I write it down for you?'

'When this is over, I'll take great pleasure in having you kicked out of the company,' Miles hissed at Tamira, looking over at Miko as he finished. 'Both of you.'

'Get real!' Miko laughed, pointing out of the broken window. 'We're not getting out of this! The only way this is over is when the mad fucker over there gets bored with his entertainment and starts popping us in the head!'

She turned to face the window now.

'And we deserve it!' she shouted. 'This company's so toxic, so evil, I would do literally anything to leave!'

'Oh please,' Devin sighed. 'Enough with the martyr shit, yeah? You've been here ten minutes and already you're the voice of our conscience? I don't think so.'

'And why shouldn't I be?' Miko looked over at him, raising an eyebrow.

'You can't be a voice if you have something stuck down your throat,' Devin smiled.

'What, and you're all so pure of heart?' Miko laughed. 'Don't make me laugh!'

'Well, we don't … don't do those things!' Hayley insisted, still at the other end of the table.

At this, Miko turned and walked back to her chair, her mannerisms more of a predator stalking her prey than of anything else.

'No,' she said, now beside Hayley, staring down at her.

'Sweet, innocent, butter-wouldn't-melt-in-her-mouth Hayley Moran. You're the worst here. I know what you did.'

'Wait, what did Hayley do?' Jason looked around, interested now. 'Tell me it wasn't something sexual. I might puke.'

'I didn't—' Hayley stuttered, her eyes wide open and fearful. 'I wouldn't—'

'She could, and she did,' Justice's voice echoed around the room once more. 'In fact, all of you have secrets, ones that, if they came out could embarrass you, way more than Miss Tanasha's oral exploits.'

There was a pause as he let that sink in.

'And, with just over an hour and a half left on the clock, let's look at a couple of those.'

101.49

'Let's play a game.'

Justice's voice was almost sing-song in style as the members of the Board stared warily across the table at each other.

'What kind of game?' Eddie was the first to ask.

'A "getting to know you" game,' Justice replied conversationally. 'Yes. This would be the perfect time for that. Up you get, all of you.'

'I'm not moving anywhere—' Jason began, but his voice trailed off as the red dot appeared on his shirt.

'Fine, whatever,' he grumbled as he rose, standing beside his chair. 'Now what?'

'Mister Fenton, can you walk to the cabinet, and pull the item from door number seven out from inside it?' Justice asked. Looking at the others before shrugging and making his way over to it, he searched the cabinet for the right number, opened the door once he found it and pulled out a metal ball, sized somewhere between a baseball and a soccer ball.

'Are we playing catch or something?' he muttered as he turned it around in his hands. 'That stupid game we do in team building sessions, where we have to say our name and department when we catch it?'

'Bravo, Mister Fenton. That's exactly what we're doing,' Justice replied.

'Well, that's just stupid,' walking to his space at the head of the table, Miles grimaced. 'We know each other.'

'Humour me, then,' Justice continued. 'I'd like to know more about you. So, we're going to play a game of catch with a difference.'

As Justice said this, a line along the seam of the metal ball lit up with blue LEDs, and with a yelp, Miles dropped it from his hands, the ball landing heavily on the table.

'You maniac!' he exclaimed, rubbing his hands. 'You shocked me!'

As Devin looked down at the ball, having rolled across the desk towards him, the voice of Justice gleefully explained their situation.

'Each of you, one by one, will hold the ball in both hands,' he stated. 'You will then keep hold of the ball for a further five seconds before passing it on. During this time, I will feed an electrical current through the device, on a scale of one to five.'

Miles blew on his fingers, as if they were burned.

'The shock your CEO had was a two,' Justice continued. 'Five is … difficult.'

'I could have held it if I knew it was coming,' Miles, chastised at the low level, explained huffily.

'Who decides the level?' Eddie asked.

'I do,' Justice replied. 'And the level is based on how well I feel you're playing the game. If you follow the rules, then you get level one. If you task me, then it's higher.'

'And what if we don't?' Victoria folded her arms. 'What if we drop the ball like Miles did?'

'If you don't last the five seconds, then you're out of the

game,' Justice replied. 'You can sit down, the task over for you.'

'So, what's the point of this, then?' Miles shook his head in confusion. 'We drop the ball, sit down, the whole thing's over.'

'Ah, but then you don't win.'

The members of the Board looked at each other as this line was spoken. There was a powerful element of competitiveness here, that was for sure, but not masochism.

'And what does the winner get?' It was Jason who asked the question.

'The winner gets a veto.'

'A what?' Miko frowned. 'Are you saying they can veto a vote?'

'Exactly,' Justice replied. 'The winner, the last person holding, gets to veto one candidate at any point of their choosing.'

Eddie nodded, understanding.

'That includes themselves, I'm guessing?'

'Yes.'

Devin looked back at the ball. This was a literal "get out of jail" card; whoever used this could make sure, even if they were unanimously voted out, they couldn't be removed.

As currency went, this was big.

'Okay, so what do we do?' he asked, picking up the ball. 'Hi, I'm Devin and I work in Oil and Gas Investment?'

'Nothing so crass,' Justice was amused as he spoke. 'Just your name … and a secret.'

'A secret?' Devin narrowed his eyes as he turned the metal globe in his hands. 'What kind of secret?'

'Your choice,' Justice's voice echoed around the room. 'Tell a secret, and then hold the ball for five seconds. But if I deem it to be a boring one, or maybe not even a secret at all, I'll up the power level.'

Devin nodded.

'I'm Devin Macintosh,' he said. 'And I …'

He paused, unsure of what to say.

'I spend an inordinate amount of time watching TikTok videos of horses being hooved,' he said with a chuckle – and then yelped as the ball shocked him. He lasted the five seconds, however, his teeth gritted as he forced himself to take the pain, and then tossed it to the table once it stopped.

'That wasn't a level one,' he grumbled.

'That wasn't a good secret,' Justice replied. 'Do better next time.'

Victoria picked up the ball, staring at it in the way someone watched a poisonous snake.

'I'm Victoria Harvey,' she said cautiously. 'And I … I sometimes don't like my daughter. Like I wonder if she was swapped at birth, or how I could be her parent. I blamed my husband until he left. Now I blame myself. I feel like a failure. It's probably why I'm fucking my driver.'

She looked around the room, confused.

'It's not buzzing?'

'Your secret was very good, so I decided you didn't need a shock,' Justice replied. 'Interesting motherly love aspect. The cheap seats will love that.'

Unsure what Justice meant by this, Victoria passed it over to Eddie.

'I knew you were sleeping with your driver,' Devin crowed.

'It's not exactly been that hard to work out, Columbo,' Victoria sniffed as Eddie straightened, the ball now in his hands.

'I'm Eddie Purcell, and I say go fuck yourself,' he said, instantly stiffening, gritting his teeth as the blue LEDs lit up, far higher than they had been with either Miles or Devin. And, after five seconds, his body relaxed, as he let the ball roll to the table.

'That the best you have?' he asked, but his bravado seemed

forced somewhat. 'I expected a challenge. You might as well just give me the veto.'

Now it was Hayley's turn.

'Hayley Moran, and I sometimes claim expenses for lunch when I shouldn't—'

She yelped, dropping the ball.

'Shit.'

'Miss Moran, your secret was boring, and you failed to hold the ball,' Justice intoned sadly. 'Please sit down.'

As Hayley sat, Tamira picked up the globe.

'Tamira May, and I haven't liked any of my assistants since I've been here. They've all been insipid, ambitious back-stabbers.'

She winced as the blue LEDs glowed, but it was obviously a low dosage, as she held it for five more seconds, passing it to Miko.

'I thought we were doing secrets?' Miko smiled. 'Everyone in the company knows that.'

Tamira ignored her, and so Miko turned to the Board.

'Miko Tanaka,' she said. 'And you already know my secret.'

'No,' Justice's voice echoed. 'I want a new one.'

'Fine,' Miko sighed. 'When I'm really hung over, or I know I'm about to have a really nasty shit – you know, the ones that really stink the place out, I always use the men's toilets.'

She looked around.

'No pain,' she smiled. 'Looks like I gave a good one.'

She tossed the ball to Jason.

'I'm Jason Barnett, and my secret … My secret is that I lied to get the job when I started,' Jason said. 'I claimed I'd interned at one of Wrentham's rivals, but I hadn't.'

He flinched and dropped the ball.

'What the hell!' he exclaimed. 'I played your stupid game!'

'With a boring secret,' Justice replied calmly. 'Sit down. You're out.'

As Jason sat down, Miles picked the ball up.

'I'm guessing I get another go?' he asked. 'I'm Miles Fenton, and sometimes I sit in this room alone, imagining Board meetings.'

He twitched as the LEDs lit up, but managed to hold on.

'What, and that wasn't as boring as my secret?' Jason moaned.

'No,' Justice replied. 'Because I know your real secret.'

Jason closed his mouth and glowered at the floor, while Eddie grinned.

'Hell, now I want to know *that* secret,' he said.

'You do?' Justice said, as if this was a surprise. 'Well, fine, then. Mister Barnett gets a lifeline.'

'Now what?' Devin asked as Jason, grinning widely, rose back up. 'We played the game. Do all seven of us get to veto?'

'No,' Justice replied coldly. 'Now we move on to round two. This time, you hold the ball for ten seconds, and the power range goes up to ten.'

'So, a bigger secret?' Devin reached for the ball. 'Okay then. I—'

'No,' Justice interrupted. 'This round is different. This time, you name another of the member of the Board, including the ones no longer in the game – one you dislike. And you tell us why you dislike them.'

There was a murmuring around the table at this.

'And if they don't dislike anyone on the Board?' Jason asked, but was cut off by Miko, laughing.

'Come on, Jason, be serious,' she mocked. 'We all hate each other.'

She motioned for the ball.

'I'll go first.'

'The hell you will,' Devin replied, holding up the ball in both hands. 'I choose Miko, because she can't bear to be second, and always has to take the lead—'

He jerked as the LEDs lit up, but after four seconds dropped the ball, his face covered in a light sweat.

'Bastard,' he growled at the window. 'I did what you asked.'

'You did, and thank you,' Justice replied. 'But you couldn't hold the ball, and therefore you're out.'

'That was way higher than before!'

'And he said it would be, you pussy,' Victoria said as she picked up the ball. 'I nominate Devin because he's such a fucking whiner.'

She also jerked back as the lights went on, but kept a grip for the full ten seconds. After this, she threw the ball to the floor, growled a sound that sounded vaguely like a triumphant insult to the others, and then slumped into her seat.

A second later, realising what she did, she stood back up.

'Too late,' Justice said, with a hint of sadness in his voice. 'You sat down. You're out.'

'But I held the ball!'

'And you sat down.'

Victoria slumped back into her chair as Miko leant over and picked up the ball.

'Your go,' she said, passing it over to a reluctant Miles.

Miles stared in horror at the device in his hand.

'I don't need the veto,' he said, chucking it back to Miko, and sitting down. 'I know I won't be picked.'

Miko looked at the ball, now in her hands, and Devin, watching from across the table, knew she was weighing up how much she needed this.

'I choose Victoria,' she said. 'She has too many vices that people aren't told ab—'

She jerked uncontrollably; the ball sliding from her hands, still buzzing as it rolled over to Hayley.

'You prick,' Miko snarled. 'I did what you asked.'

'You were vague,' Justice said. 'I don't like vague. Sit down.'

Jason reached over, picking it up.

'I vote for Eddie,' he said calmly. 'He caused the death of someone I liked—'

'You lying shit!' Eddie cut him off, swatting the ball out of his hand. 'You say something like that and it'll be *your* death I cause!'

'Mister Barnett gets through by default,' Justice said, as Jason walked over to the ball, picking it up, and rolling it over to Hayley.

'Thanks,' he smiled at Eddie. 'You were a real help there.'

Eddie just glowered back, as Hayley looked over at him.

'You want to …?' she offered.

'Ladies first,' Eddie smiled darkly.

With great trepidation, Hayley picked up the ball, staring down at it.

'I nominate Victoria,' she said.

'Surprise surprise,' Victoria muttered.

'She thinks that everyone in the company works for her, and treats the business development people like they're printers, like they're office equipment,' Hayley said. 'She doesn't thank them, she expects them to do all her work, and when they don't, she talks behind their back, making sure they don't get promoted by blocking any attempts, or worse still, actively trying to get them fired from their roles.'

'Bullshit.'

'I'm HR, bitch,' Hayley snapped. 'I see it all the time.'

She looked up, confused.

'I think this broke when Jason dropped it,' she said.

'No, I chose not to shock you,' Justice said. 'You did what I asked, and more besides.'

Smiling widely, Hayley rolled it over to Eddie.

'I don't know why you're grinning,' Eddie said as he

picked it up. 'Jason's still in, too. Which means you'll have to go another round.'

'Mister Purcell, when you're ready?'

Eddie held the ball up, turning to face the window.

'Again, fuck you,' he said, spasming back immediately as the current ran through the device, the blue LEDs now flashing wildly. He staggered against the edge of the table, but still kept upright, and by the end of the ten seconds, he dropped the ball.

'Th-this is a st-stupid game,' he stuttered, shivering.

'Congratulations.' If Justice was impressed, he didn't show it. 'Mister Purcell, Miss Moran, and Mister Barnett will go through to the next round.'

'And that's what, exactly?'

'The same, but you can only choose a rival player,' Justice replied. 'And the power rises again.'

Hayley grabbed the ball before anyone else could do so.

'I choose Jason because he plays the martyr all the time—' she started, but then yelped, dropping the ball as it pulsed energy.

She stared at it for a long moment.

'Fuck,' she said, sitting down.

Jason, sighing, picked up the ball.

'I won't be knocking it out of your sticky little hands this time,' Eddie growled. 'I'm going to watch you burn.'

Jason swallowed, looked around the table, and then, as quickly as he'd picked the ball up, he placed it back down, sitting back in the chair.

'No,' he said. 'I'm not playing anymore.'

'Then I win by default?' Eddie punched the sky. 'Yes!'

'Only if you last longer than Miss Moran did,' Justice replied, and Eddie grimaced.

'Fine,' he said, pulling off his tie. This done, he looped it around his hand, securing the ball tightly to it.

'Let's see the ball drop now,' he said, taking the free end of the tie and placing it in his mouth, biting down hard on it.

'*Uck hoo,*' he said through gritted teeth, holding the ball up in one hand while simultaneously flipping his middle finger at the sniper across the street.

If Justice had a breaking point, this seemed like it, as the lights on the ball flicked up to possibly the maximum it could take, and Eddie, through clenched teeth, biting down on the tie, screamed as the power pulsed through him. There was the smell of burning flesh, or possibly the tie burning, and then after ten seconds the ball fell dead, and Eddie slumped across the table, only just managing to stand.

Spitting the tie from his mouth, he glared at the others around the table.

'Pu-pu-pussies,' he said, not daring to move.

'Congratulations,' Justice said after a moment's silence. 'You win the right to veto someone later today.'

'Can I s-sit?' Eddie untied his necktie, tossing the ball across the room.

'Of course.'

Eddie collapsed into his chair, his face covered in sweat, his hair damp and lank.

'You look like shit,' Victoria mused.

'Rather that and with a chance to survive, sweetheart,' Eddie muttered, looking across the table.

'And, I don't know about you, but I really want to know why Miko thinks *Hayley* is worse than she is.'

96.49

Miko stared daggers at Hayley as she leant forward in her chair.

'Miss Bullshit here says she wouldn't do the terrible things I've done, and I reckon she's right,' she said. 'Because what I did was personal, intimate, and only involved one person. Whereas Hayley …'

She turned and smiled at the woman beside her.

'You just embezzle from your bosses, don't you? Something far less intimate, and far more damning and destructive.'

She looked around the room.

'I gave secrets, but she screws over actual employees.'

'What?' Miles leant forward in shock.

'Ask her,' Miko sat back in her chair, smiling evilly as she stared at Hayley. 'Let her tell you all about it.'

'She's just deflecting to save her skin!' Hayley protested, looking around the boardroom, looking desperately for someone to believe her. 'She's screwing her way around Manhattan's elite, and now she's trying to throw shit on other people rather than taking the blame!'

'I'd rather screw one man than an entire company,' Miko looked down at her nails as she smirked.

Devin shook his head at this.

'Don't belittle what you did,' he said icily. 'You didn't just have some kind of passionate affair, you sold out the company you work for, whose Board you're on, and whose loyalty you should be giving!'

'Yeah, that Board is a really great thing to be on right now, isn't it?' Miko pointed out of the window. 'Oh, *please* let me stay on the goddamned Board, I do so love these moments of terror and certain death.'

Devin went to snap back a reply, but Miles held a hand up to stop him.

'Hold on one moment,' he said, looking over at Hayley. 'We're not finished with you.'

Hayley paled slightly, looking back at Miles as he waggled his hand, continuing.

'You said deflecting. You didn't say lying.'

'What?' Hayley looked confused at the statement.

'You said she's just deflecting to save her skin,' Miles continued. 'You didn't say she was *lying* to save her skin.'

'What's the difference?' Hayley licked her lips nervously now, her eyes glued to her CEO's.

'You didn't say her comment was a lie,' Jason, seeing where this was going, nodded, turning in his chair to face her. 'Which means it wasn't a lie, and you have been stealing from us.'

He leant closer, Miko leaning back in her chair to move out of the way, and allow him to face Hayley.

'You lied, or you didn't. Which was it?'

Hayley opened and shut her mouth a couple of times, before pointing over at Eddie, her eyes widening as she spoke.

'Eddie beat an intern up!' she admitted. 'Put him in the hospital!'

'Hey!' Eddie now straightened in his chair, his eyes narrowing. 'Don't you dare throw this at me. He came at me when we fired him, and it was self-defence.'

'He was half your size!' Hayley, realising she had an opportunity to divert the attention away from her, pressed on with her tactic.

'So's Jackie Chan, and he could kick the shit out of me,' Eddie was now the one looking around the boardroom, looking for allies. 'I had no reason to believe that the intern couldn't.'

It was a terrible excuse, and watching his expression, Devin could see that even Eddie didn't believe it.

'But you liked it, didn't you?' Tamira said as she walked over to the side cabinet, pouring herself a glass of water, taking the opportunity to step forward and quickly check out of the window.

'You don't have a clue what you're talking about,' Eddie growled. 'So how about you shut the hell up and sit your ass back down?'

'I don't?' Tamira walked back to the table, sitting back down in her chair and watching Eddie across the table. 'Let's see, shall we? A chance to dominate someone, to be the big alpha? Sounds just like you.'

She held her hands up in triumph, nodding around the boardroom as she continued.

'Tell me I'm wrong,' she said with a smile. 'Come on, someone tell me *that* isn't Eddie Purcell.'

'I don't need shit like that to get me off. I'm not you.' Eddie pushed away from the table now. 'And why are you even kicking off at me? Miko's betraying the company and Hayley's ripping it off, so why am *I* suddenly public enemy number one?'

'Because nobody likes you,' Victoria smiled. 'And we like the idea of seeing you eat shit for a global audience.'

'If I eat shit, I'm saving a ton of it for you,' Eddie was

clenching and unclenching his fists in unconscious anger as he replied. 'I know what happens here. I know where the bodies are buried.'

'Don't worry, you'll be joining them real soon,' Victoria replied sweetly, pretending to shovel imaginary food into her mouth. 'Nom nom nom. That's some tasty shit you're eating right there.'

'Fancy words from the woman who may need me to help her with my veto later on,' Eddie grumbled, retreating into his chair.

'He's right though,' Jason said, stopping the argument as the other members of the Board turned back to face him. 'Embezzling is a big issue.'

'Thank you!' Eddie fist-pumped as he pointed at Jason. 'This man gets it! Yes! Justice for men, and fuck this "me too" shit.'

'I didn't say you weren't to blame, or not some kind of alpha male misogynistic prick,' Jason replied tartly. 'I just think we need to look into this more.'

'Look into what?' Hayley looked horrified at this. 'At his violence against weaker men being less important here than—'

'Than you stealing money from the firm?' Devin offered. 'Is that what you were going to say?'

'I was going to say, "less important here than the allegations thrown baselessly against me," you arrogant shit,' Hayley stiffened as she raised her hand and flipped Devin off with her middle finger. 'I can't believe you all believe that these accusations are stronger than the terrible things he did.'

'It was self-defence,' Eddie, realising the tide was turning against Hayley now, spoke far calmer than he had before, buffing his nails on his lapel as he continued, his voice now mocking. 'And it's kinda my job. You know, security and all that.'

Hayley looked like she was going to throw up now, shaking her head as she looked at the others.

'It's not fair,' she said. 'They're just accusations.'

'You still haven't said they're lies,' Miko grinned. 'Go on. Tell them I'm lying. Get off the fence. Or are you too scared to be caught out when you're *actually* revealed to have been embezzling?'

'Oh, and how would you do that?' Hayley snapped. 'I'd love to know. We'd all love to know.'

'Just ask the mysterious voice on the phone,' Miko chuckled. 'He probably has records. Or Miles has a fucking camera in your room, too.'

'You didn't, did you?' Hayley swivelled to face Miles.

'Shit, Hayley. Looks like it's between you and Miko for the scapegoat,' Victoria purred, with more than a hint of triumph. 'I'd like to say how sorry I am for you, but I've never liked you, and I utterly detest that bitch, so I'm ready to vote right now.'

'Now hold on,' Miles held his hand up. 'We can't just take a vote on baseless accusations—'

'Why not?' Devin asked. 'We do it all the time in the other meetings.'

'Because someone's life is about to be ruined!' Miles replied.

'Why do you care?' Devin pressed on. 'It won't be your life, and let's be honest, *you're* the only person here that you give a shit about.'

'Hear hear,' Victoria banged her hand on the table like a makeshift gavel. 'Let's vote so we can get out of here. All those in favour of Miko taking the blame for being a back-stabbing, blow-jobbing bitch, say aye?'

There was an uncomfortable moment of silence as the other members of the Board delayed from answering.

After a moment, Victoria drew air in through her teeth.

'Fine, I'll start. Aye. That is, I'm saying "aye" to Miko being thrown to the sharks.'

'"Let's vote, so we can get out of here,"' Hayley quoted, mimicking Victoria's accent. 'Christ, you really are a piece of work. You're so desperate to get back to a recital you utterly hated, or a driver you hadn't quite finished with his "happy ending" yet, you'd damn one of us to hell, is that right?'

'Yes,' Victoria nodded. 'I might have hated the bloody thing, but she's still my daughter. Someone I actively tolerate and sometimes like. Love, even.'

She stopped, letting the moment draw on, building up the next line she spoke.

'So, as I'd rather spend time with her than all of you bastards in this room right now, I'm more than happy to pick either of you, actually, to take the blame … because honestly … I detest both of you equally.'

She stopped, pursing her lips as she rocked her head from side to side, considering this.

'Nah, fuck it,' she finished. 'I hate Miko more. She takes the blame. Who's with me? I need five people to make this pass.'

'What about Diana?' Miko replied. 'Did she die for nothing?'

'Princess Diana?' Victoria frowned.

'No, I mean the secretary!' Miko snapped.

'For God's sake, Miko, it was *Donna*,' Jason shook his head. 'If you're going to go for the sympathy vote, then at least get their bloody name right.'

Miko crinkled her nose as she looked away, obviously angry she'd screwed up a simple fact. Hayley, however, took the ball and moved on.

'Miko might have got the name wrong, but she's right,' she insisted. 'Victoria wants to end this quick and pretend it doesn't exist, convince everyone that it never happened. But out there, in the hall, is a dead secretary named Donna, and if we leave now, without properly discussing all aspects here, then we do her a disservice.'

'We have cleaners,' Victoria replied calmly. 'By tomorrow, you won't even know she died there. And if the blood doesn't go, we'll just replace the carpet tiles.'

'Jesus, Victoria!' Devin actually moved away from her as she spoke this. 'Have a little heart here!'

'I don't mean immediately!' Victoria protested. 'I mean after the police have done everything, and you know, taken the body and all that.'

She looked over at Hayley again.

'The cleaners can wipe up the blood, and you, as our HR angel, can call her next of kin, and tell them how bravely she died, trying to save our lives.'

She glanced about the room.

'You know, lie, to make them feel so much better about it. And then you can make some kind of donation in her name, or make an award, or some kind of HR bullshit to make everyone feel better.'

She paused, an expression of concern now on her face as she held a hand out across the table, towards Hayley, placing it down as she finished.

'Unless you're the one taking the blame, of course. Who we vote for. Because, I mean, I know Miko's in the lead already, but you're not liked either.'

'Takes a bitch to know a bitch,' Hayley growled, finally dropping the "nice girl" impression.

At this, however, Victoria smiled, pulling the mink closer to her skin.

'Thank you,' she smiled. 'I like to think so.'

She looked around the boardroom now.

'I've voted,' she said. 'Any of you gutless pricks joining me?'

Slowly, and with great deliberation, the Board looked

around at each other. Watching this, Hayley chuckled to herself, but it turned more into a sob, as she realised that even though Miko already had the first vote, she was likely to be the one voted out of the boardroom.

However, Miles raised his hand.

'I should go first,' he said. 'Being CEO and all that.'

'But you didn't,' Victoria replied. 'I just did.'

'But mine should be the first vote given—'

'Listen, you fossil!' Victoria snapped. 'I've already voted! I said it aloud! To everyone! You can't gaslight us all into thinking you're some kind of decisive expert, when we all know you're only here still because you *don't know it's time to die!*'

She stopped, gathering herself together as she realised with horror that everything she said could actually turn his vote against her instead.

'Sorry,' she muttered. 'Stress.'

'Anyway, as I was saying,' Miles glared at Victoria as he continued. 'As hard as it is for me to even consider such a thing, and I want to ensure for the record—'

'There is no record,' Jason grumbled. 'He shot the secretary. Shame that, too. She was hot.'

'That's what you took from the death?' Devin sighed, shaking his head. 'Prick. Massive, useless prick.'

'Do you mind?' Miles looked at both men. 'I'm about to give my vote.'

'You're about to vote for Miko,' Devin replied.

'Everyone knows you're about to vote for Miko,' Jason agreed.

Miles took a deep breath, centering himself before continuing.

'As I was saying, I want to make sure, in front of witnesses, as there is nobody here to record this—'

'There's the maniac on the phone,' Tamira suggested. 'He seems to love noting down things.'

'*For Christ's sake!*' Miles shouted. 'Can you just let me—'

'Just get on with it, you gutless little prick,' Miko snapped. 'And that's for the record, too. Gutless, little, prick.'

Miles glared at Miko as he continued, his voice icy yet calm as he spoke.

'I vote Miss Tanasha,' he eventually said. 'I feel that she's been here less time than others on this Board, and during her brief but volatile period at Wrentham Industries, we haven't really felt the loyalty from her – loyalty that others around this Board table have given over many years of service – that we would have expected from someone who we had such glowing expectations for.'

'Jesus. "Glowing expectations," indeed,' Devin chuckled. 'Also, "We haven't felt the loyalty from her". You're just pissed she didn't offer to suck your cock, too.'

'Maybe she did,' Victoria smiled. 'Maybe he couldn't get it up for her.'

'I feel she's been disloyal to the company by looking to move elsewhere,' Miles ignored Victoria. 'Disloyalty should be punished.'

'You're fucking kidding me!' Miko rose from her chair, staring around the room in fury. 'People leave jobs all the time! They don't consistently steal money from the firm or beat up people!'

'Nevertheless,' Miles raised a hand to halt her oncoming tirade. 'I find that I – reluctantly, of course – agree with Victoria, in voting for you as the scapegoat.'

'Racist,' Miko snapped as she sat back in her chair, folding her arms. 'The pair of you.'

'I beg your pardon?' Miles looked horrified at the accusation. 'I'm the least racist person here! I have friends who are … well …'

'Black?' Miko latched onto his trepidation and pulled hard on it. 'Asian? Not white? What was the term you were going to use? Ethnic? People of colour? Maybe the "n" word?'

'Miko, that's enough,' Hayley interrupted now. 'Miles has always been inclusive, diversity wise. He's created several outreach programmes over the years.'

'I'm sure he's very good at not being a racist publicly,' Miko placed her hands on the table as she leant closer. 'But privately? I'm just saying it's convenient that I'm the only Asian here, and I'm the one he has a problem with.'

'Don't play that card,' Eddie muttered. 'It's beneath you.'

His face brightened.

'Oh, sorry, I didn't think. Apologies if me saying "beneath you" triggers anything.'

'Fuck off, Purcell.'

'He's just saying, live by the cock, die by the cock,' Devin added.

Victoria looked across at Miles, speaking before Miko could retaliate.

'Okay, so we're two votes done,' she said. 'How about you be the CEO and force the rest of them to make their decisions, so we can get out of here?'

There was a cold gust of wind passing through the broken window, and Miles shivered as he nodded.

'Who's next to cast their vote?' he asked.

DOWNTOWN BLUES

'HEY, KOEBEL! CALL ON LINE TWO!'

Detective Nina Koebel did her most glowering gaze at Sergeant McClusky as he grinned across the bullpen at her.

Forty years old and currently feeling every day of it, she'd spent most of the Sunday filling out reports and fixing issues with Narcisco's seemingly broken memory.

He'd been her partner for five years now, and Koebel didn't think he'd filled one of these damned things out correctly once in all that time.

And of course, it was super convenient he wasn't here the exact moment he needed to do these.

'Who is it?' she asked, straightening on the chair. Sunday evenings weren't usually busy in the 1st Precinct; serving an area that pretty much consisted of a square mile on the southernmost tip of Manhattan, most of their call outs involved the World Trade Center, SOHO, Tribeca, and Wall Street – most of which were closed on a Sunday night.

Koebel liked the Sunday night shift.

She could get her admin done.

'Front desk,' McClusky waggled the phone in his hand.

'Says there's a woman out there looking for a detective. Claims she called nine-one-one but nobody did anything.'

'Why did she call nine-one-one?'

McClusky looked at the phone for a moment and then turned back.

'I don't know, I didn't talk to her.'

'Why not?' Koebel was enjoying this. McClusky was a massive douchebag at the best of times, and delaying him from doing whatever he was doing, even for a few moments, was time well spent.

Of course, there was also the fact he was likely trying to get shot of a call sent to him, so the longer she could delay, the more likely the prospect of him simply giving up and taking the damned thing himself was.

'Because she asked for you.'

'By name?'

'Well no, but she wants a detective,' McClusky made a pantomime of looking around the bullpen. 'And you're the only one here.'

'Glad you finally realised you're not one, Sarge,' Koebel couldn't resist making the jibe, and kicked her feet under the table as she turned back to her desk. 'Okay, send it through.'

McClusky shook his head.

'She's downstairs,' he replied. 'Came in personally.'

Koebel let out an audible groan. She'd hoped to push this away with a quick call, but when they came in personally, it meant it was more important to them, and unlikely to be removed with a few kind words and a hand wave.

'Why's she even here?' she grumbled as she dialled the front desk. 'There's like a dozen other precincts around us.'

The line connected as she hunched forward over the desk.

'Kyle? It's Koebel. What's this about some woman?'

'Claims she called an audible in about half an hour back, but heard nothing, so thought she'd come in.'

'What was the call?'

There was a rustling of notes.

'Her boss sent her a text.'

'She called nine-one-one because of a text from her boss?'

'Yeah.'

'Jesus.'

'Apparently her boss sent some message saying she was being held hostage.'

Koebel considered this.

'So, this was a ransom text?'

'That's the problem, no,' Kyle replied down the line. 'Just seemed to be letting her know. "911 Board hostage sniper." That's what it said.'

'And where's the boss?'

'The woman reckons she's in a boardroom at Wrentham,' Kyle said. 'That's why she's here—'

'Because it's Wall Street,' Koebel pinched the bridge of her nose as she closed her eyes. 'If it's been half an hour, did we send anyone?'

'Yeah, Peroni and Jeffers.'

'And?'

'They reckoned it was a bum call. Reckoned the noise was a firework or something.'

'Noise?'

'Yeah, someone spoke to them while they were sniffing around, claiming they heard a gunshot in the area. But it's Manhattan on a Sunday. You always hear gunshots. Anyway, they're in the break room if you want to chat.'

Koebel was already rising as she finished the call.

'Put the woman in interview room two, tell her it's because it's chaos up here.'

'You don't want her at your desk?'

'No, I don't want her at my desk!' Koebel snapped back. 'If she sits at my desk, she becomes one of those people that constantly stays at your desk until whatever this is becomes sorted. Tell Peroni I'm looking for him.'

She stopped.

'Actually, don't,' she smiled. 'He still owes me money from the Mets game. If he hears I'm looking for him, he'll probably run. I'll go down there now.'

Disconnecting the call, Koebel grabbed a notebook and pen and turned towards the elevator. McClusky, sitting at his desk and watching her, gave Koebel a little wave.

'Enjoy the work,' he said with a smile.

'I don't know why you're so cheerful,' Koebel said as she waited for the elevator to arrive. 'Narcisco's not in tonight, and I'll have to go out there alone. You'll be doing his admin, Sarge.'

And, before McClusky could argue this, Koebel entered the carriage, flipping him the finger as the doors closed.

———

Officer Michael Peroni was still in the break room facing the microwave when Koebel walked in, and he made a terrified little yelp when she spoke his name.

'I don't have the money on me,' he apologised as he turned to face her, skinny and rodent-like, a half-eaten pop tart in his hand. 'I can get it—'

'Don't piss your uniform, I'm not here about that,' Koebel decided to let him off the hook for the moment. 'This woman, the nine-one-one at Wrentham. You take it?'

'For what it was, yeah.' Visibly relaxing, Peroni walked over to the table and sat down, still munching the pop tart as he continued. 'Call came in, something about her boss being a hostage or something. Jeffers and me were down the street, so we drove up.'

Resisting the urge to correct his grammar, Koebel waved for

him to continue.

'That was it, really,' Peroni looked at Jeffers, a large, terrifying black man who glanced up from his copy of *The Art of War*, as if to look for confirmation of this. 'We pulled up, the lights were on, we walked in, there were two security guards at the reception. We explained about the call, they told us it was likely a false alarm, called upstairs, checked the CCTV, said everything was fine. Had a quick look about, then left.'

'You spoke to this woman's boss?'

'Tamira May?' Peroni shook his head. 'Security did, I think.'

He looked at Jeffers for confirmation, but the partner shook his head.

'Nah,' he replied. 'They couldn't get through. But they said this was always the case, as when the Board was in session, they didn't speak to anyone. I talked with one of the drivers, said he brought one of them in from her daughter's recital. Apparently, something bad's going on.'

He sniffed, returning to his book.

'And I say good.'

'Good?' Koebel frowned at this. 'How so?'

'You remember that shit in Mercy Falls?' Peroni wiped pop tart crumbs off his uniform. 'Couple of years back?'

'Sure, I think.'

'These guys funded that clown car,' Peroni replied knowledgably. 'Buddy of mine was in the fire department that cleaned it all up. Said it was obvious they underpaid for things. Guilty as hell, and never even got a slap on the wrist. If they're having problems? Then it's on them.'

'Problems like a sniper?' Koebel leant back on the chair, watching the two officers.

'We reckon it's code,' Jeffers placed the book down now, realising he wasn't going to get a chance to read it while Koebel was there. 'Board hostage sniper – the Board is being held hostage by a sniper, picking them off one by one. It's *Twelve Angry Men*, ain't it? The film? They're trying to get something signed off and one of them isn't playing nice. They're stuck there until this person signs off on whatever it is. Held hostage by a sniper.'

'Or, like, there's an actual sniper trying to shoot them?' Koebel offered. 'Did you even bother to look at the other buildings?'

'It's Sunday,' Peroni moaned at this. 'Nobody's in. You can't get into most of the damn things.'

'Apart from the Wrentham building.'

Peroni and Jeffers looked awkwardly at each other, and Koebel knew without a shadow of doubt it was because they hadn't even tried.

'Right,' she looked at the two officers as she rose. 'Tell me about the gunshot.'

'Homeless guy, down the street from the building reckoned he heard a gunshot,' Jeffers continued. 'But he reckoned it was more a *phut* sound than a bang. But it's New York, you know? Cars backfire, there are fireworks—'

'Why would a firework be heard on a Sunday night?' Koebel asked.

'How the hell do I know?' Jeffers argued. 'Manhattan people be crazy.'

Koebel carried on staring at the two officers, moving her gaze between them slowly.

'So let me get this right,' she said. 'A woman sends a nine-one-one call in, saying her boss is trapped in a Board meeting, held hostage by a sniper. The same building where, at the same time, a homeless person hears a gunshot—'

'A *phut* sound—'

'I don't give a damn what it sounds like!' Koebel shouted. 'That's enough for me to demand to go see for myself, not let some rent-a-uniform tell me it's all fine!'

She paused, noting the look the two officers gave each other.

'What?' she continued. 'What am I missing here?'

'Security for Wrentham is top-notch,' Peroni replied. 'They use a firm that hires ex-Secret Service guys. High-end military, you know?'

'They're better than Presidential security, and they know how to keep their people alive,' Jeffers added. 'If they reckon it's nothing, I'm leaning to believing them.'

Koebel stared at the two men.

'I'm going to speak to the witness, the woman who called this in,' she said slowly and coldly. 'Meanwhile, you two—'

'We're going back there, aren't we?' Peroni sighed. 'Okay, sure. And when we find nothing?'

'I'll owe you both a beer,' Koebel said as she walked out of the break room. 'But I'd rather we could claim we tried everything when they start falling out of windows, like that other guy did a few months back. Wrentham has priors for that.'

As Koebel left, Peroni turned to Jeffers.

'So much for an easy Sunday,' he griped.

The woman, an executive assistant named Penny Martin was sitting in the interview room, gazing at the mirror along the west wall when Koebel walked in through the door.

'Sorry for the location,' she said, waving at the glass. 'There's nobody in there. Even if you were super important in a case, it's a Sunday night.'

Penny nodded, and Koebel sat opposite her.

'Why are you here, Miss Martin?' she asked.

'It's Ms,' Penny replied. 'Not Miss.'

'Okay,' Koebel pretended to write this down in her notebook. 'Why are you here, *Ms* Martin?'

'Because you're not doing your job,' Penny leant back, folding her arms as she glared at the detective facing her.

'I'm not?' Koebel raised her eyebrows at this.

'Not you, but the police,' Penny grumbled, pulling out her phone. 'I had this message almost forty minutes ago.'

She showed the message on her phone, as if this somehow validated her.

'I called front desk – *Wrentham's* front desk about fifteen minutes ago,' she continued. 'They said police came in, looked around and then left. Said nothing was wrong, and that the meeting was still going on.'

'And you didn't believe them?'

'They couldn't get through to the Board!' Penny replied brusquely. 'Nobody could even check in!'

'Is that because it's a Sunday though, and nobody's in, perhaps?' Koebel offered.

At this, however, Penny deflated slightly.

'Look, I just want to make sure my boss is okay,' she said. 'If she dies, they'll kill me.'

At Koebel's intrigued expression, Penny waved her hands.

'It's a term of phrase. I mean, if it comes out Miss May told me and I did nothing, or just let someone else do nothing, it'd go on my permanent record.'

'Yeah, I get that,' Koebel looked up from her notepad. 'Okay. So, we sent someone to look, they saw nothing, but we have had a witness claim to have heard some kind of noise, like a gunshot, so they're checking again. In the meantime, can you give me anything else?'

'Like what?' Penny frowned.

'Like if any of the people in the room don't get on with the others? Whether there could be additional friction?'

At this, however, Penny laughed.

'Are you asking me if the Wrentham Board don't like each

other?' she smiled. 'Detective, pardon my language, but they all fucking hate each other.'

Koebel nodded, writing this down.

'And did anyone – *could* anyone – have a problem with them that could lead them to doing such an act? Holding them hostage?'

'Lady, take a number and join the line,' Penny shook her head. 'They're probably some of the most hated people on Wall Street right now. And they're in survival mode.'

Koebel closed her notebook and looked at Penny as she worked through the potential scenarios.

'I've been told the security is top-notch,' she said. 'They hate them too?'

Penny nodded.

'They're ex-military, or Government,' she replied. 'They knew people who were killed in Mercy. It's been tough. Miss May even had her own security team removed, as she didn't trust them.'

'So, hypothetically, if I was speaking to one of the front desk security, and they told me everything was fine, even though they're super-bright, top-notch guys, they might not actually care about the Board's safety as much as I would?'

'Pretty much.'

'Do they know you?'

'In as much as I'm Miss May's PA, sure,' Penny nodded. 'I think they probably feel sorry for me.'

'Well, let's use that to our advantage then,' Koebel said, rising from her chair. 'Care for a drive over to the Wrentham building? I think I'd like to see for myself if your boss is okay.'

Penny almost jumped from her chair.

'I'd like that,' she said. 'I'd like that a lot.'

And, with Penny following her, Detective Koebel left the interview room, heading down to the car park, ruminating on the fact she'd expected today to be a quiet, slow one, and if she was lucky, this was all a mistake, and it could still be one.

But, deep down, she knew in her police gut that something was *off* here.

She just hoped it wasn't too late to do something about it.

———

87:28

MIKO LEANT BACK IN THE CHAIR, NOW FOCUSING HER ATTENTION on Devin, staring uncomfortably back at her.

'Die by the cock. That's rich coming from you,' she smiled.

'Why?' Devin pursed his lips together as he tried to work out Miko's revised game plan. 'I'm not like Eddie.'

'I don't know what you've heard, but Eddie's not like that either,' Eddie commented from the other end of the boardroom table.

'Live the dream, princess,' Devin smiled coldly as he glared back at the beefy, older man.

Eddie, in response went to rise, but then thought better of it, perhaps still trying to make the others forget the recent accusations against him, simply smiling back, and giving Devin both fingers, revealed in an over-the-top way.

'You're a prick, Macintosh,' he said, his voice light, but his intent darker, and plain for all to see. 'I can't wait to veto anyone in your way to the firing squad. You know, make that route nice and easy for you.'

'Oh, he's much more than that,' Miko purred, looking from Eddie to Devin. 'Aren't you?'

'Seriously, I have no clue whatsoever as to what the hell you're going on about,' Devin was getting angry now, and was shifting in his seat as he spoke. 'Is it my turn to vote? I—'

'Can I table a motion?'

Miko's voice was clear and determined, cutting across Devin as she suddenly stood up, facing the other members of the Board.

'I think we've gone past the point for motions,' Miles replied. 'We're in the voting stage now.'

'But I think you'll want to hear this,' Miko told him.

'I don't think there's anything you could say to me I'd want to hear,' Miles retaliated. 'Especially since you called me a racist.'

'I think you'll want to *hear* this,' Miko repeated, this time more determined.

'Fine,' Miles sighed. 'Go on, table the bloody motion, for all the good it'll do you.'

Miko looked around the table, spending a couple of seconds locking eyes with each person there, before eventually returning to Miles.

'I'd like to table the motion, here and now, that we add Devin Macintosh to this vote,' she said.

'Oh, for God's sake,' Devin exclaimed. 'I thought this was going to be something revelatory, not you being a bad-loser bitch who can't take being beaten!'

'He's right,' Victoria commented. 'This is as bad as Hayley trying to throw blame on Eddie.'

'I wasn't doing anything of the sort,' Hayley protested. 'I was making sure all the facts were stated.'

Miko, however, was ignoring Hayley's outburst, instead staring down at Devin with a knowing, mocking smile on her lips.

'You've been a naughty boy,' she said, almost jokingly. 'I know what you've been up to.'

'You know nothing,' Devin growled, tiring of the game. 'You're just trying to save your own skin.'

'You sure?'

'Sure,' Devin glowered.

Miko's smiled widened.

'*Really* sure?'

At this, however, Devin paused. There was something in Miko's tone, an assurance she hadn't had a moment ago.

Shit. She knows.

'Ah, this is stupid,' he muttered, waving dismissively at Miko as he looked around the boardroom table. 'We're wasting time here. I say we veto the motion and carry on with the vote, before the maniac across the street gets bored and accidentally pops one of us.'

Miko stared at Devin, catching his gaze for a long moment before looking back to Miles.

'Hey Miles, where's your wife tonight?' she asked innocently. 'Oh, wait, what was it you said? I'd ask Donna to read it back, but she's dead. You said she was out with friends, right? What was it you said … "My wife's out with friends, so she won't even know I'm gone until tomorrow." That sounds about right. Care to confirm or deny?'

'I don't know what your game is, Miss Tanasha, but I'm not playing,' Miles slammed his hands on the table in anger. 'Where my wife is, or who she's seeing tonight, is nothing to do with you or any of this Board.'

Miko moved away from her chair now, walking over to Miles, who, unsure how to react to this, simply stared up at her in confusion.

'You sure about that, Miles, old boy?' she whispered. 'You sure it's nothing to do with *any* of this Board?'

'Look, can we just get on with voting?' Devin snapped. 'I vote Miko. That's three now. Can we get two more?'

'I mean, it's a shame, you being all "team Devin" as well,'

ignoring Devin's outburst, Miko continued talking to Miles. 'But then betrayals are quite common for this Board, I suppose.'

She walked to the window now, staring out at it, across the street, the wind from the broken pane to her left ruffling her hair as she smiled.

'And Caesar believed Brutus was his brother, right until the knife went deep into his back,' she finished.

'What's that supposed to mean?' Miles, confused by this, looked around at the other members of the Board. 'Brutus? Caesar? What's she saying? Spit it out, woman!'

Devin rose from his chair now, visibly sweating as he spoke.

'Ignore her, she's just trying to save her traitor skin,' he said, his words coming out fast and almost unintelligible. 'We're three against Miko right now. All those in favour of continuing with her being removed—'

'No, Mister Macintosh. Let's discuss this some more.'

The voice coming through the phone speakers made everyone in the room jump. Justice had been quiet for a while now, and for a moment, the people in the boardroom had all but forgotten he was even there.

Devin, however, wasn't happy with this reply, and turned to face the window, following Miko as he gazed out across the city, towards the unknown assassin.

'You told us to vote!' he protested. 'We're voting! We're doing what you wanted, and in a minute you'll have your fucking scapegoat! Just let us do our job!'

'I told you to be democratic. This doesn't feel democratic.'

'And being held by *gunpoint* is democratic, you insane bastard?' Devin almost shouted now, his voice rising in a mixture of anger, fear and desperation. 'Come on! Where's the laser pointer? Yeah, I'm calling you out! This is bullshit!'

'Devin, sit down,' Jason said, nervously.

'What, you scared he'll shoot me?' still staring out of the window, Devin answered.

'No, you prick, I know that if he misses you, he could hit me, as I'm directly behind you,' Jason was already moving to the side.

Looking back at him, Devin deflated.

'We were taking a vote,' he whispered as he sat back down.

There was a moment of silence, a held breath by the Board as they waited for something else to happen.

Eventually, the voice of Justice broke the quiet once more.

'Mister Fenton, please answer the question. Where is your wife right now?'

Miles looked at the window and the sniper across the street.

'Why?' he asked, irritably. 'This is just another of your stupid games. And Miko's just trying to save her skin, so this is utterly pointless.'

'Mister Fenton, please answer the question,' Justice repeated. 'You said your wife was out with friends. Where is your wife right now?'

'You're just repeating yourself!' Miles was flustered now. 'Just tell me why!'

'Because if you don't answer the question, I will find her myself and *kill* her.'

The voice through the speakers was calm and relaxed, and nobody in the boardroom believed for one second there was any falsehood in the statement.

Miles, hearing this, shook his head, tears welling up as he continued to stare across the street at the mysterious killer.

'You leave her out of this!' he wailed. 'She's nothing to do with whatever this sick game is!'

Miko smiled now, the only person in the room to be enjoying this moment.

'Oh, she really is,' she purred. 'In fact, she's everything to do with this, if you look deep enough into it.'

'Shut up! Just shut the hell up!' Miles turned his anger onto Miko now, looking across the table at her as she chuckled.

'Don't you want to know the truth?' Miko continued, ignoring the order. 'Tell the nice sniper what she's up to, and we can all go home.'

'How do you work that out?' Victoria frowned. 'When you're currently on three votes?'

'Because I think Miles might change his vote real soon,' Miko shrugged.

'Mister Fenton, please answer the question. Where is your wife right now?' the voice of Justice spoke once more, and Eddie shook his head.

'Is that a recording?' he asked, softly, almost to himself.

'I assure you I'm right here,' Justice replied. 'But soon I won't be so relaxed about this, if Mister Fenton doesn't answer my question.'

'Just answer him!' Hayley, seeing an opportunity to save her skin again, insisted across the table.

'Do it!' Eddie added, looking around the room. 'You piss that maniac off, he's likely to start shooting at us.'

'Fine!' exasperated, Miles rose from his chair, facing the Board, rather than the window now. 'She's having dinner with an old school friend.'

'Hah!' Miko exclaimed. 'She's definitely been eating, but I don't think it's quite the meal you think it—'

'Shut your mouth!' Miles slammed his fists against the table, his face red with anger now. 'Shut your cock-ridden whore mouth! You don't know my family!'

Miko nodded at this, as if agreeing with his statement.

'You're right, boss,' she smiled. 'I don't know your family. Never met them. Never cared to meet them.'

'Then shut up and keep your nose out of my goddamned business!'

Miko cocked her head to the side at this, giving a sympathetic expression, like she was sorry for Miles, but hadn't explained why yet.

'But you see, I don't need to know your family. I just need to know your wife. You know, like Devin there does.'

Devin held his hands up, a confused expression on his face.

'Of course I know Gina!' he replied, looking around the Board as he did so. 'I've known Miles's family for years! His children hang out with mine! We've all met her! The only reason Miko hasn't is because she doesn't give a shit about this company, and is too busy doing tricks for our rivals!'

'There, are you satisfied?' Miles shouted at the window now. 'I answered your stupid bloody question.'

'How do you know she's out with an old school friend, Mister Fenton?' Justice seemed almost amused at the CEO's outburst, the voice almost mocking as it spoke through the speakers.

'We share an online diary,' Miles explained. 'We have calendars that are linked, as we have mutual friends' birthdays and anniversaries to remember. And it's easier to plan future events together when we know there's no double booking.'

'Wow, thanks for explaining how shared calendars work,' Tamira mocked, her voice monotone. 'How have I lived my life without knowing that?'

'They're great,' Miko smiled at her fellow Board member. 'And they're always one hundred percent accurate. I mean, nobody would ever lie about something, and put it into a diary, would they? You know, if, for example, they were going somewhere, or doing someone their partner might disapprove of?'

She smiled at Miles now.

'Did I say, "doing someone?" my mistake, I meant doing some *thing*.'

'When you're thrown to the wolves, I'm going to wait until they're done with you,' Miles replied coldly. 'And when the scraps of you are left, I'm going to gather them all together and take a massive shit on them.'

There was a strange sound through the speakers; a kind of staccato bark.

'He's fucking laughing!' Jason was the first to identify it. 'Justice is laughing at us!'

He looked around the table at the others.

'Look, he's just screwing with us, getting in our heads,' he said, nodding across the street. 'Don't give him the pleasure.'

'What pleasure?' Miles looked confused at the comment. 'I'm telling the truth about this! It's that bitch there who's getting in your heads about this!'

'And that's because your word's worth fuck all,' Miko sat back in her chair, rocking back and forth on it now, toying with Miles as she spoke. 'Always has been. You go where the money is, or where the wind's blowing. You never tell the truth. You're like a well-dressed scorpion whose sting got snapped off.'

'I think you'll find my sting is more than adequate,' Miles snapped back.

'Cool,' Miko smiled. 'Prove it.'

'Prove what?'

'That you're telling the truth,' Miko looked at Devin now as she spoke to Miles, watching his expression. 'Call her up. Let's see if she's where you claim she is.'

'I'll do no such thing,' Miles folded his arms. 'I'm not playing your games anymore.'

'Oh, I wasn't talking to you,' Miko looked at the window now, a dark smile on her face. 'I was talking to our friend with the sniper scope. I'm sure he has her details on file.'

As if by magic, the phone in the middle of the table clicked, and the television screen once more burst into life, this time with the contact details of Gina Fenton on it.

'No, wait!' Miles looked horrified.

'As requested, the phone is now ringing,' Justice replied through the room speakers, over the ringing of the phone. 'But if you say anything about your current predicament to your wife once she answers it, I *will* find and kill her. Do you understand?'

'You listen here, you piece of shit,' Miles growled. 'I'll—'

He stopped as the line clicked once more.

'Hello?' The voice of Gina Fenton echoed around the room. 'Miles?'

'Gina!' Miles sounded relieved his wife was all right. 'Oh, thank God.'

'Are you okay? Is there a problem?' Gina's echoed voice seemed concerned. Whether she was concerned for Miles, or concerned for herself, was still unknown.

'No darling. I just wanted to check in,' Miles, his voice now relaxed, his body language showing a man now relieved, sat back in his chair. 'Could you hold on for a moment?'

Quickly, he leant across the table, muting the call.

'Fuck you,' he said to Miko, before looking at the window. 'And fuck you. I told you she was with friends.'

'I listened to an audio drama once,' the voice of Justice continued. 'It was amazing. It sounded like the characters in the drama were on a submarine, in Victorian times. But they weren't. They just sounded that way.'

'What are you saying?' Miles's relaxed expression was rapidly retreating.

'He's saying just because she tells you on the phone she's somewhere doesn't mean she is,' Miko replied tartly.

'Indeed,' Justice continued. 'Turn off mute, Mister Fenton, and ask her how her dinner is. The one she's having right now with her friend.'

Miles went to respond, but instead nodded, clicking the speaker button again.

'Sorry, darling, I'm in a meeting,' he said.

'On a Sunday night?' Gina was shocked. 'How terrible! Can you get out?'

'I'm doing my best,' Miles said, glancing at the window before adding 'I thought I'd call during a break, and see how your dinner is going. With your friend.'

There was another flash on the television screen, and now the information was gone, replaced by a CCTV camera's footage of a hotel suite. In the suite, lying on the bed in nothing but her underwear, Gina spoke into the phone, the movements matching the audio that now came through the speakers.

'Oh. It's fine, we're about to order dessert,' she said, stretching out, sprawling on the bed as she continued. 'To be honest, I can't decide between the cheesecake or the crème brûlée.'

Miles paled, staring at the screen.

'Joanne's having issues with her husband,' Gina's voice continued through the speakers. 'She's quite distressed. I might stay the night with her if it's okay with you?'

'I ... of course,' Miles replied weakly.

'You're an angel,' Gina smiled on the screen, still on the bed. 'I'll be back as soon as I can. Snuggles.'

'I ... I love—'

Miles never finished his comment, as before he could complete the declaration of love, the phone clicked off as, on the screen, Gina disconnected the call and tossed the phone onto the bed beside her.

'Now, let's ask again,' Justice spoke one last time. 'Mister Fenton, please answer the question. Where is your wife right now?'

78:02

THE TELEVISION SCREEN CONTINUED TO SHOW GINA, SPRAWLED out on the bed, but the sound was muted, the call ended, as Miles opened and shut his mouth several times now, looking around the boardroom.

'Where is that?' Eddie asked, growling at the screen. 'It looks familiar.'

Hayley was also staring up at the image, reddening.

'Can we turn this off?' she asked, looking back at the Board. 'I mean, she's in her … her skimpies.'

Victoria laughed at the innocence of the woman opposite her.

'I like it,' she smiled, looking over at Miles. 'This way, we all get to see what he paid for.'

'And what's that supposed to mean?' Miles snarled, both embarrassed and angry at this turn in the situation.

'Look at her,' Victoria chuckled. 'There's no way those tits are real.'

'That's the Madison Hotel!' Eddie blurted out in surprise as he finally worked out what had been bothering him. 'One of the executive suites we get to use!'

He spun now to face Miles.

'And you stuck a fucking camera in it?' he asked, a mixture of incredulity and anger flitting across his face.

'Are you surprised?' Miko replied, enjoying this immensely. 'He stuck one in my office, after all.'

'Yeah, but you deserved it,' Victoria said, leaning closer. 'On account of you being a traitorous little bitch.'

'You stuck a camera in the executive suites,' Devin now looked at Miles, a slow realisation now dawning. 'You record everything that goes on there.'

'Of course I do,' Miles snapped. 'You think Wrentham gives you these suites as a perk? They wanted you off your guard! They wanted you to think you weren't being watched; that you could be honest in what you said and did! This way they could gain leverage!'

'Who the fuck is the "they" you're talking about?' Miko frowned now as she looked at Miles. 'We're the Board, you're the CEO. We're at the top of the mountain, nobody else.'

Miles couldn't help it; he began to chuckle.

'We're middle management, nothing more,' he said. 'Once you peek behind the curtains, you realise we're nothing in the grand scheme of things. There are people above us. Secret people in the shadows. Powerful people.'

'Makes a lot of sense, actually,' Hayley said.

'Oh yeah? And how do you work that out?' Victoria snapped.

'Because I never understood how a vacuous cretin like Miles made it to CEO of this company,' Hayley replied, shrugging. 'That was it, really.'

'Look, all that matters here is that Miko was right,' Tamira said, waving at the screen, where Gina Fenton was still lying on the bed. 'Mrs Fenton definitely isn't with a school friend named Joanne. Unless it's a vibrator, and it's appearing very soon.'

'This isn't true,' Miles shook his head. 'This is fake. It's his games.'

'It's your CCTV!' Jason exclaimed. 'Christ, I've been in that room. I thought I ...' He trailed off, as he realised where he was going with that comment. 'You can't call this fake when it's your balls on the line,' he finished instead.

'I think Miss Tanasha may be owed an apology,' the voice of Justice, obviously enjoying this, came through the speakers once more. 'It seems that she might, after all, be correct here.'

'It's a lie!' Miles shouted. 'It's a deep fake, or something like that!'

'Can you deep fake those tits?' Victoria clicked her tongue against the roof of her mouth. 'If so, can someone do mine?'

'Would you like to call her again? We could watch her answer,' Justice suggested.

Devin shook his head. 'Turn it off, please,' he replied sadly, placing a hand on Miles's shoulder. 'I think you've done enough, don't you?'

'I haven't even started,' Justice replied in a sing-song manner. 'Nobody has asked the question yet. The one about access.'

'How is she in there?' Miko replied helpfully. 'I mean, you're the one with the executive suite pass, Miles. Did you let her in? Did you tell her she was being filmed?'

'Of course I didn't!'

'Which one?' Miko smiled. 'The letting her in part, or the Fenton "wank bank" home movie collection part?'

'Both!' Miles snapped. 'I never let her in because I know not to go in there!'

'Because you know there's a camera there,' now Eddie was joining in. 'Oh, you're a piece of work.'

'Then who let her in?' Victoria looked around the room. 'One of us had to. We're the only ones with passes.'

'Corey had one too,' Devin suggested. 'Maybe that's why he isn't here.'

Miles, however, was looking back out of the window again.

'You're controlling the feed now, aren't you?' he asked.

'I am, and thank you,' Justice replied through the speakers. 'Without you, I would never have thought to do such an underhand thing.'

'Do you control the playback?'

'Miles, don't do this,' Devin pleaded. 'Don't play his little games.'

'I said, do you control the playback?' Miles shouted.

'Yes.' Justice spoke the word with an almost sadness.

'Then show me who she's with.'

'She's not there with anyone!' Devin replied desperately. 'We'd have seen them by now, and we're all here! She's probably stolen your key and gone there for some alone time!'

'Alone time my ass!' Miles was almost frothing with rage now. 'Who is she seeing? Is he there? Show me!'

'Miles!' Devin was shouting himself now, forcing himself to calm down. 'Miles, this isn't good for you.'

He looked to the window.

'You've done enough. Turn it off.'

'You're right,' the voice of Justice seemed almost apologetic now. 'I should turn it off. Here, let me do that right now. Everyone say bye bye to Gina now.'

There was a flicker on the screen, but then the footage rewound instead, and Gina, on the bed, reached out, the phone jumping back into her hand. The video kept rewinding, now up to four times the speed, as Gina, on the screen, lay on the bed, before disappearing quickly backwards away from it.

'I'm sorry, you have a new machine,' Justice apologised. 'I don't know the buttons yet.'

'Turn it off!' Like a horror movie fan, scared of the film but afraid to look away, Devin stared at the still rewinding scene. 'Turn it off now!'

'There's no need to take that tone with me, Mister Macintosh, I'm doing my best,' Justice replied, and now the voice was back to its normal, almost mocking self. 'Ah. Here you go.'

With a last flicker, the rewinding stopped, and on the screen the Board could see Gina, on the bed, topless, talking to Devin as he pulled his shirt on, walking away from the bed.

And then the screen turned to black.

'There,' Justice stated happily. 'I turned it off.'

As Miles slowly turned to face Devin, the other Board members following suit, Devin slowly backed away in his chair.

'It's not what it looks like,' he said softly, hands up in a surrender motion.

'You sure about that, you prick?' Eddie smiled. 'Because it looked to me – hell, it looked to all of us – that you've got the CEO's wife as an executive benefit.'

'Shut it, Eddie,' Devin growled now, turning to face the older, stockier man.

'Hell no,' Eddie grinned. 'You've been giving me shit all night. Opportunities like this are rare.'

Miles rose from his own chair now, backing away from the boardroom table as he glared at Devin.

'How long?' he asked.

'Miles, please—' Devin returned his attention to Miles, but the CEO threw up his hand to stop him.

'*How long have you been sleeping with my wife?*'

The room was silent for an uncomfortable amount of time. And then, slowly, Devin sighed, looked to the floor and spoke.

'Three years,' he replied, his voice only a whisper.

Miles stared at Devin, his expression one of incomprehension, before he staggered backwards, eventually backing into the side cabinet, the broken cell phones still in the microwave on top, no longer able to back away any further.

The members of the Board stayed still, unsure what was about to happen next.

'I can play you some audio, if you like,' Justice spoke now. 'Your camera, the one you placed in the room, is very good. Almost as good as the one you placed in Miss Tanasha's office. It has video and audio capabilities. You captured the whole thing in four-k.'

'*And you can go to hell too!*' Miles screamed out of the open, shattered window, tears of betrayal streaming down his face.

If Justice considered this, he didn't comment on it, instead continuing on regardless.

'At one point, he calls you a "cuck," to your wife,' he continued. 'Says you have no dick.'

There was a pause, and then Justice's voice became more inquisitive as he asked another question.

'That's not true, is it, Miles? Are you a dickless little cuck?'

Miles was still leaning against the side cabinet now, tears streaming down his face.

'Gina ...' he groaned.

'Please don't cry,' Justice said, his voice softer now. 'I mean, feel free to cry, but not like that. You're "ugly crying", Miles. It's not attractive. What would your wife think?'

There was a pause.

'Oh, wait. She won't care. She's screwing Mister Macintosh.'

'We can discuss this when we get out, yeah?' Devin rose from his chair now, and for a moment it looked as if he was about to walk over to Miles, maybe comfort him in some kind of sick, twisted way, but eventually he stopped himself, settling for a nervous shifting from foot to foot as he watched the CEO.

'Of course, it's always the family that suffers,' Justice added.

'What do you mean?' Victoria asked, looking from Devin to Miles. 'It doesn't look that way right now.'

She stopped, though, as the television screen lit up once more. The CCTV video had stopped, thankfully for both Miles and Devin, but now the screen had new contact details on it.

```
Devin Macintosh — Home
```

Devin stared at the screen in abject terror.

'Please, don't,' he pleaded.

'I think it's only fair for Mister Fenton to inform everyone of this current predicament, don't you?' Justice asked as, in the background, the line rang. 'Your wife Mary works so hard. She waits for you. What did you say in the car tonight? When you were travelling to this meeting from your tryst with Mister Fenton's wife?'

'Please—'

'That's right. "*It's gonna be a late one, so kiss the boys for me and I'll see you when I get home. I love you too.*" That was a lie, wasn't it? You didn't expect to go home tonight.'

'I did!'

'But Gina Fenton told her husband she was staying the night,' Justice replied. 'You're still lying, Mister Macintosh. Time to come clean.'

'How do you know about my call?' Devin glared at Miles. 'You bugged the fucking cars too? You idiot! All these things you did, he's using them to kill us!'

Miles looked up silently, his eyes red-rimmed as the phone clicked and a voice answered.

'Hello?'

'Mary! *Put the phone down!*' Devin almost fell onto the table as he leant across to the phone, screaming as loudly as he could. 'Don't listen to them!'

'What?'

'I said don't—'

Click.

'Hello, Mary. Pleasure to meet you,' Justice spoke now, and Devin realised with a collapsing sensation in his stomach that the speakerphone was no longer connected to the conversation. It seemed that Justice wanted to chat to his wife alone. 'I've sent you an email. There's a link on it to a video. Miles and I think you should watch it.'

'Shut up, you sick fuck!' Devin shouted, but his voice had lessened with the realisation this was a futile endeavour. 'Please, no …'

Mary, however, was confused by this.

'Wait, Miles sent this?' she asked. 'Miles, are you there?'

Devin looked at Miles now, as the older man straightened his tie, standing straighter as he walked to the boardroom table.

'Don't, Miles,' Hayley warned, but as Miles reached his original spot at the table, the same *click* Devin had heard when his microphone connection was cut was heard again.

Miles was live.

'Please, Miles,' Devin whispered.

Miles, however, stared straight at Devin as he spoke into the phone.

'Watch it, Mary,' he said coldly. 'See what kind of man your husband is.'

'I don't under—' Mary started, and Devin went to scream out once more, to shout at her not to do this, but there was another *click*, and the phone connection ended.

Listening to the dial tone, Devin slumped into his chair as Miles looked down at him.

'Well, that was all very exciting,' Justice said, the excited voice echoing through the phone's speakers.

'Please, I beg you, reconnect.' Instead of looking out across the street, Devin was now looking at the ceiling, almost as if he was asking God himself to reconnect the call to his wife. Which, in a strange, roundabout way, he was. Because, currently, to everyone in that room, Justice was God.

'You won't want me to,' Justice replied.

'Why?' Devin held his hand against his mouth, partly to stop himself from puking onto the table. 'Why not?'

'Because your wife will have questions,' Justice explained calmly. 'She's just clicked the video link.'

'What's on the video link?' Miles, strangely calm about all this, asked.

'Are you sure you want to know?' Justice seemed actually concerned.

'Yes, I want to know,' Miles nodded. And, as he said this, the screen opened up once more, showing CCTV footage of Gina and Devin, together, on the bed. And Devin looked away as the sound could be heard, their conversations echoing around the room.

'Happy anniversary.'

'Ow! You bitch! Dammit Gina! Don't leave marks! I exercise with the Board tomorrow morning! How will I explain teeth marks to Miles or the others when we're on the treadmill?'

'Tell him you have a very healthy sex life, while your CEO's cock is covered in cobwebs?'

'Jesus,' that was Jason, commenting.

'You should punish me. Punish me, Daddy.'

The sound stopped, and as Devin looked up, he saw that, mercifully, the video had ended. But it was enough. And if Mary saw it, their marriage was over.

Getting up from the chair, he pushed past Miles, walking to the broken window, feeling the wind blowing on him as he stared out across the street, his face set in anger, his voice only a growl.

'I'm gonna find you and kill you,' he snarled.

'What was it you told Miss Tanasha?' Justice asked merrily. 'Those who live by the cock, die by the cock …?'

Devin went to speak, but stopped himself.

Justice was right. He'd brought this on himself.

He looked back at Miko, currently enjoying the show.

'And you're fucking ended. Everywhere. You're toxic,' he said. 'I've got contacts. Big ones. They'll make sure you never work anywhere again. The only thing you'll be able to do is put your cock-sucking mouth to work in back-alley whorehouses.'

'Shut up and sit down, you goddamn drama queen,' Miko wasn't bothered in the least by his threat as she waved at his recently vacated chair. 'Buy her a car, a pony, something. She'll come running back.'

'Oh, she'll run, alright, but not to Mister Macintosh,' Justice spoke up again, and Devin spun back to the window.

'And what's that supposed to mean, you sick bastard?' he said coldly, watching across the street for any form of movement, anything that could show him where the bastard currently dismantling his life was situated.

'I didn't just send the video,' Justice replied. 'I sent the address of the Madison Hotel and the suite number. She's on her way there right now. She left very quickly.'

There was a pause, but then Justice continued.

'I do hope she doesn't know the combination to your gun safe.'

Miles and Devin looked at each other, both realising the potential for carnage and murder that was about to happen, but before either could say anything, Justice continued.

'Mister Fenton. Number six.'

Miles frowned as Devin walked back to his chair.

'What do you mean, six?'

'Behind you, on the drawers of the side cabinet, are little brass numbers,' Justice explained. 'Just like the one you opened earlier. I really hope your short-term memory loss isn't serious.'

'I've had a lot on my mind!' Miles snapped back.

'Yes, you have. And I don't really care. So, I'd like you to go over there and open number six, please.'

Devin stared at Miles as he walked over to the cabinet, looking down at the numbers. He remembered thinking Miles had placed the numbers on, but it seemed that he was wrong about that assumption.

Eventually, after much searching, Miles nodded to himself and, opening the drawer with a brass "6" on it, he looked into it, paling.

'Remove the item, please.'

Saying nothing, Miles reached into the drawer, and pulled out a wicked-looking kitchen knife, turning it around to show the Board, his eyes narrowing.

'What the fuck?' Eddie half rose from his chair at the sight. 'Why did you give him a knife?'

'In olden days, confrontations weren't settled with conventional discussion, or with lawyers in a boardroom,' Justice explained. 'They were settled man to man, and to the death.'

As Miles, knife in his hand gripped tightly and with his face still flushed with anger, stared daggers at Devin, Justice finished his explanation.

'Maybe you should regain your manhood, you gutless little cuck, by cutting off *Mister Macintosh's*.'

69.21

MILES STARED AT THE KNIFE IN HIS HAND, TURNING IT AROUND AS he contemplated what Justice had just said.

'Miles, whatever you're thinking right now, I really think you should *not* think it,' Victoria whispered, staring in horror at the CEO. 'I'm sure this can be resolved with some grown-up conversation—'

'Fuck my wife, will you?' Miles growled as he looked up from the blade, staring icily at Devin now. 'Call me a cuck, will you?'

Devin looked around the room for support, and, seeing none, straightened his shoulders.

'Honestly, if I'm being serious? I can't remember,' he admitted. 'But it's possible. I have to say, though, if the shoe fits—'

He laughed, ducking to the side as Miles, his face purple with anger, charged at him, knife out, intending to impale his rival on the razor-sharp tip. As Miles moved past the laughing Devin, however, it meant the next point of contact was Victoria, still sitting in the chair beside him, who jumped up, screaming in fear as the furious Miles speared the back of her chair.

'My mink!' she cried out. 'You cut my fucking mink!'

'Calm down, you drama queen!' Eddie said, also backing away now as Miles, his eyes wide, spun around to make another attack. 'It's not on the chair. You're wearing it, remember?'

'It's the principle!' Victoria cried as Miles charged Devin again, swinging wildly as Devin, still laughing, stepped nimbly backwards, allowing Miles to overbalance with his forward momentum and stumble into the wall, hitting it with a solid *crump*.

'Give it up, old man!' Devin laughed, his arrogance and cockiness showing now, as he danced around the office. 'You think you're the only one wronged here? So, I had an affair! Miko gave trade secrets! Victoria's shagging the driver—'

'Shut your lying mouth!' Miles slashed up with the knife, quicker than Devin had expected and, as he yanked his head back to avoid the blow, the tip of the blade nicked his cheek, scoring upwards as Miles carried on, drawing a thin red line of blood along it, the cut only a couple of inches long – a blow that, if Devin hadn't whipped his head back quickly, would have blinded him in his right eye.

By this point, however, Jason and Eddie had both run in, charging at Miles, grabbing him from behind, Eddie pinning Miles's arms to his side to stop him slashing wildly.

'That's enough!' Eddie yelled.

'Get off me!' Miles was frothing now as he stared at Devin, holding a hand to his now bleeding cheek, staring at his bloodied hand in a mixture of surprise and anger. 'I didn't get his eyes! I want to blind him before I kill him!'

'You *cut* me!' Devin looked at the knife-wielding CEO in utter shock. 'Jesus Christ, Miles!'

'What did you expect?' Jason snapped back at Devin, struggling with Miles as he tried to attack again. 'You fucked his wife, and then you started playing dickhead matador, with him as the bull! Of course you were gonna get cut!'

Devin once more stared at the blood on his hand.

'Does someone have a handkerchief?' Hayley asked, looking around. 'Or a napkin? Something for Devin's face?'

She saw a small pile of napkins on the side cabinet and pointed at them.

'Could someone get—'

'*Motherfucker!*' Devin screamed as he charged into the restrained Miles now, landing a solid right hook on the CEO's chin, knocking Miles's head back with the force of the blow. Jason, letting go of Miles, tackled Devin, with Tamira running from the other side of the table to assist him in pulling the fighting Board members back from each other, Miles now bleeding from his cut lip as Eddie yanked him backwards towards the window.

'I'll gut you!' Miles screamed, blood mixing with spittle as he screamed maniacally at Devin. 'I'm gonna geld you like a stallion! Then I'll turn you into glue!'

'We should have put you out to pasture years ago!' Devin screamed in response. 'Two in the back of the head and good night, you old fucker!'

'Guys!' Jason was now joining in with the screaming. 'You're playing his game!'

'This isn't a game!' Miles was shouting and his face was purple with rage, but tears were flowing down his cheeks now, and not because of the pain of the punch. 'Let's see you call it a game when it's your wife being filmed, or your life being destroyed!'

Miles relaxed, slumping slightly in Eddie's grip.

'Oh, wait,' he continued mockingly. 'You don't have one.'

'What, a wife or a life?' Jason looked back at Miles as he still struggled with Tamira to pull Devin back, the blood from

Devin's cut now wiped on Jason's suit and collar. 'Shit, I only just bought this!'

'Both!' Miles howled. 'No woman would take you, and you've got no friends! All you do is sit in your office and sulk!'

'I'm always in my office because I'm always fixing your fuckups, you old dinosaur!' Jason was loosening his grip on Devin now, as he turned to face Miles. 'Maybe you shouldn't be a bastard to the guy holding back the man who wants to kill you! Maybe if you did your job correctly, I wouldn't have to spend my life—'

He stopped as Devin, now only held back by Tamira, lunged at Miles, his arms outreached, his hands stretching for the CEO's throat. Only Hayley, now joining in and helping Tamira pull him back, stopped the attack which was unfortunate, as Miles – elbowing Eddie in the kidney, the bruiser staggering back and having let go of his target – now charged at Devin as well, his blade rising to stab his rival …

Who wasn't there.

Jason, however, was.

'*Gargh!*' Jason screamed out, lurching back from Miles, the kitchen knife now rammed into his right thigh. 'You stabbed me!'

'You were in the way!' Miles protested, looking around. 'He was in the way! I didn't see him!'

Jason looked down at his leg, the knife jutting awkwardly out. Devin, his fight now dissipated, pulled away from Tamira, staring down at it as well.

'That's bleeding badly,' he muttered, the concern clear in his voice. 'That shouldn't be bleeding that hard.'

'What, and you're an expert on knife crime now, Rambo?' Jason said, but his face was paling, as his blood loss was becoming more than he'd expected. Stumbling back, he looked confused around the room.

'He might be right …' he groaned, as Hayley, moving from

behind Devin, ran to him, examining the wound before looking back at Miles.

'You useless bastard!' she shouted. 'You've probably nicked an artery! Someone give me a belt!'

Frozen to the spot, the men stared around the room at each other, unable to make any kind of decision.

'Or a tie! You're all wearing them!' Hayley manhandled the fading Jason to the table. 'Move the chairs! Get him onto the table!'

'Who the hell do you think you are?' Miko stood back as Hayley pushed past. 'The office first aider or something?'

'Yes!' Hayley replied curtly. 'Because I am! Quick! And someone grab me those napkins!'

With Jason now badly injured, the fight seemed to have disappeared from both Miles and Devin and, although still on opposite sides of the boardroom, all they did now was stare at the body on the table, groaning in pain as his leg bled out. In the end, it was Eddie who pulled his tie off, tossing it over to Hayley.

'Here, it's ruined since I chewed on it,' he said.

Hayley nodded thanks as she turned back to Jason.

'This is going to hurt like a bastard, but I need to cut the blood flow,' she said, sweat pouring down Jason's face as he nodded, his eyes clenched shut. Wrapping it around his thigh and securing it with a knot, Hayley pulled hard at it, the tie cutting into Jason's thigh as he screamed.

'Hold this knot!' she shouted at Eddie. 'You can tighten it more than me!'

Eddie agreed, pulling harder at the makeshift tourniquet. As he did so Hayley took the opportunity to pull the blade out, using it to slice down the suit leg, revealing the vicious wound, but at the same time also allowing the blood to escape the confined area it'd been trapped in, the boardroom table now becoming covered in it as Jason writhed in pain.

The flow, however, lessened as the blood, stopped by the tourniquet could no longer escape, and Hayley padded the wound with napkins, looking around and clicking her fingers at Devin.

'I'm not a dog,' he snapped, but then realised what she was pointing at, and pulled his tie off. 'Yeah, sorry. Here.'

Hayley took the second tie and wrapped it around the napkins, bandaging the wound and holding them in place as she tied a second knot.

'We need to get him to a hospital!' she shouted out to anyone listening, before looking at the window and the sniper across the street. 'You hear me? He needs a hospital! He's lost a lot of blood.'

'He's not lost any blood,' Victoria muttered, staring in horror at her stained mink jacket. 'That implies we can't find it. And we can see it everywhere.'

Miles, watching the scene on the boardroom table with a growing sense of desperation and despair, stared down at his blood-covered hands, stained when he'd stabbed Jason.

'I'm sorry, Jason,' he whispered, his voice almost inaudible. 'I didn't mean to …'

'Didn't mean to what?' Miko, now standing in the opposite corner, shouted across the room at Miles. 'Didn't mean to stab him? Didn't mean to try to geld Devin? What the fuck, Miles!'

'He …' Miles looked imploringly at Devin, as if hoping the man he'd tried to kill moments earlier would somehow assist him. 'I was angry …'

'You were fucking played, that's what you were,' Victoria muttered, turning away from the carnage behind her, and staring out of the window in her blood-stained mink coat. 'Okay, you sick, nameless bastard. We've played your game, it's gone badly and now Jason needs medical help. So can we end this?'

There was a crackle on the phone's speakers.

'Do not fret, for Mister Barnett *will* receive medical care,' the voice of Justice spoke.

'Oh, thank God,' Hayley almost whimpered, leaning closer to Jason. 'Did you hear that? He's getting you medical attention.'

'Indeed, we will do just that,' Justice continued. 'As soon as one of you admits to a wrongdoing.'

'You *what?*' It was Tamira who now stared at the window in utter disbelief. 'He's dying here!'

'No, he's bleeding there,' Justice replied calmly. 'And Miss Moran's timely efforts and first aid skills have made sure that currently, he's not dying. But he could still die. If he gets no medical care. All you need to do is admit to a wrongdoing. An admission of guilt. Any guilt, so far unspoken.'

There was a moment of silence as the boardroom members took in the request's enormity.

'Do this, and I will provide medical assistance.'

Miko sat back in her chair, staring across Jason's moaning body at the window.

'This is sick!' she exclaimed. 'You're sick!'

Eddie looked at Hayley, a helpless, "what do we do" look upon his face.

'I'll do it,' Miles spoke softly, still staring at the ground.

'What did you say?' Victoria looked at him, unsure if she'd heard him correctly.

In response, Miles raised his head to face her.

Gone was the anger, gone was the fury. All that was left now was sad resignation.

'You want guilt?' he asked, looking out of the window. 'I'll give you some. I've got loads to spare.'

'What are you talking about?' Hayley frowned, looking back at Devin. 'You should be doing this, not him! You're the one who started it!'

'How did you work that out?' Devin snapped back. 'He tried to stab me!'

'Because you were having an affair with his wife!'

'*Enough!*' Miles's voice was surprisingly loud and commanding, and the rest of the Board stopped their bickering as they all looked at him.

Realising all eyes were on him now, Miles cleared his throat and straightened his tie.

'The fire wasn't the only issue we had to sort out after Mercy,' he said, his voice calm and unwavering. 'People got sick after it happened.'

'Miles, shut up,' Devin spoke softly, cautiously. 'You don't know what you're saying.'

'Oh, I know exactly what I'm saying,' Miles replied, shaking his head. 'And I should have said it earlier.'

Hayley, still standing beside the groaning, pale form of Jason, rose, facing Miles now.

'What do you mean, sick?' she asked. 'What kind of sick?'

'Miles, don't,' Devin pleaded.

'Really sick. The kind you don't get better from,' Miles admitted, taking a deep breath and letting it out before continuing. 'The doctors believed it was from the fire, that maybe the smoke and chemicals had mixed up into something, or maybe there was some kind of allergy to the smoke.'

He shook his head sadly.

'It wasn't.'

'Miles!' Victoria had turned back from the window now, staring across the room at her CEO. 'For the love of God, shut the fuck up!'

'No!' Miles spun to look at her now, and tears ran down his face once more. 'Don't you see? I've spent so long dealing with these lies, it's destroyed my life! It's probably what drove Gina into his bed!'

He punctuated this last line by pointing over at Devin once

more.

'Now wait a moment!' Devin shouted back. 'You want to throw yourself to the wolves, that's your call, but don't blame me for this! Or Gina!'

Tamira shook her head, walking back to the chair, sitting down in it, at a right angle to the table, one of the napkins in her hand, held under the lip.

'Let him finish,' she said, nodding at Miles. 'He started it, he can end it.'

As everyone looked at Miles, Tamira took a pen from her pocket, writing carefully, without looking down, onto the napkin, her face set in a neutral pose. If you looked at her, say, from across the street and through a sniper rifle, you'd never think she was doing anything except for listening.

Miles, nodding at her, did as she suggested.

'The press thought that the sickness was because of the fire, but they couldn't prove it. That's why it was never revealed,' he continued.

'Was it?' Eddie growled.

'Hmm?'

'Was it connected to the bloody fire?'

'No, it wasn't anything to do with it,' Miles shook his head. 'We didn't lie about that.'

'For God's sake, Miles, shut up!' Devin said, pointing at the phone on the boardroom desk. 'He's listening to us! He's hearing all of this, you dopey prick!'

'And I don't care anymore!' Miles yelled back at Devin before looking back at Eddie.

'It wasn't anything to do with the fire, because Protex was dumping toxic shit into the water supply,' he admitted. 'They'd been doing it for years, on our suggestion.'

Eddie stared in utter disbelief at Miles before looking slowly around the room.

'You are shitting me,' he replied, looking each Board

member in the eyes before continuing. 'And we knew about this?'

'Come on Eddie, don't play the guiltless innocent for the cheap seats,' Victoria muttered. 'The refinery site ran out of space, and we couldn't get the funds together to build additional storage. So we told them to do what they needed to do, and we'd back their play, as long as it didn't cost us anything. We all knew about the waste dumping.'

'Not the fucking illnesses!' Eddie was livid as he stared down at Victoria. 'How many?'

Victoria didn't answer the question, and so Eddie turned to face Miles now.

'How many?' he repeated angrily.

'I don't understand—'

'How many *kids?* How many deaths in the last two years?' Eddie looked around. 'You're saying "people", but that's not that, is it? You'd have explained away people, but when it's kids, you really don't want that out there. So how many kids died?'

Miles looked at Devin, and then Victoria, before turning slowly to face Eddie.

'… Four deaths,' he admitted, his voice raspy as he spoke. 'All children.'

Eddie staggered back from Miles as if he was suddenly radioactive.

'Jesus Christ,' he mumbled to himself before looking around the boardroom, at the other members watching him. 'Who else here knew about this?'

'Does it matter?' Victoria asked irritably.

'How can you be so cold? You're a mother!' Eddie was shaking his head now, unable to process what was being said.

'And?' Victoria folded her arms, her body language shifting more defensively as she scrutinised Eddie. 'They weren't my daughter. They were nobody to me.'

'And if it was your daughter?'

Devin chuckled.

'She wouldn't have to endure any more recitals, for a start,' he replied glibly.

At this, however, Eddie now turned the full intensity of his anger onto Devin.

'Oh, you're a real funny man,' he thundered. 'You absolute waste of oxygen.'

If Devin was concerned at Eddie's anger, he didn't show it, turning to fully face the larger man.

'You want some? Come get it!' he declared loudly. 'You want to know why you didn't hear about this before? It's simple! You're not part of this!'

To emphasise his point, he waved around the room.

'You're a gorilla in a suit that we tell to hit things!' he continued furiously. 'Don't make out you're anything more!'

'You know nothing about me!' Eddie screamed back, his face reddening.

'No?' Devin couldn't help himself, he'd gone too far, and the line was way behind him now. 'I know *you killed Ryan what-shisname!*'

It was as if Devin had pricked Eddie with a pin; the anger and bluster simply deflated away as Eddie, his face stricken, collapsed into the empty boardroom chair behind him.

'Ah, shit, sorry,' Devin, realising he'd gone too far, shook his head. 'No, I am. That was a dick move. The pressure …'

He trailed off, looking away as Victoria, her arms still folded, turned to the window.

'There you go, you bastard!' she yelled. 'We've given you a secret! Now give us a paramedic before Jason dies of blood loss!'

The boardroom was quiet; the members of the Board waiting for a response.

Eventually, Justice replied, the voice calm, almost angry as it echoed around the speakers of the room.

'Did the paramedics come when the people burned to death?' he asked. 'Did the paramedics come when children coughed up toxic blood?'

There was another pause, and then Justice finished with one last word, spoken harshly.

'No.'

Hayley looked up from Jason, her eyes wide in shock.

'But you promised!' she pleaded. 'You said he'd—'

'I didn't promise a paramedic,' Justice interrupted, his voice now cold and icy. 'I said he would receive medical attention. And he will, in approximately one hour.'

'You son of a bitch!' Tears were running down Hayley's face now, as she looked around the boardroom in desperation. 'He won't last that long!'

'Then you'd better find a way to ensure that he does.'

'How the hell do I do that?' Hayley moved away from Jason now, facing the window, but Justice had disappeared once more, the line quiet as the grave.

Hayley turned to Miles.

'How the hell do I do that?' she repeated, but this time it was soft, almost as a plea.

In return, Miles shook his head, tears streaming down his face.

'I did what he asked,' he moaned. 'It's not my fault!'

Hayley turned her attention back to Jason, still groaning on the table, his face now ashen, his leg still bleeding through the napkins, although at a far more reduced rate than before.

'What the hell do we do now?' she muttered.

Nobody answered.

Because nobody had a clue.

ON THE STREET

Koebel had arrived in a police car a few minutes after leaving the precinct, and, with Penny beside her, she had walked along the outside of the building, checking the ground while Penny looked up at the surrounding buildings.

'Why are you looking at the ground?' Penny asked irritably. 'He's up there! They're up there!'

'Where, exactly?' Koebel asked, returning her attention to the PA. 'Where is the boardroom?'

Penny paused, looking up at the building looming above her.

'It's on this side of the street, twenty-third floor,' she said, pointing high up the side. 'It'll be further on down, maybe there?'

Koebel looked up at where Penny was pointing, and then followed the line of windows back down, pausing at a spot on the pavement at the base of the building. Walking swiftly over, she crouched down, pulling on a glove as she picked up a piece of shattered glass.

'There's glass here,' she said, frowning. 'But it's sheet glass.

Not the tempered stuff you'd expect to see on a high level floor.'

She rose, looking up at the building, squinting as she tried to see up to the twenty-third floor.

'Why do you care about glass?' Penny was looking at the buildings on the other side.

'The witness said they heard a rifle,' Koebel explained, returning to the shards of glass on the floor. 'If someone shot at the Wrentham Board, then the glass would break. Or, with tempered glass, crack at least.'

'You think they shot the window, and it fell to the street?' Penny now looked around, seeing the fallen glass all around her.

'I think they definitely broke a window,' Koebel stroked her chin. 'Have you had renovations recently? In particular, the boardroom?'

'Yeah, about a week back,' Penny nodded. 'I remember seeing workmen. Or a workman, I can't remember, but they were in the boardroom. I think they were in several.'

'Several boardrooms?'

'Detective, we have hundreds of people working here,' Penny couldn't help herself, and a hint of pride slipped through as she continued. 'We need more than one boardroom.'

'And the Board, the one your boss is part of, would they meet in these?'

'Oh no, just one,' Penny shook her head. 'It's always … oh shit, that's how they knew?'

'I think there's a chance whoever did this got into your company building somehow, and while there they replaced the windows with glass more inclined to shatter when struck,' Koebel mused, looking back up at the surrounding buildings. 'They wanted to make sure the bullets hit home.'

'So, you think this is real?' Penny asked, but Koebel was already walking towards the main entrance.

However, before she got there, Officers Peroni and Jeffers walked out, the latter looking concerned as they walked over to Koebel.

'Security showed us the boardroom CCTV footage,' he said. 'They have a camera in there; apparently there's been some loyalty issues, and Miles Fenton, the CEO, placed a few on the entire floor.'

He showed a print out; on it was an image of a Board in session.

'This was taken from the screen, we took a copy—'

'I understand how "print screen" works,' Koebel said, showing it to Penny. 'Who are these people?'

'That's Miko Tanasha, Hayley Moran, Miss May's there – that's my boss – then there's Jason Taylor. Miles Fenton's at the head, then you have Victoria Harvey, Devin Macintosh, and Eddie Purcell.'

'You missed someone,' Koebel pointed at a young woman. 'Who's that?'

'No idea, she's probably there to take the minutes,' Penny frowned. 'I think the usual woman's on holiday? There's one missing, though. Corey Gregson. He usually sits beside Purcell.'

'Maybe he's late?'

Penny shook her head.

'This is a Sunday night meeting, which means it's important. Potentially career ending. Gregson would be there. And if he was late, he'd be around here, trying to get in.'

Koebel nodded.

'Seen a lost millionaire?' she asked the two officers.

Peroni shook his head. 'No,' he replied.

'And in this footage, they didn't look scared?'

Peroni looked a little queasy at the question.

'No,' he replied. 'But that's because I – I don't think it's real.'

'How do you get that from the footage?' Koebel frowned.

'It's a loop, from early in the meeting,' Jeffers replied. 'When we watched it, I noted a very small jump where the footage returned on itself.'

'Nobody else noted this?'

'Nobody monitors the boardroom,' Jeffers made a shrugging motion. 'If Miss Martin here hadn't called, nobody would notice. The guards didn't notice last time, and we didn't see it.'

'But we realised when we saw the other footage.' Peroni didn't look happy.

'Go on.'

Peroni now passed a second screen print. This time it was in an open-plan office.

'This is the office and corridor outside the boardroom,' he said. 'Also on a loop, we think, but obviously later on.'

'How do you know that?'

Peroni pointed.

In the corner, on the floor, there was a half-visible head lying there.

'That's the woman you couldn't work out,' he said. 'The security reckon she must have been running from the boardroom when she was shot and killed.'

'The bullet sound,' Koebel started towards the entrance once more. 'We need to get up there and see what's real—'

'I wouldn't do that, detective,' an unfamiliar voice spoke, and Koebel looked up to see a stranger walking across the street, towards them. Moustached and in his mid-thirties, in casual clothing, baseball cap and shades, he looked like an average man on the street, but the FBI windbreaker jacket he wore, and the badge he held up spoke otherwise.

'Hawthorne, FBI,' he said to Koebel, but showing his ID to all three officers.

'FBI. Great,' Koebel moaned. 'We only just worked out this is an active crime scene. How the hell did you get here so fast?'

'You Detective Koebel?' Hawthorne ignored the question for the moment.

'You already know I am,' Koebel muttered. 'Let me guess. McClusky.'

'They said you'd give me all the help I needed,' Hawthorne continued.

'Help?' Peroni was surprised at this. 'You taking the case over?'

'No, not yet, but we're involved,' Hawthorne nodded towards the lobby. 'Let's get the guards out of there, slowly and quietly, yeah? And if there's anyone else in the offices, let's evacuate them too.'

'Why?' Koebel planted her feet firmly on the ground now, stubbornness oozing out of her. 'This is a sniper all the way up on the twenty-third floor. What aren't you telling us?'

Hawthorne looked at Penny.

'And you are?'

'Miss May's PA,' Penny replied. 'I'm the one who called in the nine-one-one.'

Hawthorne nodded.

'I'm sorry, Miss PA, but you need to walk across the street, where this guy—' he pointed at Peroni, '—is about to set a police line, and call this in to block off all passing traffic.'

Peroni looked at Koebel, who shrugged and nodded. Sighing, Peroni motioned for Penny to follow him across the street.

'Go on then,' Koebel sighed. 'What's the story here?'

'Let me tell you what we know,' Hawthorne nodded. 'That way, we're all up to speed. The Wrentham Board meeting started just over an hour ago, according to one driver. And just *under* an hour ago, that assistant, Penny Martin, received a text from her boss.'

'That's right,' Koebel, eager to prove she wasn't on the back foot here, added. 'Around the same time, witnesses heard what sounded like a rifle firing. There's glass on the street, maybe from one of the boardroom windows, where it shattered, possibly from a bullet striking it.'

'So, someone's using them for target practice?'

'I bloody hope not. We think the sniper's in a building across the street,' Koebel nodded with her head. 'But there's something off. The glass isn't the right window glass for a building like this, so I think it was set up in advance. Which means whoever this is, isn't just some maniac with a gun. This has been planned.'

'Oh, that's a definite,' Hawthorne nodded. 'And that's also why I'm here. You can't check the buildings, and I want everyone out, because we received an anonymous message.'

'From who?' Jeffers asked before wincing. 'Sorry.'

'It's fine,' Hawthorne replied. 'Asking the question means you're interested in the answer. I'd rather that than a bored officer. Especially with what I'm about to show you.'

He opened his phone and scrolled to a photo. It was of a parking garage, and in the middle, in focus, was a package wrapped around the concrete pillar with a mixture of clingfilm wrap and duct tape, a small stick poking out of it.

'Damn,' Koebel whistled.

'Yeah,' Hawthorne put away the phone. 'The message we had with it said the whole of Wrentham's building is wired with enough C4 to take out the street.'

'And we believe them?'

'Photo looks pretty realistic. There's twelve of these bastards down there. We do anything, they'll detonate.'

He looked up at the surrounding buildings.

'They also said if we enter any buildings, they'll detonate as well. Basically, we go near them or the Board, they blow the building up. And, if they're organised enough to change windows in a boardroom, then they're organised enough to set up a kill-switch.'

'Can we contact any of the Board members?' Jeffers asked.

'The PA tried that on the way here,' Koebel replied. 'All went straight to voicemail.'

'Helicopters?'

Hawthorne shook his head.

'He sees one. Boom.'

'So, he's male?' Koebel asked.

'We're assuming,' Hawthorne replied. 'They usually are. No offence.'

'None taken,' for the first time, Koebel smiled. 'I rarely enjoy being placed in the same box as mental domestic terrorists.'

'We've forwarded the message, sent on WhatsApp, to our cybercrime department,' Hawthorne mused, looking up at the building beside them. 'They traced the phone that sent it.'

'And?'

Hawthorne swallowed.

'It's Corey Gregson's phone,' he said. 'One of the board-room members.'

'Who's not there,' Koebel's eyes widened. 'Christ, is Gregson the sniper?'

'No idea,' Hawthorne replied. 'It's a possibility, though. But apart from that—'

'We think he's already killed,' Jeffers showed the printed screenshots. 'These are looped, but the second one shows the secretary from this one on the floor. We think she may have tried to run and was shot.'

'Dead?' Hawthorne peered at the image. 'Damn. We can't go up and check. Find her name; let's see if we can get hold of her family.'

'I thought you weren't taking over?' Koebel raised an eyebrow.

Hawthorne smiled, holding up his hands.

'Sorry, force of habit,' he said. 'How do you want to play it?'

Koebel looked across the street at Peroni, currently speaking to Penny while watching them suspiciously.

'He could be watching us right now,' she said.

'I'd pretty much guarantee he's watching you and the officers right now,' Hawthorne said, literally forcing himself not to look up at the buildings. 'Me, I'm just some FBI guy with a cap on, inserting myself in whatever's happening. I'm interesting, but you're the ones in charge still, so he's watching to see what you do next. Do we ignore his message and storm in? Do we sit back and let this unfold?'

'We need to block the traffic,' Jeffers replied. 'I'll park across the street up there.'

With a nod from Koebel to send him on his way, Jeffers walked off.

'Personally, I'd wait,' Koebel said once Jeffers was gone. 'He's contacted us once, he'll do it again. There has to be some kind of demand made. We might even work out if it's Gregson or not.'

'Or it's not him, and he just really hates them,' Hawthorne suggested. 'We don't know what his problem is right now, but we do know it's big enough to wire up twelve chunks of C4 under the building. And, if you're right, replace all the windows in the room with easy-to-break-through glass.'

'We need to start some kind of dialogue with him,' Koebel puffed out her cheeks, releasing the air slowly as she thought. 'What about calling Gregson's phone?'

'Tried it, not responding,' Hawthorne replied. 'Happy to send it to you guys, but we've been trying for a little while to no response.'

Finally, he looked up at the Wrentham building.

'There's eight people in that room who could be dead very

soon,' he said. 'And I wouldn't lose a minute's sleep if it happened.'

'Don't you mean nine?' Koebel looked at the photo, but Hawthorne tapped the secretary.

'She's not one of them,' he said. 'She's collateral damage.'

'And likely dead.'

'We don't know that,' Hawthorne mused. 'If he's looped the footage, it's because he doesn't want us to know for sure. She might even be part of it.'

Koebel shook her head.

'You FBI guys must be great fun at parties,' she said.

In response, Hawthorne shrugged.

'In my version, at least she's alive,' he replied.

'I suppose so. It'd be nice to not have to visit the morgue here,' Koebel nodded as, across the street, Peroni went to assist Jeffers, Penny taking the opportunity to run back over to them.

'So, what the hell is going on?' she asked testily. 'What was so important I had to be dumped over there?'

'It's a police matter, and you're not police,' Koebel replied icily. 'But if it makes you feel better, congratulations. You're not mad, and you did the right thing calling it in.'

Penny looked across the road now, watching Peroni, having spoken with Jeffers, run into the building, waving at the guards.

'It's a bomb, isn't it?' she asked. 'It's not bad enough it's a sniper, he's blowing the building up, too.'

Hawthorne pulled his phone out, watching Peroni as he spoke to the guards.

'I need to call in what I know,' he said, nodding across the street. 'I'll be over there if you need me.'

He stopped.

'One other thing,' he added. 'Expect press to turn up soon.'

'Because of the road closure?'

'No, because he's loving the attention,' Hawthorne nodded

at the buildings the other side of the street. 'He's got a high-level Board dancing to whatever tune he's playing right now, and all we can do is sit on our thumbs and wait for his next move. He spent a lot of time planning this, and in my experience, the people who do that always want an audience.'

With this prophetic statement made, FBI Agent Hawthorne walked off, phone to his ear as he looked for a quiet place to speak to his superiors.

Sighing, Koebel looked up at the Wrentham building, wishing she'd gone with her gut and taken the day off, just like her partner did. Now McClusky would turn up in his best suit, and claim all the attention.

Koebel couldn't help herself; she smiled at the thought. If McClusky wanted the exposure, he could have it. And when the building started raining millionaires on him, he could take the blame as well.

'Something amusing?' Penny, seeing the expression, frowned.

'Let's hope not,' Koebel replied cryptically, before walking off towards the main entrance. 'Come on, Miss Martin. You know a lot of these people, you can help me evacuate any of them still inside. And, while we do that, you can tell me everything you know about Corey Gregson, and why he might hypothetically want the Wrentham Board members killed.'

60:26

HAYLEY WAS FROZEN IN PLACE, STARING DOWN AT JASON, STILL bleeding from the stab wound, his trouser leg ripped away and revealing the now drenched in blood napkins.

'He's losing too much blood,' she said, moving in finally, twisting the knot on the tourniquet, trying to tighten it. All this did, however, was wrench on the wound itself, causing Jason to almost sit up, doubling over in pain as he screamed out.

'Ahh! You bastard!'

'That doesn't sound good,' the voice of Justice spoke through the speakers. 'That sounds like he's dying.'

'He's losing too much blood,' Hayley repeated, this time to the window. 'Help us!'

'He won't help us,' Victoria snapped. 'He wants us dead.'

'That's not fair. If I wanted you dead, I would have already done it,' Justice replied. 'Through the head, from a distance. But I don't want you dead, Mrs Harvey—'

'I told you, it's *Ms*,' Victoria snapped back.

'Christ's sake!' Miles cried out. 'Why does it matter?'

'I don't want you dead, *Ms* Harvey,' Justice was almost mocking in his response. 'I want you paying for your crimes.

One of you will take the blame, sure, but the rest of you will find yourselves hounded by the press for the rest of your lives, and to die right now is just escaping the storm that's coming.'

'Well, you should have thought about this before you gave that stupid old bastard a knife!' Eddie shouted in response.

'Hindsight is always twenty-twenty, Mister Purcell,' Justice replied calmly. 'As well you know. But, if it helps, let me make this perfectly clear. If Mister Taylor dies, Miss Moran, I will kill you as well.'

There was a moment of stunned quiet in the room.

'You literally just said you didn't want us dead!' Devin shouted.

'I don't *want* you dead,' Justice explained. 'But that doesn't mean I won't do it to get what I want. And right now, I want Mister Barnett alive.'

'I can't save him!' Hayley cried. 'I don't have the tools!'

'Oh, is that the only reason?' Justice replied in a sing-song manner.

'Yes!' Hayley spat. 'If I had the right equipment I could save him, so how about you let us save him and stop playing these games!'

'There. "Let us save him." That's what I wanted to hear,' Justice seemed almost proud of Hayley's response. 'Why call upon medics when you can do it yourself? Ms Harvey, open draw three, remove the contents – there's two in total to be removed – and place them on the boardroom table. Do *not* open them.'

Looking confused at the others in the room, Victoria walked over to the cabinet, looking along it until she saw the brass "3" attached to a door.

Opening it, she reached in, pulling out a first aid box.

However, when she reached in again, she pulled out a second, identical box. Both were about the size of a shoe box, and as she picked them up with a frown on her face, she walked back to the table.

'Pass me one of those, quickly,' Hayley begged.

'No,' Justice ordered. 'Not yet. *Ms* Harvey, please place them on the table.'

As ordered, Victoria did so, giving an apologetic look to Hayley.

'Now what?' she asked aloud.

'Now it's up to Mister Barnett,' Justice replied.

At this, Jason, fighting through the pain in his leg, his hair drenched in flop sweat and his eyes tight in agony, forced himself to rise to his elbows.

'Up to me?' he groaned. 'What do you mean, it's up to me?'

'I'm afraid that it's time for you to tell everyone your secret,' Justice explained. 'Clearly and slowly, if you would.'

Jason looked around the table, his eyes wild and terrified at the people watching him, licking his lips nervously as he shook his head through the pain.

'I-I don't know what you mean,' he protested.

'Jason, don't do this,' Eddie moved in now, placing a hand on Jason's shoulder. 'If you have a secret, just tell us. Then we can patch you up. You'll live. If you don't, he's not gonna let us. And you'll bleed out.'

'He's screwing with you,' Jason groaned through clenched teeth, the effort of speaking without screaming in pain visible on his face. 'He didn't know this would happen! Miles said it was an accident!'

'That's true,' Justice replied. 'I didn't know it would be *you* injured, but I always knew someone would be. And I always knew you'd have to tell everyone your secret, eventually.'

Justice sighed through the speakers.

'Come now, this is not the time for being shy,' he continued. 'Especially as your life depends on it.'

'Fuck you!' Jason shouted at the ceiling as he fell back onto the table in pain. 'I don't have any secrets!'

'Such a shame that you want to do it this way,' Justice replied. 'Oh well. Looks like I'll have to do it for you.'

Jason spun to face the window, pulling himself up on one arm.

'What do you mean—'

He didn't get any further, as behind him the television screen burst into life once more, and across it the members of the Board could see the blank screen becoming populated with photos of children.

Young children.

They were varied; taken at different times of the day, and in differing locations. Some were taken from a distance, some were across a park, others on the street, or through a window, either of a car, or a building, in both day and night situations.

Always candid. Never posed.

Eddie stared up at the screen, his forehead crinkling.

'What the hell?' he asked, vocalising the question many others in the room also had, but hadn't spoken out aloud.

'These? Oh, these are photos from Mister Barnett's personal and encrypted hard drive. Aren't they, Mister Barnett?' Justice replied with a totally inappropriate amount of jollity for the moment. 'Or would you prefer me to call you "Uncle Jason" from now on?'

On the screen, the photos kept appearing.

Looking away from it, Eddie glared down at Jason.

'What the fuck?' he hissed. 'You're a kiddie fiddler?'

'He's a goddamned paedophile!' Miko laughed. 'All this "holier than thou" bullshit he was spouting, all the sob stories about being here on his own, fixing our messes, when actually he's just whacking off to Disney videos!'

She looked at Miles, who in turn was fixated on the now crying Jason.

'Tell me you have that on CCTV,' she said, mimicking a man masturbating. 'Oh yeah, Wednesday Addams! Do it harder, Kevin McAllister!'

'No! It's not like that!' Sweating harder now, Jason was once more trying to rise as he protested. 'It was research! Data gathering!'

Miles shook his head in disbelief.

'Why would you need photos of children as research?'

'Blackmail,' Eddie growled. 'He wanted to blackmail us with whatever he found. Didn't you? Or is Miko correct?'

Hayley had been staring up at the screen as the others spoke, but now she stopped, a little yelp escaping her lips.

'That's my niece!' she exclaimed. 'Right there! What the hell are you doing, taking photos of my niece, you pervert? Who else did you take photos of?'

'It's not what it looks like!' Jason sobbed.

'No? Because it's not looking good for you here,' Devin replied. 'And to think, Miles gave up a secret for you.'

'If it's not what it looks like, you can answer the question, can't you?' Hayley, no longer the caring nurse, moved to face Jason. 'Tell me!'

'I can't—'

'I said *tell me!*' Hayley slammed the palm of her hand onto the bloodied napkins, digging her thumb into the wound as Jason screamed out, his voice high pitched. '*Tell me!*'

'Get off him before you kill him!' Tamira pulled Hayley off now. 'He can't tell you if he's unconscious or dead!'

'I needed leverage!' Jason finally cried out, reaching out and clutching his leg as he did so. 'I needed a guarantee for my appraisal!'

'Your appraisal? Jesus, they're children!' Devin exclaimed. 'What kind of monster are you?'

'Oh, such morality from the guy fucking his boss's wife?' Jason spat at Devin, his pain now fuelling his anger as he glared across the boardroom. 'Don't make me laugh! All of you, all of us in here, we all have something bad we've done! Mine was business related!'

'Mine was too, but that didn't stop you from going for me,' Miko snapped.

'Nah, this is bullshit,' Eddie growled. 'This ain't leverage. You're sick, Jason. Sick in the head, sick in the heart, the mind, whatever. You need help, not a folder of work colleague's kids.'

At this, the anger drained out of Jason, and he slumped back against the table.

'I'm sorry,' he moaned, tears streaming down his cheeks. 'I don't want to die! I'm scared!'

'Damn right you should be scared,' Miko replied. 'If it was my kid up there—'

'Do you have a kid?' Victoria asked icily.

'No, but I—'

'No, you don't,' Victoria held up a hand to pause her. 'So let someone with them decide what they'd do, yeah?'

'What a good idea,' the voice of Justice spoke, and before anyone in the room could say anything, the images still appearing on the television screen suddenly winked off.

'That doesn't sound good,' Devin muttered as, on the screen, new photos appeared, one after the other. These were similar in style to the ones that had been appearing already, some from a distance, some across open spaces, some through windows, all candidly taken. But this time, there was something different about these.

For a start, they were all photos of the *same girl*.

Victoria gaped in horror at them.

'That's … that's my daughter,' she breathed, her eyebrows knotted together as she broke away from the screen to stare at Jason. 'Why do you have photos of my daughter?'

'Why do you think?' Eddie grumbled.

Flicking her eyes to him, Victoria shut them, closing out the photos on the screen as she clenched them shut.

'You've been following my daughter,' she said calmly, as if stating a list of facts. 'You've been taking secret photos of her, too. Why?'

Jason was whimpering now.

'I'm sorry ...' he whispered, his voice almost inaudible over the mutterings of the other members of the Board.

Victoria opened her eyes again, turning coldly to face Jason.

'Is this why you asked about the recital?' she asked. 'Information to use while you whack off in the washroom?'

She glanced at the screen, still showing photo after photo of the same child.

'My daughter?'

Jason didn't reply, instead sobbing into his blood-covered hands.

'You can fucking die,' Victoria said. 'These first aid kits aren't for you.'

'Ms Harvey,' Justice's voice echoed once more through the speakers. 'Please open the two boxes.'

'And you can go to hell too!' Victoria shouted out. 'This isn't a game anymore! This is personal!'

'I know, better than you could ever understand, believe me,' Justice replied. 'And because of that, I'm about to give you something to help you through this difficult moment.'

Victoria started to laugh, while the others in the room observed her.

'Your game isn't going to work this time!' she cried out gleefully, and with no small amount of malice tinged within. 'I don't want to help him!'

There was a moment's silence.

'Not help him,' Justice eventually replied, his voice as calm and placid as ever. 'Help *you*.'

'Whatever this is, it'll end in pain,' Miko whispered. 'Walk away.'

'Walk where?' Victoria looked up at her. 'We're trapped in the room. We'll *die* in the room.'

'True, but we don't have to turn into *him* in the room.'

Victoria stared out of the window.

'Ms Harvey,' Justice's voice repeated through the speakers. 'Please open the two boxes.'

'Don't—'

Ignoring Miko's plea, Victoria returned her attention to the two first aid boxes, opening them both, side by side.

In one was a fully stocked first aid kit, enough to not only fix the vicious wound Jason Barnett had but also tend to Devin's cut cheek and Miles's split lip.

But in the other, all alone and resting inside it, was a butane powered blowtorch, the kind used in restaurants, and by top level chefs.

Devin, standing closest to Victoria as she opened them, saw the items at the same moment she did.

'Oh, God, no …' he trailed off. 'You sick bastard.'

'I don't understand,' Victoria shook her head. 'How does this help me?'

'Because you have a choice now,' Justice explained. 'You can now pick one of these items to assist with the medical treatment of Mister Barnett.'

Victoria looked back at the items as Justice continued.

'One, as you can see, is a fully stocked medical kit, including powerful painkillers and antibiotics, which will not only end his pain for a while, but ensure you save his leg in the process.'

There was a pause before Justice continued, and Victoria was convinced she could hear the voice become more malicious.

'Or you could choose door number two, and use a kitchen

blowtorch to cauterize the bleeding,' he added. 'Both will keep Mister Barnett alive until medical help arrives in around fifty minutes. One will help him drift off, painlessly, until they do a better job than you. The other option, however … well, that option will cause him great pain and distress, as you burn the wound closed, his skin charring as it seals over.'

Victoria returned her attention to the screen, where the photos of her daughter looked down upon her.

Laughing.

Shouting to her friends.

Playing.

Innocent and unknowing of the stranger photographing her.

A hand placed itself on hers, and Victoria was surprised to see Miles observing her sadly.

'Don't go down this road,' he whispered. 'By doing this, you'll become as bad as he is.'

He emphasised who he was talking about by nodding out of the window.

'Actually, you'll be worse,' he concluded.

'And how do you work that out?' Victoria countered, pulling her hand away from his.

'Because he doesn't know us,' Miles replied. 'We're strangers to him. He hurts us in the same way a child kills insects, like burning ants on a sunny day with a magnifying glass. You heard him. He said, "through the head, from a distance." It's emotionless, not close up and personal.'

He looked at Jason, still on the table, watching Victoria in helpless terror.

'He doesn't know you, and you don't know him. But you've worked with *him* for years.'

'He's taken photos of my *daughter* for years.'

'A daughter you've already stated you don't care about!'

'But that's my choice!' Victoria pulled her hand from Miles.

'I can love or hate my child, but that doesn't allow him to do that!'

'There might be videos, too,' the voice of Justice offered. 'I could look, if you want.'

'No,' Victoria shook her head, locking eyes with Jason as he silently pleaded with her. 'What, so I'm supposed to choose now?'

'Yes,' Justice crowed, triumphant. 'Ms Harvey, it's now your choice on which treatment you will administer to him. The medical kit … or the righteous fire.'

———

51.17

'Don't,' Hayley pleaded. 'Don't let it go down like this.'

Victoria went to pick up the kitchen blowtorch, then paused, moving back to the real first aid kit, as if unsure of which way to go.

'If you don't do it, I will,' Eddie growled.

'You're not helping!' Tamira snapped across the table, but Eddie simply scowled back at her.

'Good!' he exclaimed angrily. 'Because I ain't helping no goddamned paedo!'

'I'm not …' Jason moaned softly, tears running down his cheeks. 'It was *research* …'

'We can fix that "research" right now,' Eddie offered. 'With fire. Cleansing fire.'

He moved towards the table, but Devin moved quickly to intercept him.

'It's not your decision to make,' he whispered.

'Then she'd better make the right damn decision,' Eddie replied, backing off a little, letting Devin keep the floor. 'Tick tock. Don't want to keep the nice Mister Justice waiting now, do we?'

If Victoria was listening to Eddie, she didn't show it, as she carried on staring at the boxes.

'Victoria, you need to help him,' Hayley repeated. 'He's losing blood. He won't make it.'

'You only give a shit about his survival because that prick out there told you he'd kill you if Jason died,' Miko mocked. 'And that would be *so terrible* if it happened. Hey, Vicky, have a seat. Take your time.'

Victoria didn't react to the jibe, her attention still elsewhere.

Eventually, nodding quietly to herself, she leant over the desk, reaching into one of the first aid boxes, and pulling out the small kitchen blowtorch.

'How do you turn it on?' she asked the room.

'You press the trigger to light the flame, and then slide the regulator on the left-hand side to set the flame,' Eddie replied, glaring at the others. 'What? I cook. So what?'

'As long as that's all you use it for,' Miles said nervously, not really wanting an honest answer to this.

'What other ways are there to use it?' Eddie smiled darkly, mocking Miles. 'Oh, wait, I think Victoria's about to learn one right now. I hope you all like the smell of cooking meat. Long pig, I think the term is.'

'Long pig?'

'When you cook and eat human flesh,' Eddie bared his teeth in a smile. 'So I've been told.'

Victoria held the torch up in her hand as she observed it. It was in two parts, a black cylinder handgrip, stubby and no longer than her own hand when she gripped it, and the top part was chrome, looking more like the trigger attachment on a garden hose than a weapon of pain.

She clicked the ignition, and a thin blue flame exploded from the end, the length around two inches, before it narrowed to a flickering tip.

Seeing this, Tamira walked towards her.

'There's no way you're doing this—' she started, but stopped, hands raising as Victoria spun to face her, the torch still burning, the flame now pointing at her.

'Back the fuck off,' Victoria snarled.

The Board backed away from her as Victoria walked over to Jason, his expression terrified now, trying to squirm off the table as she approached.

'Please, Victoria,' Hayley pleaded one last time.

Instead of replying vocally, Victoria simply waved the torch once more, motioning for Hayley to move back to where Tamira now stood.

Now alone, Victoria looked down at Jason.

'My daughter,' she hissed.

Jason didn't reply, paralysed with fear as Victoria used her free hand to untie the necktie around the wound.

'Don't, please,' Miles begged. 'He'll bleed out.'

'I'm not untying *that* one,' Victoria snapped across the room, glaring over at the CEO as she spoke. 'I'm saving his life, remember? The napkins are being removed for his own good.'

She smiled, darkly.

'After all, we don't want them going up in flames as I do this,' she explained. 'That might be even worse.'

'Please, someone stop her …' Jason whispered, but nobody heeded his pleas, as the Board stood in stunned silence as, the wound now revealed again, Victoria faced Jason again.

'Tell me it was purely business.'

'It was, I swear.'

'Liar. Tell me you never spoke to her.'

Jason's eyes flickered around the room.

'I never did, honestly.'

Victoria leant closer to Jason, angling so she could speak into his ear.

'Liar, liar, leg on fire,' she breathed. 'This is gonna hurt a whole goddamn lot, so don't feel any macho need to hold it all in, okay? Instead, feel free to scream real loud as I go to town on you, yeah?'

'I don't—' Jason began, but this quickly turned into a primal, guttural scream of intense agony, as Victoria turned the chef's cooking torch onto the exposed wound, the long, blue flame licking out at the sides as the skin started to bubble and char around it.

Jason arched his back as Victoria continued to cauterise the wound with the torch, moving up and down it almost tenderly, as she watched the skin blacken and burn with a morbid fascination.

Hayley turned, burying her head into Miles's shoulder as she sobbed. And as Jason finally passed out, the screaming now stopped, Devin stepped forward.

'That's enough, Victoria,' he said.

If Victoria heard him, though, she didn't listen, continuing to char the skin, humming a soft tune, even as she did so.

'I said *that's enough!*' reaching from behind and grabbing her arms, pinning them to her side, restricting the use of the torch, Devin pulled the struggling Victoria away from the unconscious Jason, as the others, bar Tamira, moved in to stop her, grabbing and pulling away the torch as they did so.

Eddie, meanwhile, walked back to his chair and sat down, while Tamira walked back to her own place at the table, still standing, staring down at the phone in the middle of the boardroom table.

'*Burn in hell!*' Victoria screamed at Jason as Devin continued to try pulling her away.

Miles, with Hayley beside him, now grabbed the real first aid kit, moving quickly to Jason, pulling out items to use on his hideously charred thigh.

'There!' Justice exclaimed delightedly. 'Mister Barnett's bleeding has been stopped. He'll survive until—'

The voice through the speakers crackled and stopped, as

Tamira, finally reaching a decision, leant forward and wrenched the phone from the middle of the desk, pulling it out of the socket as she did so, the cable falling back onto the desk as she wrapped the broken cord around the handset. She stormed past the others in the room, handset in her arms, walking determinedly to the broken, open window and standing on the edge of the floor, facing nothingness as she screamed out across the street.

'*Fuck you!*' she shouted as she tossed the phone and its attached cables out into the air, watching it spin and tumble as it fell the twenty-three floors to the ground, before looking back up. 'Fuck you and your fucking games! Come on, shoot me! I dare you!'

Devin, having let Victoria go, pulled Tamira from the window, the force of the effort sending her tumbling backwards in the room, sprawling on the floor near the door.

'What the hell are you doing?' he yelled. 'Are you suicidal?'

'I'm saving all our asses!' Tamira shouted back as she rose from the floor, dusting herself down.

'And how did you work that out?' Devin glanced back across the street, before looking down at his chest, worried there might be another red dot on it.

'I tore the phone out, so he can't hear us now,' her voice now calm, Tamira explained. 'The call's not disconnected as it came through the switchboard, but now he doesn't have a way to speak to us, or more importantly, hear us.'

She looked around the room.

'He's been pissing about with us through it since we called Corey. Now the connection's, well, disconnected. And he can't call us back as he blew up our fucking phones.'

'In case you haven't realised, you insane bitch, removing the one way he could speak to us means he might as well just shoot us!' Miles exploded. 'Or blow us up, even! And with no goddamned phone, how do we get a message to the police to tell them we need help and a paramedic for Jason?'

'Screw Jason,' Victoria, now standing sullenly beside the wall, grunted. 'Screw you all.'

'Helpful,' Tamira said sarcastically. 'And for the record, I had a plan – and I just sent the police a message.'

'On the phone?' Eddie laughed. 'That's not how you make a phone call, Tammy. I'd hoped you'd know that by now.'

'I'm sorry, have you done anything so far? No? Then fuck off, Eddie,' Tamira said as she sat back at the table, ignoring the bloodied and burnt unconscious body in front of her. 'I told them what was going on by writing it on a napkin. I secured it with cable and threw it out.'

There was a moment of stunned, and almost respectful silence at this.

'And, as for the dickhead over there, he wants one of us to take the blame. We're still doing that, as it's the only way he won't blow us all to hell. All I've done is stop these stupid games he was playing,' Tamira waved for the others to sit down. 'So, can we get on with this meeting? I want to get the hell out of here, and Jason needs a goddamned hospital.'

Koebel was on the street, talking to McClusky on the phone when the phone smashed against the pavement.

The first instinct was to dive for cover, as there hadn't been any other missiles thrown at them so far that evening, but after a moment, Koebel looked around, decided there was nothing else coming, and disconnected the call to McClusky, who was at that point demanding to know what was going on. In a way, she was grateful to the missile, as it gave her an excuse to get off the line, and she made her way over to where the remains of broken glass still lay on the pavement, now added to with pieces of charcoal grey plastic, which, if you squinted real tightly, you could just about make out into what could have been some kind of phone, once upon a time.

Jeffers was already there, latex gloves on, picking through the wreckage.

'Be careful,' Koebel said. 'CSI will lose their shit if they learn you've interfered with their things.'

Jeffers smiled and held up a pencil, currently being used to turn over pieces of plastic.

'Not my first rodeo,' he said, nodding across the street at Peroni, on crowd duty. 'Although Peroni would be picking bits up and licking them by now.'

'Well then, let's not let him near it,' Koebel grinned, crouching down to look at the wreckage. 'A phone? Why would they throw a phone?'

'You were on a call to the precinct, so you might not have heard, but a woman was screaming out of the window as she threw it,' Jeffers pointed upwards with the pencil as he spoke. 'Dunno if she was the one who also tossed the phone out, or even what she was saying, as it was too high up, but the two things have to be related somehow.'

He stopped poking with the pencil as a flash of white appeared on the pavement, hidden under the phone's chassis.

'Boss?' he asked, looking up. 'Napkin.'

'Was it there before?'

'No. Only glass before.'

Koebel looked up at the building.

'So, someone tosses the phone out, but sticks a napkin on it,' she mused. 'Why?'

'It's got writing on it,' Jeffers had used the pencil to flip it over. Seeing it, and now pulling on a pair of latex gloves of her own, Koebel gingerly picked up the piece of tattered napkin, reading the message.

SNIPER ACROSS STREET
TWENTY-THIRD FLOOR.
DONNA KILLED, JASON STABBED
SPOKE THROUGH PHONE.

'Looks like progress,' a fresh voice spoke, and Koebel looked up to see FBI Agent Hawthorne walking over to them.

'Looks like intel,' she replied, waving the napkin. 'Pretty bloody clever, actually. Made it look like vandalism while passing us the news.'

Jeffers looked up at the agent.

'We need to know who threw it,' he said.

'Tamira May,' Hawthorne replied knowledgeably.

Koebel rose to face him at this revelation.

'And how the hell would you know that for a fact?' she asked. 'Officer Jeffers only just realised it was a woman.'

'Officer Jeffers wasn't talking to Penny Martin when it happened,' Hawthorne shrugged. 'She recognised the voice immediately. Probably because Miss May screams at her a lot, on a day-to-day basis.'

Grudgingly accepting this, Koebel passed Hawthorne the napkin. Hawthorne was already wearing latex gloves, but he used a pair of tweezers to hold the paper up as he read it.

'Yeah, okay. "Sniper across street, twenty-third floor. Donna killed, Jason stabbed, spoke through phone." Well, I think she ended that last part when she tossed the damned thing out of the window.'

He frowned.

'Who's Donna?' he asked.

'No idea,' Koebel pursed her lips. 'But apparently she's dead. Probably the secretary in the second photo, the one we saw on the floor.'

She sighed.

'I suppose we can at least consider this a witness statement confirming her state of life,' she said sadly. 'Poor girl, whoever she was.'

'And who's Jason again?' Hawthorne passed the note back. 'Is that Barnett, the sales guy?'

'Sales Director, yes,' Koebel nodded. 'And one of the Board members. Though why someone stabbed him, I have no clue. And currently, we can't do anything about it.'

Hawthorne smiled at this.

'Actually, maybe we can,' he said, lowering his voice, almost as if worried the sniper twenty floors above him might overhear.

'Go on,' Koebel raised an eyebrow. 'I'm listening.'

'I've been talking to my guys, and we think we know the building he's in,' Hawthorne explained. 'I won't turn around, as it might give us away, but it can only be one of them if he killed someone by the door, forcing them through it. And now we know the building and the floor he's playing his games from, we can get a small team in, move up to the sniper's location and take him before he can detonate the bomb.'

'He'd see us,' Jeffers replied. 'A small team is still a team. He sees any kind of armed unit, he's gonna freak out and blow them to hell.'

'Maybe not,' Hawthorne shook his head as he moved closer. 'Not if we go in through the security entrance.'

Koebel, realising what the FBI agent was saying, nodded.

'Yeah, I see what you're thinking,' she replied carefully. 'Cut all power to this side of the street. He'll think we're fishing, trying to flush him out. Meanwhile, we'll be in and out in a matter of minutes.'

The nod, however, turned into a shake of the head.

'And if it fails, we kill everyone.'

There was a moment of contemplation of this outcome before Hawthorne cleared his throat gently.

'With all due respect, detective, and officer, I think that's gonna happen anyway,' he replied ominously. 'This guy's not playing up there. We've not had a ransom message in almost an hour and a half, people are being injured up there, it looks like it's all a game to him, but I think he's looking for something big. A statement nobody can ignore. And blowing the hell out of Wrentham is just that.'

Koebel whistled as she pulled out a clear Ziplock baggie, carefully placing the graffitied napkin into it. She didn't want to admit it, but the same thought had been going through her mind, too. The only options here were catching the sniper, likely through death-by-cop, losing the sniper and seeing the building destroyed with everyone in it killed, or some sick combination of both.

'I'll get a team together,' she said.

'And I'll get the power cut,' Hawthorne replied, already dialling as he walked off, making a phone call that was about to change everything.

43.44

As the other members of the Wrentham Board of Directors returned to their original seats, Tamira relaxed back in her chair, glancing momentarily at the unconscious Jason, his leg now properly managed, the burnt skin now covered in anti-burn gel, the now cool skin covered with a sterile dressing, and secured with a bandage and adhesive tape.

'I call this Board meeting back to order,' she said.

Devin, now with a plaster over the cut on his cheek, flipped her the finger.

'You might be hot shit right now, but Miles is still the CEO,' he said.

'Christ, Devin, give it up,' Miko laughed. 'He's not going to forgive you for cucking him. And by now Gina's having the shit kicked out of her by your actual wife. Maybe even being shot.'

She looked around the table with a mocking expression of concern.

'Maybe we should send the hotel the remains of the first aid kit?' she asked. 'Oh, wait. We'd have to call them, and Tamira tossed out our phone. Maybe she could toss out the first aid box? Use the torch to burn letters into the plastic?'

'It's Gregson,' Tamira said, ignoring Miko. 'It has to be. All this, all these games. Sick bastard is laughing his guts up after calling us all in today.'

'How did you come to that decision?' Hayley asked.

In response, Tamira waved around the room.

'Do you see him here?' she replied. 'It's not us, and it sure as hell isn't that stupid prick there.'

She aimed the last part of this at Jason.

'I mean, Christ, nobody has their leg burned extra crispy because they want to stick it to the man or something.'

'People in spy books shoot themselves in the arm to look like the victim,' Hayley crossed her arms sullenly as she looked at Jason. 'I'm just saying this could be like that.'

'Wait, so you're saying he literally allowed his CEO to stab his leg in the middle of a fight and nick an artery, risked total blood loss, outed himself as a paedophile and allowed the mother of the child he was preying on to burn the shit out of his leg – all because he wanted to make us think *he wasn't the mastermind behind this?*'

Devin laughed.

'Christ, it really isn't an act, is it, Hayley? You really are that useless.'

Hayley didn't reply, still sullenly staring at the unconscious sales director.

'So, it's Corey Gregson, because he's not here?' Victoria shook her head. 'You heard the man. Gregson's probably dead.'

Eddie, hearing this, leant back in his own chair, steepling his fingers in front of his chin.

'Is he? Or is this all a sick joke?'

'It's a hell of a sick joke, Eddie,' Victoria replied. 'But hell, you could be right. We all know the two of you were real tight, so you'd be the best one to know. Why don't you go ask the dead secretary outside?'

There was a long, awkward silence as many of the people around the table, caught up in the recent actions, now remembered the woman murdered almost an hour and a half earlier, and now lying outside their door.

'He has to be connected to Gregson,' Devin continued, irritatingly scratching at the plaster on his cheek. 'He knows stuff only that prick knows.'

'Like what?' Hayley asked.

Devin glanced nervously at Miles before replying.

'Me and Gina, for a start,' he said.

Miles, looking away, had a slight tic in his eye as his wife's name was mentioned, but apart from that, he said or did nothing.

'Nah, mate,' Miko laughed as she looked across the table at Devin. 'Everyone knew about that.'

She took this opportunity to give a side glance at Miles, catching his attention as she did so.

'Apart from Miles, anyway,' she finished. 'I think that one came as a little bit of a surprise. Whoopsies.'

Miles looked away again, unable to look either Miko or Devin in the eye.

'What about your own oral pleasures?' Devin responded.

'Oh, fuck off,' Miko snapped, but Devin held up a hand to stop her oncoming rant at him.

'No, I'm serious,' he said. 'We all know you did it now, you announced it was true, and we have the footage of you shouting at Trent. But that's with hindsight. When it was shown, Miles was surprised at it, so he obviously hadn't seen the CCTV where you said it, and Eddie's the security guy, with all his greasy little snitches in the company, and he was surprised too, which means he hadn't heard the story from anyone, either.'

'He's got a point,' Eddie grudgingly admitted. 'I don't know where he's going with it, though.'

'Justice knew because he'd seen the footage, and we also know he's connected into the CCTV cameras because he's shown us the cameras in the hotel, and also files from our computers,' Devin looked around the room.

'So, he's checked through the footage,' Victoria narrowed her eyes. 'So what?'

'It's weeks, months even of boring, office-based footage,' Miles, reluctantly returning to the conversation, said. 'He'd have to watch it all. The only way he'd be able to do it quickly is if someone gave him advanced warning on where and when to look.'

'Which takes us back to you,' Devin looked back at Miko. 'Someone knew to check on your footage. Someone knew where and when you were pissed about being used by Trent Nemeth. Who did you tell? Was it Gregson?'

Miko considered this for a long moment, staring off into the distance before speaking.

'Bastard,' she said, softly nodding. 'Yeah, it was. We were drunk, laughing about it. I was telling him about it because he asked me for tips.'

'Tips on what?' Miles asked.

'Sucking cock,' Miko replied matter-of-factly. 'You know Gregson was pansexual, right?'

'What's pansexual?' Hayley frowned as she spoke. 'Is that like bisexual?'

'Don't worry, it's something you'll never need to know about,' Eddie chuckled. 'You're too vanilla for it.'

Hayley looked as if she was going to argue this point, but then retreated into the chair.

Ignoring this, Miko continued.

'Corey Gregson was the only one who knew about Trent, as it wasn't one of my prouder moments, and I needed to offload onto someone I trusted,' she said, looking back at Devin now. 'I think you're right. It has to be him.'

'What, so Gregson fed everything to this maniac across the street?' Tamira's face was disbelieving. 'Or are we saying Gregson *is* this maniac across the street?'

'He's definitely not Corey Gregson,' Eddie replied, straightening in the chair. 'He talks completely different.'

'Maybe it's Gregson putting on a fake voice?' Miles suggested.

Devin shifted in his chair at this.

'I said before he has a shitty accent, but it's still an accent,' he said. 'You'd hear it poking through. All "yee haw" and that.'

'He's also not that good an actor,' Eddie was shaking his head now. 'He would have started laughing by now, for sure. Or he'd have made more personal slurs when talking to Devin because he really hates him.'

'Corey doesn't hate me,' Devin protested. 'We play squash together.'

'Only because you're shit at it and he always wins,' Eddie grinned. 'If you had any skill, he'd be out of that court immediately. But you keep placing hundred dollars a match bets, and he likes the extra money.'

He chuckled.

'He also likes that he gives your money to homeless people,' he continued. 'As he knows it'd kill you if you found out. You know, with your hatred of poor people and all that.'

Devin looked crestfallen as he looked away.

'I thought he liked me,' he muttered, ignoring the rest of the comment.

'Why do you care? You never liked him,' Victoria sniffed. 'You told me so, tons of times.'

'Yeah, but I didn't want him to not like me,' Devin retorted.

'You know how it goes. I want everyone to like me, even the ones I dislike.'

'I've got news for you,' Miko linked her hands behind her head as she leant back in her chair. 'Nobody likes you. Especially the ones *you* dislike, because those guys fucking *hate* you.'

'It makes sense if it was Corey, though,' Eddie was still thinking through the earlier comment. 'He had access to the boardroom too, he could have set that cabinet up, even get the windows replaced. He's the infrastructure guy, after all.'

Hayley looked over at the cabinet as Eddie spoke; the doors where the first aid kits had been hidden were now open, the drawer where the knife was placed still pulled out.

'I wonder what else is in it?' she asked, rising from her chair, but Tamira placed a hand on her forearm, stopping her from rising.

'Don't,' she said through gritted teeth. 'You're facing the window. He can't hear us, but he can still see us through the sniper scope of the rifle he has aimed at our heads.'

She looked around the table.

'We need to look like we're still voting. Some of you put your hands up.'

There was an almost unconscious shudder around the table; the other members, realising they could finally speak freely, had forgotten the killer across the street could still just about make out what was going on.

Slowly, Miles and Miko raised their hands.

'This is bullshit,' Victoria stood up, leaning over the table and pointing at Miko. 'He's not going to believe we're all being good and professional. He's going to expect to see arguments. Like this cock-sucking bitch having a meltdown.'

'Piss off, you self-entitled drama queen!' Miko rose to face Victoria, but stopped as Victoria smiled, sitting back down in her chair.

'Perfect,' she said. 'He'll love that. We're still voting, and you're still bitching.'

Glowering, Miko sat back down.

'So, what do we do? Jason's gonna need a hospital,' Eddie said, aware his face was facing away from the window.

'Screw Jason,' Victoria barked. 'He can die for all I care. It's all his fault, anyway.'

She looked over at Miles.

'Well, him and the living dead over there, at least,' she finished, as Miles slowly turned to stare at her, a hurt expression on his face.

'How do you figure that?' he asked, after a moment spent most likely gathering his thoughts. Victoria clicked her tongue against her teeth, puffing out her cheeks as she worked out her next comments carefully.

'Jason was a shit sales director, wasn't he?' she started. 'Profits were tanking. We all know this because we all saw the reports. 'We needed to make up the shortfall, and the plant at Mercy was a money pit. Had been for years. If we were going to find ways to save money, we had to make savvier deals. And that was his job.'

She punctuated her point by prodding Jason's arm. He groaned, but didn't stir.

'Fucking vultures,' Miko sighed, looking around the table. 'All of you.'

'Don't you dare play the martyr,' Victoria turned her attention back onto Miko now. 'I've seen how you've voted since you got here. I've been to every meeting you have, and I've watched you like a hawk.'

'You need better hobbies,' Miko buffed her fingernails, looking down at them. 'Stalking doesn't suit you. Maybe you should take some notes on how to do it from Jason there? You know, if he doesn't end you for cooking up his leg, or ask for your daughter as payment for his lessons.'

'Deflect the point all you want, but you know I'm right, or you wouldn't do it,' Victoria smiled darkly. 'You would have done the same back then. You would have voted to cut the costs in Mercy.'

Miko's amused expression soured as she stared balefully across the table.

'Well then,' she said icily. 'I guess we'll never know how I'd vote on the Mercy situation, as I wasn't here when you voted on it. So, we'll just have to take my word on it— What?'

Victoria had chuckled while Miko was speaking, and she held up a hand to halt her.

'I know, because we all have the virtue of hindsight,' she said. 'You can be so virtuous when you have hindsight, after all. You remember the Palisades votes last month? To reduce cash flow in the mid-west?'

'Of course, I do,' Miko shifted uncomfortably. 'What about it? Are you going to tell me this was some kind of test or something?'

'That depends,' Victoria looked around the room. 'I'm sure everyone here remembers how we voted on that. But can you remember how you voted?'

'Of course,' Miko replied coldly. 'I voted with you all to do whatever was needed. The cash flow was spiralling out of control. It needed to be reined in.'

'Exactly,' Victoria was triumphant, almost pumping her fist into the air as she spoke. 'You voted with the Board, as it was the best thing to do. The most cost-effective thing to do. And what happened after that? After it went through, within a week, it decimated entire towns, employment-wise.'

She sat back down, watching Miko as she finished.

'Ten thousand people lost their jobs because of that vote.'

'Bullshit,' Miko looked around, looking for someone to tell her this was a joke.

'It's true,' Miles replied. 'Ten thousand is a low estimate, too. Probably closer to fifteen, maybe even twenty if you take in subsidies and the self-employed, even contractors who lost contracts through that.'

'And by "that", he means "through you voting to kill them all," if you needed to be told,' Victoria added.

'Yeah, but at least they can get new jobs,' Miko retorted, pushing back from the table in her chair, trying to gain some kind of distance from her and the Board, even if it was metaphorical. 'They weren't given a death sentence like the poor bastards in Mercy!'

'They might as well have been,' Devin interjected now. 'Those jobs kept two mid-west towns afloat, before we took them away with a wave of our hands. There's no other work for them down there.'

'Shit,' Miko whispered. 'And you didn't tell me this?'

'It was all in the report!' Tamira snapped back now, turning to face Miko. 'But you were too busy wiping the cum off your blouse to read the bloody things, weren't you? Oh, it was beneath the mighty Miko Tanasha to read such tat, wasn't it? Those poor people in their poor houses, while you lived in your Manhattan penthouse, looking for a better payout!'

'And you're all fine with this?' Miko stood now, hands on the table as she replied. 'You're happy to kill these people in Mercy, and to destroy jobs in the Palisades?'

'We killed people there, too,' Eddie muttered. 'Reports are saying almost a hundred people have committed suicide there since they lost their jobs.'

Miko looked over at Hayley, who had been strangely silent up to this point.

'Surely you can't be happy about this,' she said.

In return, Hayley looked up at her, fresh tears in her eyes.

'Do you remember that vote?' she asked. 'I mean, really remember it?'

'Not really,' Miko sighed. 'But I'm sure you're about to tell me something revelatory.'

'I voted against it,' Hayley replied coldly. 'I explained how people would die. And you? You laughed at me. Told me I was being a drama queen, that they'd all be fine.'

She stood, her face flushed, her hands clenched tight.

'How's that working out for your guilt complex now?' her eyes narrowed as she glared at Miko. 'You know what? Screw it. I vote for Miko Tanasha to take the blame. And, with Devin, Miles and Victoria already casting their vote, that means we need one more, before Mister Justice can take what he needs from your ending, and be damned with you.'

35:45

'IT WAS A SHORT-TERM PLAN.'

Miles wasn't looking at Hayley as he spoke, instead staring off across the room.

She wasn't even sure he knew he'd spoken aloud, and so waited a moment, in case this was the start of another revelation.

However, when no more words seemed to be forthcoming, she frowned, looking at the other members of the Board.

'Am I dreaming?' she asked. 'Did the old man of the sea just say something?'

His eyes red and tired, Miles now glanced up at Hayley, slowly and imperceptibly nodding at her.

'I said it was a short-term plan,' he breathed. 'Mercy, I mean. We knew we needed to do something quick to gain back some finances, you know – put us in the black, move us from danger. So, whenever we had a tender, we'd publicly state we were looking purely at the welfare of the people involved, but when they weren't looking, we'd put in cheap alternatives, with the plan to return and repair it all properly once the government grants came in.'

'For God's sake,' Miko shook her head in disbelief. 'You're telling us you literally stuck duct tape on this and hoped it'd last until payday?'

She puffed her cheeks out as she took this in.

'That's what students do to their cars!' she exclaimed. 'Not what companies do to billion-dollar processing plants!'

'We were desperate!' Miles exploded. 'We were getting pressure from the shareholders, the reports weren't looking good, we needed to keep our heads above water! The costs were like weights, attached to our legs, pulling us under, drowning us.'

'So what, Mercy paid the price for your overspending?' Miko shouted back. 'You're telling me that Mercy paid the price because of *his* shitty salesmanship?'

She pointed at Jason as she rose from her chair.

'Come on! You can't blame all this on him,' she said. 'You knew about this years ago, and he's been working with a solid handicap since then.'

'What handicap?' Miles asked, confused now.

'*You!*'

Miko punctuated the shout with a solid slap to the face, a vicious, open-palmed right hand that sent Miles staggering backwards a couple of steps.

'You're the handicap here!' Miko continued, her anger still rising. 'You've been CEO for almost a decade, and that's almost a decade too long! Every shitty thing that Wrentham's done, every person who's died, or watched their fucking child die; all of these can be laid right here at your feet!'

'That's unfair!' holding his cheek, Miles shook his head defensively. 'I'm not king! I'm not some kind of dictator! I don't make the rules! We do! All of us here!'

He waved at the table, showing the other Board members.

'Every single one of you voted with me on these! And even

though you're newer, Tanasha, you jumped right in, siding with us on every major change!'

He looked up at the corner of the room for a moment, but then returned his gaze back to the Board.

'And yes, the insane maniac across the street wants us dead, or destroyed, and he's not the only one, but we've done good work too! We've given millions to charity! We've started outreach programmes! When Mercy started having problems, we sent people in—'

'We sent people in to fix our screw-ups!' Hayley joined in now, returning to her original point. 'We caused the problems that we then came in to sort out, problems we never intended to fix in the first place! That's the same as an arsonist taking credit for putting out the house fire he started!'

However, after finishing, she paused, looking up at the corner of the room.

'Why were you staring up there, anyway?' she asked, moving from the table, waving away the protestations from the other members of the Board as she squinted up at it. 'Is that a camera? Did you stick a goddamned camera in the boardroom?'

'It's not like the others!' Miles defended. 'It's for security!'

'What the hell security are you talking about?' Eddie was angering now. 'I'm the security director! I wasn't told about this!'

'It was a management decision!' Miles shouted. 'It's so if there's a fire, the people by the monitors can click through the cameras to make sure nobody is still in the building!'

'This is how you managed to stick your own ones in, wasn't it?' Miko replied now. 'How you could spy on me? Are these in every office?'

'Cameras, yes, but they don't have sound,' Miles sounded defensive as he replied.

'Mine had fucking sound!' Miko raised her hand again, but forced herself to stop, as a realisation struck her.

'Oh, you utter prick.'

She turned to the others.

'He was so busy making sure he could sneak in on us, so desperate to hide his own screwups while gathering all our secrets, he connected his cameras into the main network. The same fucking network that lunatic across the street is linked into!'

'How was I supposed to know?' Miles protested. 'It was for your safety!'

'Your safety, more like,' Devin growled. 'You're the ultimate stalker. How does it feel to be so paranoid that you need to spy on all of us?'

Miles went to say something, but then he paused.

Slowly, his expression changed to one of arrogance, with a sneer crossing his face.

'It felt powerful,' he replied. 'I got to see everything. Miko shouting at the man she sucked off, Victoria coming into this very room to take a little nose candy—'

'Shut your mouth,' Victoria hissed. 'You have no—'

'Oh, come on, we all know!' Miles replied. 'If you're not snorting a line in here, you're knocking back some ketamine.'

He moved closer, his voice lowering, his eyes narrowing.

'Tell me, Victoria, how many of these boardroom meetings have you been too,' he asked slyly. 'And how many votes have you taken, while utterly mashed on "K", eh? Maybe all these problems we're having right now, maybe they're all due to you having some kind of bad trip while raising your hand?'

'Come on, Victoria, we all know it's true,' Devin leant closer now. 'Like I know that wasn't really a tablet for acid reflux you took in the elevator, and you were just strapping in for the ride, like you do every time you think nobody's watching.'

Victoria went to protest, but instead just waved a hand in a submissive gesture.

'Do you blame me?' she asked. 'God, these things are so boring. I need something to help me through, or I'd end up slitting my wrists.'

She looked over at Jason.

'Still, this meeting has been more eventful than usual,' she admitted, pulling out her tiny silver box from the inside pocket, opening it up and taking one tablet out, popping it into her mouth and swallowing, without the need of water.

'Ah, that's the good stuff,' she smiled, offering the box around. 'Anyone want some? No?'

Eddie had been watching the conversation intently, but now rose from his chair, walking past Miles, over to the corner of the room, staring up at the hidden camera in the corner.

'He's been watching us through this all along,' he said. 'Balls to the sniper rifle. He didn't need it. Miles gave him a fucking guest pass to the meeting.'

He turned back to Miles.

'No audio, right?'

'He can't hear us, if that's what you're thinking,' Miles shook his head. 'In here, I made sure the cameras never had microphones. Or are you worried about something else?'

'Like what?' Eddie moved towards the CEO now, his body language more feral, like a tiger stalking his prey. 'Go on.'

'Like what you did in here,' Miles folded his arms defiantly. 'You know that time when you spoke to Ryan by the window; an hour before he died.'

'You were in here with Ryan?' Devin frowned. 'Why would you be in here?'

'It was personal,' Eddie spat. 'And we came in here because Ryan wanted to talk where nobody else came.'

He looked at Victoria.

'Unless they were filling their boots,' he added, as Victoria gave him the finger.

Ignoring this, Eddie crouched down, picking up the blade from where it'd been thrown, after Hayley had pulled it out. Now, rising back up, blade in hand, Eddie stared at Miles.

'What are you doing?' Miles looked horrified at the knife in Eddie's hand.

'Confirming a theory,' Eddie said calmly, pointing the knife at Miles. 'He can't hear us, but he can see us. If he can hear us, he'll know I'm doing this for show, and he'll call my bluff, wait me out. But if he can't, then all he's seeing is me, angry, with a knife, about to gut his CEO—'

He stopped, smiling as the red laser dot appeared on his chest.

'And there's the warning,' he smiled. 'The "drop the weapon" or the "stop whatever you're doing" warning.'

Tossing the blade onto the side cabinet, Eddie held his hands up to the window to show they were clean.

A second later, the red dot winked off.

'Ryan was a whistle-blower,' Eddie continued now, walking back to his seat, outwardly calm, but obviously forcing himself to hold everything together. 'I'd known him since college, even brought him over here when I was hired. He was twitchy after Neil Haskell died, saying it was too convenient, that Neil had been drunkenly spouting his mouth off, saying how we needed to pay for what we did at Mercy – what *he* did, even - and after the crash, Ryan decided he wanted an exit plan that *didn't* involve being offed. So, he contacted the FBI, offering to tell them about how we deliberately left the pipe-cladding to fail, how we ... well, how we allowed the other stuff, too.'

'You *what?*' Victoria turned to face him now, leaning forward as she continued. 'He was grassing on us and you knew it? And you decided to only tell us about it now?'

'There was no need to make it public, because I talked him out of it,' Eddie replied. 'In here.'

'You did nothing of the sort,' Miles muttered. 'You threatened him.'

'I thought you couldn't hear what we said?'

'I didn't need to!' Miles laughed. 'Gregson was checking the feeds and called me to come see it. You had your hands around the poor bastard's neck, and you had him against that window, a foot off the ground!'

'As I said,' Eddie replied calmly. 'I talked him out of it.'

'You talked him into jumping from the roof an hour later,' Devin stated, before looking back at Miles. 'Hold on. Corey Gregson had access to the CCTV?'

'Yes.'

'Why Gregson?'

'Because I trusted him a damn sight more than I trust all of you bastards,' Miles sniffed. 'I'd worked with him in our old company. When I was established here, I made a case to poach him. An ally for when I had to face the Board.'

He smiled.

'And he told me constantly you were a prick,' he said. 'Now I understand why.'

'Some ally,' Victoria muttered. 'Sitting next to the sniper, for all we know.'

'Gregson has access to the footage, and Mister Justice has access to the footage,' Miko nodded slowly. 'Victoria could be correct, as much as I hate saying that. There's a feeling like they're connected.'

'Are there cameras on the roof?' Tamira asked now.

'No, they're only for internal use,' Miles replied. 'Why?'

'Because if there were cameras on the roof, we'd know if Ryan jumped, or if Eddie threw him off the roof.'

'He was a friend!' Eddie slammed a fist on the table.

'Who, an hour before his death, was held against a window

by the throat!' Tamira shouted back. 'By you! It's easy to say a dead man is your friend. He can't repute it!'

She nodded to the others at the table.

'I have a confession,' she said, suddenly serious. 'Ryan and me, we were lovers. My daughter? She's secretly his.'

'Bullshit,' Eddie replied, a smirk on his face.

'Ah, but you can't prove it, can you?' Tamira settled back in her seat. 'He named her and everything. I know the rumours that I had a sperm donor for the baby, but the only sperm donated was Ryan Blake's.'

'Actually, I can prove you're lying,' Eddie sneered.

'Go on,' Tamira smiled darkly.

'Ryan Blake was gay,' Eddie replied, before glancing over at Miko. 'But *you* knew that, didn't you?'

Miko nodded.

'Corey told me when he came out,' she replied. 'Told me he had a fling with Ryan.'

She looked over at Tamira.

'And as butch and manly as you are, you're missing the one thing he'd be interested in.'

She waggled a finger between her legs.

'But I'm told medical science can work wonders these days, so keep taking the hormone tablets,' she finished.

'*Bitch!*' Tamira yelled as she launched off her chair, slamming into Miko, taking her off her own seat as they fell to the ground.

As Devin, Miles, and Hayley pulled them apart, her eyes were wild as she pointed at Miko.

'I've risked everything trying to save us!' she shouted. 'All you've done is make snarky comments! I'm sick of you!'

'You threw a phone out of a window!' Miko replied. 'How is that saving us?'

'I also sent a message to Penny,' Tamira, her anger fading,

shook Hayley away. 'Before we threw the phones into the microwave.'

'You sent a message?' Miles was aghast. 'You could have killed us all!'

'But I didn't, did I?' Tamira picked up her chair, setting it back down as she sat on it. 'And she's such a little suck-up drama queen, I knew she'd call the police the moment she got it. She's so eager to please, the thought of being able to claim credit for my life being saved. God, that's got to be giving her the tingles.'

'I thought you hated her?' Hayley frowned. 'You said you've hated all your assistants since you've been here. You called them all insipid, ambitious backstabbers.'

'I don't think that when they actually save my life,' Tamira shrugged. 'Okay, maybe a little. She thinks she'll get a promotion for this, I'm sure. But I'll probably fire her for this.'

'Why?' Miles was confused by the direction this was taking.

'She's supposed to fall on grenades for me,' Tamira replied. 'But I seem to be sitting on a pretty big fucking grenade right now, and she should have seen this coming.'

Eddie shook his head.

'And I thought I was a prick to the lower levels,' he muttered. 'You take it to a whole new level.'

'Yeah well, anyway … the police cars down there? They're here because of me,' Tamira leant back in the chair. 'You're all welcome, by the way.'

'What police cars?' Miles looked confused now.

'The ones on the street,' Tamira replied triumphantly. 'I saw them when I tossed out the phone. You could see the lights.'

'I've got one question,' Victoria raised a hand. 'Have we ever met Penny? Can we trust her not to screw this order up too?'

Devin went to reply, but paused, frowning.

'Actually, yeah.'

'She's my assistant, and although she's shit most of the time, she's not comatose,' Tamira replied. 'God, Devin, she's even sat in meetings with you, by my side.'

'Yeah, but I usually call them things like "assistant one" or "assistant two", as they're always interchangeable,' he replied, his eyebrows furrowing as he considered this. 'You know, I don't think I actually know the names of my current PAs.'

'That's a shame, as they'll be the ones releasing your public apologies tomorrow,' Miko smiled.

'I vote Miko,' Tamira suddenly said, holding up a hand. 'That's five, a majority vote.'

She looked over at Miko now.

'Bye bye, bitch—'

'I'm changing my vote,' Miles muttered. 'I'm not voting for Miko anymore.'

'You're *kidding* me!' Devin's eyes widened at this. 'What, you're going to vote for me instead?'

'Yes,' Miles folded his arms, sitting back in his chair. 'I think it's best for everyone if you take the blame. Poor Miko here was correct. She wasn't here at the time, like us. She wasn't as guilty about what happened as we were. As *you* were.'

'Bloody hell, you've changed your tune!' Victoria laughed. 'An hour ago, you were all about company loyalty!'

'Miko makes a good point, though,' Miles shrugged. 'She was correct when she likened us to people duct-taping their cars. We dropped the ball, and we deliberately didn't pick it up. We knew nobody would be able to accurately pin the blame on us.'

'You just want her to change her vote from you,' Devin muttered irritably. 'Fine. I change my vote too. I vote Miles.'

'So, why didn't you?' Eddie said, and the conversation paused as everyone looked at him.

'Why didn't I what?' Miles looked confused now as Eddie pointed at him. 'I didn't vote?'

'I'm not on about this stupid favouritism thing,' Eddie waggled his finger. 'I'm going back to what you said earlier. That we'd use cheap alternatives, and then repair it all properly once the government grants came in.'

'And?' Miles asked. 'What's your point, Purcell?'

'Why didn't we fix it when the grant came in?' Eddie continued. 'I know for a fact that we hit a profit three years ago. It was one reason Ryan was nervous. He said to me the profits were in, and we could have easily sorted it all back out, months before the fire happened.'

He stood up, the finger still pointing.

'So, tell me, Mister CEO of Wrentham fucking Industries, *why the hell did we let those people die?*'

27.39

MILES LOOKED AROUND THE TABLE.

'You know why we didn't do it,' he replied coldly. 'Something came up.'

'Something came up,' Eddie stood, shaking his head. 'Something always bloody comes up, doesn't it?'

'No, he's right,' Victoria spoke now. 'Our South African assets were drying up. Profits in Europe started falling with all that Brexit fallout. We used the grant money to shore up other holes that appeared in the system.'

'Wait, you knew this too?' Eddie looked around the room. 'Am I the only one who didn't know this?'

'You weren't in the meeting,' Devin turned to face him now. 'You were on vacation.'

'I don't take vacations.'

'Well, you were out of the office for some other bloody reason!' Devin snapped. 'Hayley, too.'

'Jesus Christ,' Hayley whispered. 'You voted without a full Board present.'

'Of course we did!' Miles thundered. 'You don't wait for stragglers when a decision needs to be made immediately!'

'It was an accounting problem, anyway,' Victoria added. 'So mister punchy and the HR queen weren't high on our list of—'

'An accounting problem?' Tamira held a hand up, shaking a finger at Victoria. 'No way. Don't you dare fucking throw this on me. You gave me numbers, not facts!'

She looked over at Eddie.

'If I'd have known the truth, I'd never have allowed it!'

'And that's why we gave you numbers and nothing more,' Victoria replied. 'At the time, we couldn't allow you to stop it – allow you to keep the money in Mercy, rather than open it up for international use. To do so would have killed the company.'

'What, instead of hundreds of people?' Eddie objected. 'You placed Wrentham above them?'

'Fuck those people!' Victoria defended. 'What's a hundred nobodies, chosen over ten thousand employees? A hundred nobodies that we could easily shift the blame on. Only an idiot doesn't take those odds!'

She leant closer.

'And you're forgetting that when we did this, there hadn't *been* a fire. There would never *be* a fire. We believed we could ride it out another year or two, easily.'

'You kicked the can up the street again,' Hayley replied.

'Yes, but we always meant to return to the can!' Miles protested at the end of the table. 'We were never just going to leave it.'

'Bullshit,' Victoria folded her arms. 'You literally just said you *deliberately* didn't pick up the ball you dropped. You never intended to fix this, no matter what we said officially. *We* never intended to do anything. We stuck our heads in the sand and hoped it went away, and when it burned down, we sent in lawyers to shut people up.'

Hayley gazed at Victoria quietly, the intensity of this enough to pause any other discussion in the room. It was as if everyone knew something bad was about to happen, but at the same time, they couldn't stop themselves from changing it.

'I always knew you were a bitch, Vicky,' she eventually hissed through clenched teeth. 'I didn't realise you were a sociopath too.'

Victoria rose to stand facing Hayley, her arms no longer folded, her hands slamming down on the table, making everyone jump at the suddenness of the action.

'You know what, Hayley? I'm sick of your holier than thou attitude,' she exclaimed. 'Sitting there in judgement. Human Resources? That's not real work! That's a goddamned part-timer's role!'

'Oh, there she is! Queen psycho!' Hayley laughed bitterly. 'Blaming everyone else for her fuckups once more!'

'Damn right I'll blame others! One reason we were in a hole was because of you!'

Hayley opened and shut her mouth twice, her face paling slightly.

'Me?'

'Yeah! You!'

Hayley looked shocked, thrown, even. She glanced around the table nervously, realising everyone was watching her, waiting to see how she'd answer this.

'And here we go again,' she muttered. 'Trying to throw blame on me before people ask more questions about you!'

'If the shoe fits!'

Hayley stepped back from the table now, shaking her head as she continued.

'That's a pretty big accusation,' she said, her voice quavering, even though her attitude was one of righteous indignation. 'You got proof to back that up before I call my lawyers?'

'With what?' Devin interjected. 'I microwaved the phones, and Tamira threw our only other way to contact anyone out of the window.'

'I meant when we get out of here, obviously!' Hayley sneered at Devin, but her eyes betrayed the fear inside her.

She was about to carry on, but Miko started laughing at this, clapping her hands slowly.

'Oh, perfect. "When we get out of here." Absolutely nailed it,' she said, slowly turning in her chair, still slow-clapping as she faced Hayley. 'Nobody's getting out of here, sweetheart. By the end of this, in what, just under half an hour or so, he's going to get bored with watching without hearing what's going on, and start popping us off, one by one. *Pew. Pew. Pew.* Or he'll blow up the building for shits and giggles.'

She waved a hand languidly at the others.

'We're eating popcorn and watching the show while sitting on death row,' she finished. 'To think anything different is just insanity.'

'Well, I don't care! I'm not having this bitch slander my name!' Hayley replied, before turning back to Victoria. 'Prove it, or shut your damn mouth.'

Victoria said nothing, staring coldly across the table.

'That's what I thought,' Hayley nodded. 'You can't prove it. You're just doing what you always do, shouting loudly and pointing blame at others before you become the next target.'

Once more, Victoria didn't reply, her lips tight.

'I'd like to hear the proof of that, actually,' a voice spoke through the television surround sound speakers, and at the sound, pretty much all the members of the Board reacted in varying methods of shock.

'I'm sorry, did I surprise you?' Justice continued, obviously amused.

'Motherfucker,' Devin grumbled. 'Looks like the phone plan was as shit as your other suggestions, Tammy.'

Tamira, in return, looked mortified as the voice continued.

'You look so surprised,' Justice said calmly. 'Did you seriously think the phone was the only way I'd be able to hear you? I've been listening to every single word you've spoken.'

Victoria looked nervously at Miles, who looked like he was about to have a stroke.

'It's amazing what people say when they think they're on their own,' Justice crooned. 'All the nice, juicy gossip starts to reveal itself. All the secrets spill out.'

Tamira slumped in the chair, beaten.

'And Miss May? Your ruse to get a message out worked, so well done you,' Justice continued. 'In fact, your little assistant Penny is downstairs right now, helping the police and the FBI with their enquiries. She's very loyal.'

There was a pause.

'I wonder how loyal she'd be if she knew the truth?'

Through the speakers a new voice spoke. Tamira, from moments before.

'And she's such a little suck-up drama queen, I knew she'd call the police the moment she got it. She's so eager to please, the thought of being able to claim credit for my life being saved. God, that's got to be giving her the tingles.'

'I thought you hated her? You said you've hated all your assistants since you've been here. You called them all insipid, ambitious backstabbers.'

'I don't think that when they actually save my life. Okay, maybe a little. She thinks she'll get a promotion for this, I'm sure. But I'll probably fire her for this.'

'Why?'

'She's supposed to fall on grenades for me, but I seem to be sitting on a pretty big fucking grenade right now, and she should have seen this coming.'

'Oh shit,' Miko looked over at Tamira. 'Looks like the president of your fan club may want to stalk someone else when she hears that.'

'Unfortunately, the chances are she won't,' Justice replied

conversationally. 'Because I'm likely to drop a building on top of her very soon. I wonder if she'll get a nice funeral if she's died on Wrentham's dime? Probably not. The deaths in Mercy didn't, after all.'

'We need more time,' Miles spoke up now.

'What, so the police can find me?' Justice asked. 'It won't matter. They've seen the explosives, too. And the FBI. They won't come near me in fear of detonation. And even if they find me, it'll be too late for you, as you've got just over twenty minutes remaining. Unless you've made a choice?'

'We had a choice,' Devin muttered. 'But Miles changed his mind.'

'Discovering you've been made a fool of does that,' Miles replied, his eyes flashing angrily. 'But I seem to recall you changed your mind, too.'

'Look, let's just get this done,' Devin sighed. 'Table vote. All give an answer, right now. Loser takes it on the chin and goes apologise, or whatever this mad fuck wants.'

He held up his hand.

'I'll go first. I say Miles.'

'I say Devin,' Miles replied. 'Miko?'

Miko looked at both men.

'I second Devin,' she said.

'Wait,' Devin held a hand up. 'What does that even mean? You second my vote? Or go against me?'

Miko considered the questions.

'Which one hurts you the most?' she asked. 'I'll go with that one.'

'That's two for Devin, then,' Miles smiled darkly. 'Not looking too good for you, you adulterous little shit.'

'If it all goes wrong, and I end up taking the rap, I want you to know something, Miles,' Devin said sincerely. 'I always felt bad about lying to you. Sure, I still stayed with Gina, because let's face it, the sex was incredible and the breasts you bought her were a chef's kiss, but I always worried how you'd react, and whether it would be the last nail in your overly high-cholesterol coffin.'

He leant closer.

'But after all the things I've learned about you today? I *really* want you to stay here, when we all leave, and go down with the ship. And I don't mean go down in the way Miko likes, I mean go down crying and screaming as this whole fucking building collapses around you.'

'How poetic,' the voice of Justice echoed around the room now. 'Currently, Mister Macintosh has two votes, while Mister Fenton has one. Ms Harvey, could you continue?'

Victoria looked over the table at Miko, puffed out her cheeks, clenched her eyes tight and groaned.

'I really want to say Miko, but I'm going to have to vote for Jason,' she muttered.

'Aw, you love me,' Miko mocked. 'Look everyone, she loves me.'

'Don't make me change my mind,' Victoria growled.

'I vote for Victoria,' Hayley said sternly. 'Because she's a drug-using, lying, two-faced sociopath.'

'I vote Miko,' Tamira said sullenly.

'I vote for Jason,' Eddie finished, staring at the body on the table. 'I know Miles screwed the company over, and God, I hate Devin, but what Jason did … it's sick. Wrong, even.'

There was a long moment of quiet.

'That's one each for Victoria, Miles and Miko, and Devin and Jason have two each,' Hayley was counting on her fingers. 'It's a draw.'

'I could veto Devin, so Jason gets it,' Eddie mused.

'Not yet,' Justice's voice echoed through the room. 'Mister Barnett hasn't given his vote yet.'

'You're kidding!' Devin shouted. 'Look at him! He needs medical help, not a vote option!'

'You're just saying that because he won't vote for himself,' Miles chuckled. 'And if he votes for you, then you're it.'

'He wouldn't vote for me,' Devin replied uncertainly. 'You're the one who stabbed him, remember?'

'I'd like to see who he votes for,' Justice reinforced his decision. 'One of you, please wake Mister Barnett up.'

'Come on!' Eddie spun around to face the window. 'This is sick! He's out for the count, and he's not in pain while he's unconscious! Let him—'

He stopped as the red targeting dot appeared on his chest.

'Oh, here we go again,' Eddie rose now, arms outstretched. 'Let's go then! Come on, shoot me, you mad bastard! Come on!'

'Eddie, don't!' Devin snapped.

'He won't, because the glass here isn't changed from the tempered glass the building was built with!' Eddie gloated. 'I saw the shards on the floor there, and he didn't have the time to change all of them. So, I reckon he wanted to make sure we couldn't run, so he changed the window in front of the door. But here, at the other end of the room? Bring it on!'

'Eddie,' Miko was looking at the window as she spoke. 'How do you know the glass is the original tempered one?'

'There's a brand mark in the bottom corner!' Eddie pointed into the corner of the frame. 'All of them have it! You can see it right—'

He stopped.

The maker's mark wasn't there.

He looked up, the red laser glinting across the street.

'Shit,' he whispered. 'He changed all the windows.'

'No, he didn't do it,' Miko contradicted.

'What do you mean, he didn't?'

'I mean that man out there, he didn't change the windows,' Miko repeated. 'It was Gregson.'

Eddie stared at Miko, his mouth opening and shutting as he did so.

'Why would Corey do that?'

'Because he wanted to blackmail us all,' Miko sighed. 'It was you and Ryan that started the whole bloody thing, actually.'

'How do you get to me and Ryan from Gregson changing the goddamned windows?' Eddie was angering now, glancing back at the street outside.

'Because Ryan gave him the idea,' Miko sighed. 'Back when he was talking to the FBI. The problem with the windows, you see, was the type of glass they were. If you changed the tempered glass to something thinner, you could get good audio from them when using a directional microphone. And although Miles put a camera in here, he didn't add sound, because he didn't want people hearing the shit he was saying in the meetings.'

'That's …' Miles started to argue, but stopped.

'Actually, that's a fair point,' he admitted. 'Why damn your own soul when you're collecting others?'

'So what, Ryan was going to change the glass?'

'Yeah,' Miko continued. 'Well, that's what he'd said to Gregson. Change the glass so the FBI could listen in to the highest level boardroom meetings, and in the process catch us talking about Mercy.'

She stared out of the window, across the street.

'Just like we're doing now,' she said. 'But then a few days later, he jumped off the roof. Or was thrown.'

'I never threw him off anything.'

'So you keep saying,' Miko shrugged. 'Anyway, when Ryan Blake died, Corey got super paranoid. He was convinced you knew he'd spoken to Ryan, and that you'd be looking to toss him off a roof next, and so he got people in quickly to take out the frames and fix them up. It was when some of you were in

Davos.'

'Sneaky shit,' Eddie muttered, glaring back at the windows. 'But this wasn't for the FBI?'

'No, this was purely for himself,' Miko admitted. 'He wanted solid blackmail information, and for the same self-prioritising reasons Jason did, but instead of shitting the bed royally like the idiot on the table, Gregson arranged to change the glass to one that people could hear through.'

'Which means he had to need an office across the street to aim the microphone from,' Eddie ran through the logistics in his head. 'Bloody hell, you are still alive, aren't you, Corey? Goddamned sneaky bastard.'

'Why did he tell you this?' Devin asked Miko now.

She shrugged.

'I already told you we'd talked. When I explained I wanted out, and showed him how far I'd go to do it, I think he saw a kindred spirit there.'

'Is this you, Corey?' Eddie asked, facing the window. 'Is this you being too gutless to face us?'

'Wake him up, please,' the voice of Justice continued.

'Go to hell,' Eddie said, pausing when the red dot appeared on his chest once more. 'We want to speak to Corey.'

'Your faith in the strength of this glass is gone, Mister Purcell, so are you sure you want to push me further, now you know the bullet will easily cut through this window?' Justice asked. 'Wake. Him. Up.'

Justice's voice was cold, emotionless. The conversational style he'd had before was now gone. Swallowing, and conceding the moment, Eddie nodded.

'Hayley, could you …?' he whispered. As he did so, the dot disappeared, once more winking off, and he slumped back into the chair, swearing softly to himself.

'"And lo, the mighty warrior faced death, and found

himself wanting",' Miles intoned quietly. 'Don't be too hard on yourself. We all want to live, after all.'

'Jason, can you hear me?' Hayley was lightly shaking Jason now, watching him carefully as she shook a little harder. 'Jason, it's Hayley. You need to wake up now. We need you.'

'Need … why …'

'You need to make your voting choice now,' Hayley continued soothingly. 'Just tell us who you want to vote out, and we'll let you go back to sleep. Deal?'

Jason nodded, his eyes still clenched tight.

'It hurts …' he moaned.

Glancing balefully at Victoria, Hayley forced her voice to calm again.

'I know,' she cooed. 'But who do you want to vote for? We're tied between two, it's—'

'Don't you fucking dare rig this vote!' Devin shouted. 'Don't give him options! Let him choose for himself!'

'Fine,' Hayley pouted, leaning back down, whispering into Jason's ear. 'Jason, we need to know which of all of us you want to pay the price.'

Slowly, Jason opened his eyes and, with his expression showing the intense pain it took, he rose to his elbows, taking the opportunity to look around the table, focusing on each member, one by one.

'What's … the tally?' he asked.

'Don't tell him that, it'll influence him,' Devin repeated.

Eddie, however, leant closer to Jason as he glanced over at Devin.

'Bullshit,' he said. 'We all heard the votes, and we all voted accordingly, so he should get the same rights.'

He looked back at Jason, his face hardening.

'Victoria, Miles and Miko have one each, and you and Devin are tied at two,' he said. 'So—'

'That's enough!' Devin shouted. 'You told him what you wanted to tell him.'

'No, actually I didn't, and if you interrupt me again, I'll throw you out of the goddamned window,' Eddie snarled at Devin before looking back at Jason.

'So you know,' he spoke coldly, 'I was one of the two that voted for you. I think you're sick. And I think you need help. But I don't want to be the one that actually helps you get that – I'd rather be the person who sees you *burn*. Understand?'

Quietly, and with a small amount of pain clear on his face, Jason nodded.

'Now tell us who you're bloody voting for,' Devin sighed.

'Miles.'

The room looked at Miles, who frowned.

'Me?' he questioned. 'Why me?'

'There's so many reasons,' Miko mocked.

'Because … you stabbed … me.'

'Sure, but that was an accident!' Miles spluttered. 'What about Victoria? She set you on fire! She burnt you! Why am I being punished?'

Jason nodded at this, a small, tight nod, before releasing a pent-up breath.

'Because … Victoria … well, I deserved it,' he whispered.

'Great. Hear the great martyr to the cause,' Miles shook his head. 'Giving us his wasted vote.'

'Wasted in this round,' Hayley said, standing. 'The count is two for Devin, two for Jason. So, Devin, Tamira, Jason and I, as people who didn't vote for them before, enter the second round of voting, the subjects being Devin and Jason. Who—'

'Wait a moment!' Devin held his hands up. 'That's unfair! What if someone wanted to change their vote for someone else?'

'It's how the British Governments choose their party leaders,' Hayley protested. 'You weed out the lesser-needed people, and then you vote for the top two. If they're in power, and the current Prime Minister quits, that's how they also pick the new one.'

'Yeah, but that's with people who *want* the job!' Devin protested. 'This is different! And we're not in bloody Britain!'

'What, so you want to do it like we do here?' Victoria chuckled. 'Did you see how many times the last Speaker of the House votes took before they had a decision?'

'Not everyone has voted,' Eddie whispered.

'Of course they have,' Hayley looked around the room. 'The dead secretary outside doesn't get one.'

'Gregson hasn't voted,' Eddie replied.

'Gregson's dead!' Hayley frowned at this. 'The man—'

'What, the strange, unknown man, who knows so much of what Gregson knows, told us he was dead, so we obviously believe it?' Eddie spun back to the window. 'We need proof of death.'

There was a silence from the other end of the conversation.

'I know you can hear us, with your microphone, the one Gregson spoke of,' Eddie continued.

'That's why you shot the window, wasn't it? Far better to listen through an opening.'

Again, silence. Eddie looked over at Tamira.

'That's how he could hear us when you tossed the phone,' he said. 'Hacked into the visuals Miles kindly placed in for him, while earwigging across the street.'

'You're correct, Mister Purcell,' Justice finally agreed. 'But Mister Gregson is unfortunately unavailable—'

'*Bullshit!*' Eddie screamed, and even Justice paused, so surprised was he at the interruption. 'You have the TV under your control, you're obviously tech-savvy, so show us a photo. A video. Anything that proves Gregson is dead! Otherwise I use my goddamned veto!'

There was a long pause, and then a slight chuckle.

'He isn't dead,' Justice admitted. 'Yet. You're right. I needed him for what he could give me. And, as he's just as guilty as you for the crimes, perhaps his vote should be heard.'

'So, you agree that he's still a current Board member?' Eddie asked.

'I will accept that.'

'Good.' Eddie nodded at the others. 'Then I change my vote. I now vote for Corey Gregson to be the person sent out.'

Nobody said anything for a long moment.

'Oh, clever,' Miles said, a smile breaking out on his face. 'Yes. I too vote for—'

'Unfortunately, although Mister Gregson will give his vote, he cannot attend any press conferences, as his time on this planet is finite,' Justice replied.

'Or he's helping you do this,' Tamira muttered.

Justice, however, didn't answer this.

'You just don't like us beating you at your own game,' Eddie muttered. 'If it's between anyone and Gregson, I'll veto them off the list.'

'The important point here, Mister Purcell, is that it is indeed my game,' Justice replied sharply. 'And regardless of your veto, I make the rules. Now finish the voting, please.'

'Right then,' Hayley continued after a moment. 'Devin and Jason are in the lead.'

'And we said this is a stupid way to take a vote,' Devin muttered.

'Well, as the HR director, I think this would be the safest and most sensible way to do this,' Hayley said dismissively, looking at the others. 'Now, I—'

'*No!*'

Victoria slammed her hands on the table, leaping to her feet, the chair clattering to the floor behind her as she now pointed at Hayley.

'Right from the very start, she's been playing us,' she

accused. 'She's avoided all questions as to what her terrible secret was, and she moved on every conversation when a chance to vote for her was given.'

'That's because I don't have secrets as terrible as you!' Hayley replied angrily. 'Miles, please, tell them—'

'We ended up having to go for cheaper alternatives, because we were short of funds,' Victoria interrupted, leaning over the table, almost leaping across at Hayley. 'That's why the disaster at Mercy Falls happened.'

'We've already gone over this,' Eddie replied. 'How is this relevant?'

'Because the reason for losing funds, the shortfall in revenue and the decision to alter the costs wasn't through mismanagement,' Victoria pointed her finger once more at the now worried Hayley, backing away from the table. 'It was down to Hayley goddamned Moran, and the millions of dollars she stole from Wrentham Industries.'

Hayley let out a terrified sob, as the others around the table turned between her and the triumphant Victoria.

Who, the point now made, turned around, picked up her chair from the floor and, adjusting her mink coat, sat back down, leaning back into it, clasping her hands together as she looked at the others in the room.

'So how about we take another vote?' she asked pleasantly.

NEWS VANS

On the street below the building, Detective Koebel looked up, glaring at the news vans that approached the cordon.

'Goddammit,' she muttered to herself as she walked towards the line. The police had already stopped a small crowd that had gathered, and Koebel had been expecting the press for a while now. Wall Street closed on a Sunday night usually meant a movie was being filmed, or something bad was happening.

Both of which always brought the press.

Agent Hawthorne, appearing out of nowhere like Marley's Ghost, walked over to her, nodding at the camera crews.

'Busy times,' he said. 'To be expected, though.'

'There's a lot more than *I* expected,' Koebel frowned. 'You think they know something we don't?'

Hawthorne nodded, but then stopped, staring at her.

'You've not been told?' he seemed actively surprised about this. 'I just spoke to your boss, McClusky. I thought he would have told you.'

'McClusky's not my boss,' Koebel grimaced at the thought. 'And he's a grade-A prick, so let's go with the idea I have no clue what you're talking about and move on from there, yeah? What haven't I been told?'

Hawthorne nodded, pointing at the news crews.

'Apparently our sniper contacted all of them,' he explained. 'Said there was going to be a press conference outside Wrentham at nine-thirty.'

He looked at his watch.

'That's about twenty minutes from now,' he continued.

'Who's giving the press conference?' Koebel looked around. 'Christ, is it McClusky?'

'I don't think we're invited to this one,' Hawthorne grinned. 'I think this is all him upstairs, raining judgement on people.'

'What, God?'

'Close enough,' Hawthorne replied. 'I'm not looking up at where we think he's aiming from, in case he's watching, but anyone who makes a room full of millionaires dance to his beat, and who expects the world's press to listen to him afterwards must have a little bit of a God complex, wouldn't you say?'

'Fair point,' Koebel said, still watching the press gather their things. 'But, on the subject of press conferences, we still don't have a ransom. Do you think this is where he tells us his goddamned plan?'

She spat onto the road, as if disgusted by the idea.

'He has to know that giving him a place to speak out while holding people ransom is tantamount to negotiating with terrorists, and we don't do that here.'

'To be honest, I'm a little unsure at the moment about what he knows and doesn't know, although I have people trying to contact him right now through the routes he used to call the press,' Hawthorne explained. 'All we can work out from the press, though, is that they were all told, in differing manners, that tonight, outside the Wrentham building, someone would talk about the Protex Oil Disaster and that everyone should be there to see it.'

'Protex?' Koebel wrinkled her nose as she tried to remember. 'Wait, was that the oil refinery disaster in Arizona a few years back?'

Hawthorne nodded.

'Apparently, there were connections to Wrentham, something to do with shorting the safety equipment. The Board is up there – well, the Board *were* up there discussing it, I think.'

He nodded across the street to the growing rabble of press.

'Apparently the biggest thorn in Wrentham's side is a reporter named Stephanie Blake, and she's just turned up with a full entourage, so expect fireworks.'

'So, if it's not us giving the conference, then who's the speaker?' Koebel was looking over at the entrance now, stroking her cheek absentmindedly as she did so. 'And do they know they're about to hold a press conference under a building wired to explode?'

'I'm guessing the sniper won't blow it up while people are getting the message he wants out there,' Hawthorne straightened, stretching his back out as he considered this. 'He asks for the press conference. He gets the press conference. Only a lunatic would then *blow up* the press conference.'

He paused.

'That said, he could be a lunatic,' he admitted. 'Although nothing he's done so far has been the work of a madman. He's been quite methodical.'

'Insanity doesn't equal chaotic,' Koebel muttered. 'I've danced with a few people over the years that have done crazy-ass things, and they've all been sane, while the coldest, and most planned revenge stories have all been from people we later had committed.'

Hawthorne nodded.

'Let's hope if he is crazy, there's a little chaos there,' he suggested. 'That way we might find a chink in the armour. Something to get through. Apparently, the speaker is a woman, the daughter of people who died in Mercy. I checked into her, and she seems legit. Arriving soon, I assume.'

'So, what did McClusky say?' Koebel returned her attention to the growing number of reporters amassing the other side of the cordon. She wasn't happy about this; already they were starting to film into the street, looking for a story, some aiming their cameras up at the side of the Wrentham building, likely informed about the phone that had been tossed from the twenty-third floor, still lying smashed on the pavement while CSI checked it for anything else.

'He says he spoke to your captain, who spoke to whoever their boss is, and they said to give this guy whatever they want for the moment, and let this woman speak to the press at the appointed time, or else they'll do it outside the cordon anyway. At least this way we can contain it,' Hawthorne replied, noting the expression crossing Koebel's face. 'You don't approve?'

'I don't approve of much of what McClusky suggests, but this is a bad call,' Koebel muttered, starting towards the reporters.

At this, Hawthorne nodded.

'Either way, it's out of our hands for the moment. We've been told by on-high, both my bosses and yours, that if we can bring this to an end, and get the Wrentham Board out of that room before they're shot one by one on live television, we give the crazy fucker his press conference.'

He paused, looking across the street.

'Shit.'

'What now?' Koebel stopped to look at him.

In response, Hawthorne pointed at the front entrance of the Wrentham offices.

'He wants the press conference there, right?' he said, waving in the general area of the plaza leading from the front entrance down the steps to the street. 'It's in plain view of his building.'

'So? We expected that, surely?' Koebel followed Hawthorne's gaze. 'Oh, shit. You don't mean that, do you? You don't mean he can see *them*, you mean *they'll* see you as you try to gain access.'

'Yeah,' Hawthorne nodded. 'We were planning to take out the power, but it'll be visible if we do it. And once that's down, I was going to take a small team in. But if any live cameras in that crowd follow us, we're going to be on national TV. Maybe even international.'

'And if he has a television on in his office, or even a live feed to something, he'll see it and be ready for you.' Koebel shook her head sadly. 'Gotta say though, it makes me feel a little less angry, knowing the FBI might screw up on live TV.'

'You want to lead the group?' Hawthorne smiled.

'Hell no,' Koebel shook her head. 'But here's something else for you. Say your sniper watches us. Surely he'll notice if you start warming up, or even putting on tactical gear? Also, what if he notices that the guy in the cap and FBI windbreaker has disappeared? You're likely to be a known face to him now, just like me.'

'I wasn't intending to do it within his eyeline,' Hawthorne looked back across the road. 'But yeah. Dammit, I can't do it.'

'Aw, are you pissed you won't be leading my armed response guys up into the building?'

Hawthorne looked back at Koebel, now smiling at him.

'You knew this would happen!' he exclaimed. 'That's why you offered your ESU people! You knew I'd end up having to step back, and your guys would get the win!'

'They'll be heroes,' Koebel smiled. 'Wrentham might give them a ticker tape parade.'

'Hey! Koebel!' one reporter on the other side of the line yelled out. 'What's going on?'

'Friend of yours?' Hawthorne asked, turning away so the reporters couldn't make out his face.

'You know how it is,' Koebel forced a smile and waved back at them. 'You visit enough brutal murder locations in a city, and you recognise the faces.'

'Nice,' Hawthorne smiled. 'Probably best not to mention the FBI-planned attack and the mad gunman.'

'You think?' Koebel looked back at the reporter, cupping a hand to her mouth as she shouted back. 'Your mom just called. She's telling the world all your deep, dark secrets.'

'Gonna be a long night then!' the reporter yelled back, laughing, as he turned back to the others around him.

The conversation now over, Koebel's smile faded.

'We need to get this finished soon,' she said. 'I've got a nasty feeling about this. And I'm worried the whole press conference thing is an angle where he can have some woman tell everyone how many boardroom members he's killed before we take him out.'

'Yeah,' Hawthorne looked up at the building. 'We need to get the reporters over to the entrance, but maybe to the side of it? They can set up, but it'd give us some space to get in from the back of the building across the street. We could do it in the confusion, while the journos are distracted.'

'Risky,' Koebel pulled out her phone, tapping on it. 'ESU won't be happy with that. But we could have them wandering around for a couple of minutes, tell the reporters they're around for the press's protection, then slip them in, and go hunt our shooter.'

'Keep the press contained, though, in case things go bad,' Hawthorne suggested. 'As you said, the last thing we want is a screwup on national TV.'

'And you?' Koebel asked. 'You're not going with them?'

'Nah, you're right. He's seen me. I'd rather keep his attention on me than become conspicuously absent,' Hawthorne smiled, stroking his moustache as he took one last look around the street, and the plaza beside it. 'So I think I'll use the confusion of the press to take a couple of your guys in through the side entrance, and start making our way up to the twenty-third floor, and go rescue the Board.'

Koebel raised an eyebrow.

'What if he's got cameras in the elevators, and he sees you in them? If he controls everything like we think he does, he might send you plummeting back down.'

'Only if he sees us,' Hawthorne shrugged. 'If we time it to go up as the power goes off, we can use the time to get up there. Or, we can just climb the twenty-or-so floors, maybe even check for connections in the elevators before we even get in. I know which one of the two routes I'd prefer. And by the time we get to the top, your guys will have sorted out the threat anyway, so we can get in there, check what's going on, and get the hostages out.'

'You really don't want the arrest?' Koebel asked.

Hawthorne looked over at the reporters, and then the other officers, before turning to face the detective.

'I don't need it,' he said. 'And being known by him aside, if I had to make a choice between going up against a crazy gunman, or finding myself in a room filled with incredibly grateful millionaires, I know which one I'd want.'

'You may have a point,' Koebel conceded. 'Take Peroni and Jeffers. They're good, and they'll listen to you without you having to explain who you are again. I'll distract the reporters for a while.'

'Appreciated,' Hawthorne checked his watch before shaking Koebel's hand. 'Probably won't see you until this is finished. Let's hope the next time we meet isn't you picking me out of the rubble.'

With that ominous warning made, Hawthorne whistled to Peroni and Jeffers, standing near the plaza, waving for them to follow him to the main entrance, as he causally walked away from Koebel and the awaiting reporters.

Koebel couldn't help it; she looked up at the building window they believed held the sniper. And, staring up into the now-dark sky, she almost believed she could make out the slightest red sliver of a laser.

Shaking her head, as if trying to shake the idea away, she walked over to the reporters trying to push through the cordon.

'Did I say you could come through?' she held a hand up as she stopped, the reporters pausing in their actions. 'You're being kept here for your own safety.'

'We were told to come!' One reporter, an older man with a magnificent, bushy moustache, exclaimed. 'And now we're being held back!'

'You were told to come for a press conference that isn't happening for another ...' Koebel checked her watch. 'Eighteen minutes or so. And, because of this, we're holding you in this safe area.'

'Safe area?' The bushy-moustached man was incredulous at this. 'How is this—'

'Listen, Ron, I don't want to argue, so I'll put it out there, clear and off the record,' Koebel replied, watching as several of the reporters, hearing this, turned off their recorders. 'See over there? That broken glass and plastic. That's a broken window from the twenty-third floor. The plastic is a phone unit, thrown from the same floor.'

'Did the phone break the window?'

'We're not commenting on an active investigation, but we are concerned for your safety,' Koebel lied, noting the slight smirk the officer holding the cordon line gave her. 'If these things fell, then other things could. And from twenty-three stories, something like a simple phone could reach terminal velocity by the time it hit the ground, which means if it hit any of you, we'd lose the ability to read any more of your amazing work.'

'Bullshit,' another woman reporter scoffed. 'In fluid dynamics, an object is moving at its terminal velocity if its speed is constant, because of the restraining force exerted by whatever it's moving through. That's only a hundred metres or so. You'd need double.'

'They take you off the science desk when they put you on crime, Stacey?' Koebel smiled, but there was no humour to it. Stacey, realising she'd annoyed the one officer who could probably stop her getting access into the scene, made a weak smile in response.

'Just saying, it might not kill us,' she said.

'Well, it'd bloody hurt,' Koebel grumbled. She'd hoped her science bluff would at least have held a couple of minutes. However, she was saved by a female officer, one she recognised from a few protests over the last couple of months, leading a young woman towards her.

'Civilians on the other side of the line,' Koebel said as she walked over. The officer shook her head, motioning for Koebel to follow her and the woman away from the press.

'This lady was told to be here for the press conference,' she said.

At this, Koebel looked up at the woman again, taking her in more fully this time. She was young, early to mid-twenties, her blonde hair pulled back into a ponytail, and wearing a black suit and pale shirt, although she didn't look comfortable in the clothes.

Either that, or she was uncomfortable being in a street with a sniper twenty storeys above her.

'I'm Kate Spencer,' the woman held a hand out, unsure if that was what was expected. Koebel, sensing the uncertainty, shook it. 'I was told to come by Stephanie Blake, one of the reporters over there, who was given my details by the sniper, apparently, for the nine-thirty press conference.'

'Until this is all over, you need to stand with the press, Miss Spencer,' Koebel nodded back at the reporters.

At this, though, Kate Spencer shook her head.

'No, I don't think you understand,' she said. 'My parents were Dan and Erin Spencer. They died in the Protex Oil Refinery disaster.'

'You're the speaker Agent Hawthorne mentioned,' Koebel nodded, finally realising who the woman really was. 'Okay, sure. Best we keep you away from the press. Do you know what you're speaking about?'

Spencer looked up at the Wrentham building as she continued.

'Yeah,' she said. 'In fifteen minutes, and according to the man who contacted Stephanie, the man up there, gaining confessions from the Wrentham Board as we speak, *I'm* the one giving the press conference. I'm going to talk about my parents, how the people in this building killed them, and how the world now has the proof.'

Kate Spencer straightened her shoulders.

'So, where do you want me to stay until it's time to begin?'

19.23

Hayley gathered her composure quickly; she knew she had to attack right now, rather than play defence. She had to keep everyone fighting amongst each other, force them towards an easier target, like Devin, or even Jason.

Surprisingly, it was Miles who spoke first, looking over at Victoria as he wiped at his lip, looking down at his finger and being surprised at the small amount of dried blood on it.

'Victoria,' he said slowly and carefully. 'I'm only going to say this once. That's a pretty big accusation you made there, and it's not the first time you've stated similar in this meeting.'

'Yeah, and the last time you said it, you didn't have the proof, did you?' Miko sneered. 'So, what's different this time?'

Victoria said nothing. Instead, she stood, stoic, looking at each member of the boardroom in turn.

'I was hoping the culprit would have a change of heart and admit to their wrongdoing,' she admitted.

However, at this, Hayley couldn't help herself, and started laughing.

'My lawyer is gonna fuck you so badly!' she crowed. 'I can't believe you tried this weak ass attempt again!'

'I wasn't talking to you,' Victoria replied calmly, taking a deep breath, letting it release slowly before continuing. 'All those years you padded up the contracts, taking the lower bids and altering them to make them look better … I bet you thought you were so clever.'

'What's this, story time?' Hayley looked incredulously around the room. 'She just knows there's a chance she'll be voted out! She's trying to save her hide!'

'If I was trying to save my hide, I'd just change my vote to Devin,' Victoria snapped back, looking over at him. 'No offence, Devin, but you're the likely candidate.'

'Over the stalker kiddie fiddler?' Devin still couldn't accept this. 'Jesus.'

'Yeah, sorry,' Victoria carried on watching Hayley. 'It's okay, Hayley. Getting small kickbacks here and there? Everyone did it. Hell, half of us here paid for their houses with these.'

She looked back at Devin and Miles.

'Or their wife's new tits,' she added, winking before they could protest. 'But these were small kickbacks. The odd five-figure deal, that was always a pleasant surprise, but never anything excessive, never anything that could truly screw anyone over.'

'How much did you take in kickbacks, Hayley?' Eddie asked.

'Piss off, Eddie! I never took any!' Hayley was shaking as she spoke, but her face wasn't reddening in anger, it was pale, scared, even.

Like she feared getting caught.

'I'd say about fourteen, fifteen million dollars' worth,' Victoria continued. 'Maybe a little less, maybe a little more. Would that be about right?'

Eddie leant closer, shaking his head.

'It's always the quiet ones,' he said sadly.

'Come on, Ed! I saw the security firms you hired!' Hayley turned to him, protesting now. 'Half of them were your ex buddies!'

'There's a big difference between favours and million-dollar embezzlement!' Eddie replied angrily, annoyed at being called out on this. 'Also, my friends? They all came from the US Military! They're the people we were *supposed* to be hitting on for security work!'

He looked over at Miles.

'You wanted cost cutting? I made sure *I* picked the best people, rather than paying out on expensive recruitment consultants!'

'Did any of them suck *your* cock for a job?' Miko snarked.

Eddie stopped his angry rant and slowly turned to face her.

'You should stop talking now,' he growled. 'You're in deep enough shit as it is.'

'Eddie!' Victoria barked now, bringing his attention back to her. 'She's doing it again, taking the attention away from her, pushing it back on the other arguments we have here.'

'I'm doing no such thing!' Hayley replied. 'I'm defending myself against your baseless accusations!'

'My accusations claim you not only took kickbacks,' Victoria said, her eyes narrowed and cold, 'but also that you placed people's lives in danger through your cost-cutting, especially when the company we hired for the Protex fire cladding was one of your bumped-up companies.'

Miko, who had been about to fire back a comment at Eddie, paused and turned to Hayley.

'Wait, the whole damn thing was because you went for the cheaper option? Because they were giving you kickbacks to get the job?' she asked.

'Yeah,' as Hayley wasn't replying, Victoria did it for her. 'We went for these cheaper alternatives because Neil Haskell, your predecessor, worked with Hayley Moran as they did their due diligence on them, and came up all smiles. They gave us a detailed report, pointing out how although they were more cost effective than the next tender, their quality of work spoke for itself.'

She looked back at Hayley.

'What we didn't know was that they were *way* cheaper. A good ten percent lower than the "cheap" tender they were giving us. And if we had known, we'd have looked into why, and likely learned how the difference between them and their next cheapest rival was heading into Hayley's pockets.'

'Don't you mean Hayley and Neil?' Miko asked.

'Neil Haskell died a few months after the Protex disaster,' Devin added now. 'Car accident, driving under the influence. It's why you came on around six months after it all happened.'

'But by that point everything Neil and Hayley had done, was all hidden away,' Victoria took over the narrative.

'But then what?' Miko argued. 'Going back to the tenders, if you found out the price was worryingly cheaper, you'd have taken it anyway; you'd have just told Moran and my predecessor there to share their "commission", so to speak.'

'No,' Miles shook his head at this. 'We would have asked for more details, we would have checked the cladding, and we would have realised it wasn't suitable for use. We would have gone for the next offer.'

'The hell you would!' Hayley laughed at this point. 'You were so busy counting pennies you never gave a shit about the dollars!'

'We would have turned it down if we knew!' Miles shouted back. 'We were desperate for money, sure, but we weren't suicidal! We knew that doing a poor job would get us – well, it'd get us right here!'

'And yet here we are,' Tamira said, softly. 'And we did this to ourselves. Hayley and Neil ripped off the company, sure, but you've already said you went for the cheapest option to cover your asses, and planned to fix it down the line. You just never did.'

'Where's all this "you" shit coming from?' Miles turned to face her now. 'You were in every goddamned meeting too!'

'I know,' Tamira leant her head against the back of the chair, staring up at the ceiling. 'I'm as much to blame as you. More so, even.'

'And how do you see that being the case, Tamira?' Victoria smiled triumphantly, looking at Miles, to see if he understood where Tamira was going with this.

'Hayley and you, going back and forth all night,' Tamira continued. 'You can't prove anything, as you don't have the confirmation you need. And with the paperwork gone, and Haskell dead Hayley knows this, so she constantly threatens her lawyers, knowing you'll eventually back down, as you can't prove this in a court of law, either.'

'Tamira, stop,' Hayley was staring at her now, her eyes widening. 'You need to stop right now.'

'And you need to shut the hell up, before I toss you out of a window,' Tamira snarled as she rose to face the standing woman. 'I thought I could outwit this "Justice," this voice of God, but I couldn't. We can't. We're fucked, no matter what happens.'

She looked at her watch.

'We've got less than fifteen minutes before the mad bastard blows us to shit, and nobody has gained any leverage over anyone else. Sure, two of us want Jason gone because he touches kids—'

'I don't,' the now awake Jason whispered. 'It was leverage.'

'Whatever,' Tamira didn't even look down at him as she continued. 'Some of us want to lose Devin because he's a prick. Or Miles because he's useless. Miko because she's a Judas. It doesn't matter anyway, as we'll vote on someone, and they can just say no. Or, with Eddie, he can literally say no because of his magic "get out of jail free" card.'

'But the Board will have voted,' Miles intoned.

'And it'll be just as useless as all the other votes we've made up here!' Tamira's voice was rising as she got more passionate. 'But, at the end of the day, we're talking about the Protex Oil Refinery disaster, not the other twenty or thirty smaller horrors we've all voted on, all of which we're getting some kind of pass on, right now, because the stupid bastard listening to this doesn't know they're going on as well!'

She looked around the room now.

'It's not about taking responsibility, it's about paying a price for penance!' she shouted now. 'Jason gets stabbed, and burned with fire, as the woman he's been stalking the child of gets revenge. Miles gets a chance to take out the man who's been having an affair with his wife, while at the same time learning of the affair in the first place, as proof he's out of touch.'

'And what's your penance, then?' Eddie asked. 'Because so far I've not seen it.'

'Mine's connected to Hayley,' Tamira replied. 'I—'

'*Don't you dare say it!*' Hayley moved closer, her arms coming up, as if to fight. 'Don't you dare throw me under the fucking bus! All this talk of penance! How is Victoria there suffering, eh? Her daughter being snapped by a paedo? The drugs she took in the meetings, the ones that stopped her caring about the terrible things she was voting for, why hasn't she had penance for that? This is as much her fault as ours! If she was cleaner, more focused in these meetings, maybe she would have asked more questions!'

'Maybe I am paying the penance,' Victoria sighed as she pulled out her silver box once more. 'Because the last tablet I took really didn't remove the buzzy little irritation you give me every time I listen to you—'

She stopped, staring at the box properly for the first time.

'This isn't my box,' she whispered.

'Of course it is,' Devin replied. 'You were taking tablets in the elevator, and in the room.'

'Yeah, but this isn't my box,' Victoria held it at him, as if expecting him to look at the box and suddenly realise the truth. 'I have petals in the corner. This has lines that are made to look like them, but ...'

She trailed off as she opened the box, staring at an inscription written inside the lid.

IN MEMORY OF THE LOST SOULS OF MERCY,
ARIZONA

'Oh, shit, no,' Victoria dropped the silver box onto the table, the little pink tablets scattering across it. 'The cleaner. Outside. I bumped into him, he picked the box up, gave it back to me.'

'You think he palmed and swapped it when he wiped the box?' Devin laughed. 'Come on, be serious.'

'Look at the message!' Victoria was pulling away from the table now as she realised the full impact of this. 'The tablets! They're not my ones! I took one earlier ... I wondered why it didn't work ...'

She spun to face the window.

'What did you give me?' she shouted. 'What did I ingest?'

'Are you worried about becoming sick, Ms Harvey?' the voice of Justice replied calmly. 'Perhaps you should have worried more about that when you allowed the children of Mercy to become ill, maybe even die.'

'What did you give me?'

'A little concoction,' Justice replied. 'Fatal if left alone. Think of all those poor Russian spies and dissidents poisoned over the years, who died after two or three hideous days of pain, because they didn't get the antidote in time.'

'Where's the antidote!' Victoria rose now, looking over at the side cabinet. 'Is it in there? What do I have to do to get it?'

'The antidote isn't in the room,' Justice explained. 'I wouldn't be so easy with the answer, would I? And don't worry, as long as you get medical help, once you're outside, you'll be as right as rain. As long as you vote for someone to take the blame, of course. And oh dear, we're close to ten minutes now. That's not looking good for you, is it?'

There was a pause.

'Number two,' Justice stated.

With panic on her face, Victoria ran over to the cabinet, pulling open the drawer marked with a brass "2", pulling out a zipped package. Without even wasting time walking to the table to open it, Victoria unzipped the bag, pulling out a small hand-held device; it was orange, rectangular and had a digital display on one side, with several buttons on it.

'What the hell is this?' she shouted at the window.

'It's a Geiger counter,' Justice replied. 'Turn it on and aim it at yourself.'

Victoria, her hands trembling, did so. There was no clicking like the ones she'd seen in films and television, but when she aimed it at herself, the number reading on the screen rocketed up, as the device squealed.

'Yes, you're not well at all,' Justice explained. 'Probably also because you've had them next to you for the last hour. In fact, all of you probably have some exposure, although Ms Harvey here was the only one stupid enough to *eat* one of them.'

Tamira looked at the possibly radioactive tablets on the table, stepping backwards from them.

'Oh, don't worry,' Justice continued. 'The time you have left is so short, there's not enough for you all to gain the same sickness as Ms Harvey now has running through her body.'

Victoria looked back to the room, the other members

ignoring Justice's advice and backing away from the scattered tablets.

'Well, now Ms Harvey has a reason for getting this to end quickly, let's cut to the chase, shall we?' Justice's voice echoed around the room. 'Miss May, please explain to the other members of the Board, just exactly how you helped Miss Moran and the late Mister Haskell embezzle over fifteen million dollars from Wrentham Industries, and in the process made sure the Protex Oil Refinery wasn't fit for usage, causing the deaths of three hundred innocent people, not to mention the children that followed it?'

Tamira looked at Hayley, who silently shook her head.

She looked at Victoria, still staring at the digital display of the Geiger counter, as if hoping against the odds that it would magically go down.

She looked at Jason, now turning to his side to look back at her.

And finally, she glanced at Miles, before turning to the window.

'Sure, why not?' she said. 'After all, it's time to go out with a bang, isn't it?'

13.20

'SHE COULDN'T PULL THIS OFF WITHOUT ME,' TAMIRA EXPLAINED calmly. 'But it was her plan.'

'We don't have time for show and tell,' Victoria interrupted. 'If Tamira claims she's a part of this, I trust her word. Especially as it proves Hayley is the one who started all this!'

'You knew, didn't you?' Tamira asked. 'You kept attacking Hayley, but it was me you were speaking to.'

'I suspected, knew she had help, but also believed you were a better person than she was,' Victoria shrugged. 'No, that's not quite right. I thought you were weaker than her. More likely to buckle, or drunkenly ram your car into a truck like Haskell did. Sorry.'

Tamira didn't reply, just shrugging in a "you could be right" manner.

'If she started this, then the whole damned mess is her fault,' Devin said, staring across at Hayley. 'I say we don't need to vote here. We can just throw her to the press. Who's with me on that?'

'Now wait one moment!' Hayley pleaded. 'I was brought into this by Tamira! It was her idea!'

'Don't you dare throw this on me, you lying bitch!' Tamira snapped. 'I'm accepting my role in this, and I'll tell the world what happened. But you and Neil were the ones who came up with the plan!'

'I couldn't pull this off without major help from accounts,' Hayley was babbling now, her voice high and fast as she spoke over her rival, trying to get her side out before Tamira could. 'The moment that Judas there heard how much we could make, she came right on board.'

'Nu-uh!' Tamira shook her head as she faced each member of the Board, realising that *she* was now the target of Hayley's story changing. 'I didn't know where the money came from! She told me she was skimming from the various funds involved!'

She looked at Miles.

'I didn't know she was putting lives at risk until it was too late,' she admitted. 'Neil didn't even realise what she'd done until after the disaster.'

'Oh, boo hoo,' Hayley muttered, for a moment dropping her guard.

But it was a pause in the attack she shouldn't have taken as Tamira, no longer discussing the point, turned and charged at her, spearing her in the mid-section, a physical tackle that sent them both to the floor in a flurry of arms and legs.

'We don't have time for this,' Victoria moaned as, rising first, Hayley took the opportunity to punch Tamira hard in the jaw, a solid blow from someone who, until this meeting, had been seen as a mousey, timid woman.

'*Bitch!*' she screamed.

Unlike the fight between Miles and Devin earlier, not one member of the Board moved in to stop this, as Tamira moved in, her shoulder hammering into Hayley's ribs as she grabbed her thighs and bodily slammed her onto the desk, climbing onto it, and punching down, her own face bleeding from the mouth, Hayley's nose exploding in blood as Tamira rained punches down onto her rival.

Eventually, Hayley threw Tamira off, the latter woman stumbling and crashing into the chairs beside the still vacated table, as Hayley, her face now a mess, staggered back to the side cabinet.

'You both made money from death. You should both face the press,' Devin said, as Hayley scrabbled past the still-stunned Victoria, grabbing the knife from where Eddie had tossed it onto the side cabinet earlier that meeting.

'Fuck you, Devin!' she shouted, as she waved the knife around, making sure anyone who came near her would be slashed by the sharp edge. 'I don't want no trouble! Just let me go and you can have the money!'

'You think we give a shit about the money?' Devin laughed at this. 'This whole damned thing is about Protex, and you and Tamira here are the reason it happened.'

'Bullshit,' climbing to her feet, Tamira replied. 'Bad voting and concern over profits caused it. Poor planning and failing to fulfil our promises caused it. People distracted with affairs, or drugs, or dead friends turning whistle-blower, or even goddamned self-interest stalking caused it, because not one of you bastards stopped this happening!'

'I wasn't here,' Miko added.

'So, you keep telling us!' Tamira shouted back. 'But we all know thanks to your voting record that even if you had been, you'd have voted "aye" to whatever Miles suggested! And don't tell me otherwise! We've already been over it! And Miles there was so desperate to keep his own bosses – these secret fucks counting their billions – happy, he just steamrollered past everything, gathering information on us all, purely to make sure his votes went through!'

'Look, I just want to get out,' Hayley was crying now, the

knife wavering in her hand. 'It's not fair! I'm not evil like all of you!'

As she said this, the television screen at the end of the room lit up. It had been quiet for a long time now, and the spark of life it made as the power turned on made everyone spin and stare at it, both Victoria and Miko jumping at the shock.

On the screen was a web browser page. There was no way to see if this was live, or a screenshot, all that could be seen was the bank's logo, a Cayman Islands address, a bank number and a single amount, in figures, in the middle of the screen.

$$\$14,439,347.00$$

'What's this?' Miles asked, looking at both Hayley and Tamira and, after receiving no answer, looking out of the window. 'I said, what the hell is this?'

'As much as I've enjoyed this, Ms Harvey is right, and time is of the essence,' Justice explained. 'And as you can see, Miss Moran, I don't need your permission to access the Cayman account where you placed your embezzled funds.'

Hayley's eyes darted from the other members of the Board to the number on the screen, and then back to the other members of the Board.

'That's mine,' she hissed. 'I earned that.'

'You earned that?' Eddie laughed at this. 'How did you come to that insane decision?'

'It's money I'm owed for having to deal with your shit!' Hayley shouted. 'That intern you beat up! Why do you think he never put in a complaint? Because I sorted it! When Tamira's assistants raised complaints against her, I was the one who reminded them of the NDAs they signed, and the hell that would land on them if they spoke! When Neil started talking about telling the police about the account, who helped him on his way? When Ryan was held against a window by you, who made it go away? I did!'

'You killed Neil?' Devin leant back in surprise.

'No! That was an accident!' Hayley moaned.

'He was drunk behind the wheel,' Victoria added. 'Did you do that?'

'Fuck Haskell, how the hell did she know about me and Ryan?' Eddie frowned, looking at Miles. 'Was she looking at the footage?'

'Corey told me!' Hayley was rabid now, spittle flying from her lips as she looked around the room. 'He saw the fight, and he wanted to have you kicked out! I told him I'd make sure Ryan didn't talk!'

'*You* pushed him off the roof?' Miko was horrified.

'What? No! Hell no!' Hayley shook her head vigorously. 'I didn't know he was going to do that, although I may have pushed his buttons a little, accidentally.'

'I'm gonna fucking kill—' Eddie jumped onto the table, and was about to leap at Hayley when a klaxon sounded in the room. It was instinct, as the Board members dropped to the floor, all convinced this was the moment the building collapsed, or the bullets started flying.

After a moment, the klaxon stopped, and Eddie looked up.

'If you've quite finished your histrionics, Mister Purcell?' Justice stated. 'I need you to climb down off the table, please.'

'She killed—'

'No, she didn't,' Justice interrupted. 'Ryan Blake was a very disturbed man who wanted to clear his conscience. Unlike all of you, he couldn't bear to be a part of this, anymore.'

'And so, he snitched on us to the feds,' Devin muttered.

'No, Mister Macintosh,' Justice replied. 'He snitched on you to *me*. Because I've been watching you for a long time now.'

'I thought you were working with Corey?' Devin looked out of the window. 'Or that you were Corey?'

'Would you like to know who made Ryan jump off the roof?' Justice continued. 'I have a video of them. Not on the roof, but from the floor below, minutes before Ryan jumped. It's enough to show you the truth.'

The television screen changed from the bank page, as a small window appeared in the middle, overlaying the page. It was CCTV footage, likely from another of Miles's secret cameras, and showed Ryan Blake walking quickly down a corridor, shouting at someone behind him.

After a moment, a second person walked into the picture, following Ryan as he exited the floor through the fire escape. He was a man in his late forties, his hair black, and, when he looked back the way he came, the camera showed the moustache on his face, before he turned back and, now sure he was alone, followed Ryan onto the stairwell, out of shot.

'Gregson?' Eddie shook his head in disbelief. 'You're telling me *Gregson killed Ryan?*'

'Yes,' Justice replied.

'Bullshit!' Devin snapped. 'Gregson was a prick at the best of times, but he'd never kill someone! And there's no video up on the roof! How do you know he pushed him?'

'Because he told me,' Justice continued. And, following this, a second voice now spoke through the speakers.

It was that of a man with a strong Texan accent. A real "Yee-haw" one, to paraphrase Devin.

'*You want the truth?*' the voice said, the nervousness clear in the voice's timbre. '*Sure, I pushed him off. He wanted rid of me, but he knew I was blackmailing Miles. I wanted access to the people in the actual room, sitting at the proper table. I'd helped him with his cameras, but Miles cut me out. And then Blake saw them while he was talking to the feds about Haskell's death, and Protex, and all that shit, and he got paranoid. He knew I'd done this, so he threatened to tell Purcell.*'

Eddie's fists clenched as he looked at the speakers.

'Gregson,' he hissed.

'*I couldn't let that happen,*' Gregson's voice continued. '*I mean, the man's Neolithic, an absolute lunatic. I didn't know what he'd do. But I knew the only person who could set him on me was Ryan, so I hounded him to the edge, made him back away to the lip of the building – and then pushed him over.*'

The video of the corridor had disappeared now, and the web page was back.

'Yes, it's all very sad, and trust me when I tell you Mister Gregson is about to gain his own penance, but we have other things to discuss, and we're almost out of time.'

'Just let me go, and I'll give you all the money!' Tamira shouted out now. 'Fuck Hayley! She set it all up, but I can get in and remove it!'

'I paid you for your work!' Hayley raised the knife. 'That money's mine!'

'Unfortunately, that's no longer true,' Justice replied. 'You see, I made a withdrawal from your account this morning.'

On the screen, the amount showing suddenly started dropping, until it stopped at a new number.

$500,000.00

'What did you do with my money!' Hayley screamed.

'I made a donation to the Mercy fund,' Justice replied. 'Thirteen million, nine hundred and thirty-nine thousand, three hundred and forty-seven dollars, to be exact. It's not quite the levels of a multi-billion dollar payout to the victims of the Protex disaster, but it does give each one of the victims' families forty to fifty thousand dollars. Which is a nice gesture until they club together to destroy you after the press conference. Oh, Mister Purcell, I made the donation in the name of Ryan Blake. I hope you don't mind.'

Hayley wasn't speaking, simply staring at the number still

on the television screen, licking her lips nervously, most likely trying to work out how to gain it.

Devin watched her, shaking his head. They had mere moments left, before the mad bastard across the street detonated the building, and she was still worrying about pocket change for some of the people in the room.

'Please, let me have the rest,' she whispered.

'Oh, sorry, I forgot to press the button a second time,' Justice replied, and in front of their eyes, the number on the screen dropped once more to a new number, now flashing on the screen.

$0.00

Hayley, staring at the image, shook her head, tears running down her cheeks as her hand holding the knife loosened, the blade falling to the floor.

'No …' she whispered.

'Miss May, if you could, number eight.'

Tamira looked confused at the command, but Devin nodded over to the side cabinet.

Slowly, and still watching Hayley in case she attacked her once more, Tamira walked over to the door, opening a large side door with a brass "8" on it.

Inside it, pushed to the back, was what looked to be an aluminium cabin case.

'Please bring the case to the table,' Justice continued.

Shrugging, Tamira reached in, pulling out the cabin case, noting the lack of wheels. Hefting it with an audible grunt, She struggled over to the desk, dumping it down onto the top as she straightened up, wincing as her back twinged.

'What the hell is in that?' she moaned. 'Weighs a ton.'

'Step away from the case, Miss May,' Justice ignored her question. And, shaking her head at whatever this madness was, Tamira stepped backwards, moving over to Victoria. But, as she did this, seeing the Geiger counter still in Victoria's hand, Tamira chose instead to move over to the back wall.

'Miss Moran. Can you take up the blowtorch that was used so expertly upon Mister Barnett, please, and turn it on?'

Hayley shook her head.

'I don't want to,' she said.

'Miss Moran, if you don't, I will ignore the last few minutes of life you have on the clock, and detonate the entire fucking building,' Justice's voice snapped. 'Pick up the blowtorch and do as I say.'

It might have been the tone spoken, or it might have been the words themselves, but Hayley now looked around the room nervously. Victoria, seeing the torch on the cabinet, offered it over. Hayley took it, although still keeping her distance.

Then, clicking the ignition, she looked to the window.

'Now what?'

'Open the case.'

Slowly, Hayley opened the lid of the aluminium case, and let out a yelp.

Inside it was a pile of money, roughly half a million dollars' worth, held in blocks of ten thousand.

'Please, no …' Hayley stared from the money to the torch, her body paralysed.

'The people of Mercy lost everything by fire – the fire you caused, in some small respect,' Justice stated. 'Now it is time for you to do the same. Use the torch to ignite the banknotes, please.'

'I swear I didn't—' Hayley either refused to move, or couldn't will herself to do so as she spoke.

'I will not ask a second time,' Justice replied coldly. 'Light the money. Lose everything, like the people of Mercy, or I will detonate this room around you.'

Hayley looked to Tamira, who, unable to keep her gaze, stared down at the floor.

Reluctantly, Hayley placed the torch closer to the banknotes, tears running down her face as the blue flame ignited the top notes, each one a hundred dollars. Within seconds, the flames licked up, some kind of accelerant on them speeding up the process. And the torch wasn't needed anymore as, watching her ill-gained money go up in flames, Hayley stepped back, the torch falling limply to her side.

Behind the fire, however, the television screen changed the image on it; gone was the bank statement page. Now, instead, were photos taken from the Protex Oil Refinery fire.

Burning buildings.

Burnt bodies.

Smoke, firefighters, the damage left behind after the flames were finally quenched.

The photos appeared in silent order, the message behind them powerful and sombre.

'We deserve everything we get,' Miles whispered to nobody in particular. 'Everything.'

Nobody replied to this, as they all watched the images pass by, hypnotised as they watched the screen.

'Now,' Justice started once more. 'With just over five minutes to go, I think it's time for the final vote. If one of you—'

The voice winked out, a sharp *snap pop* sound following it.

Devin was the first to tear his eyes from the screen, looking out of the window, across the street.

'The lights are off across the road!' he said, excited. 'The power, it's turned off! He couldn't finish what he was saying—'

And then the shooting started.

BREACH

HAWTHORNE HAD BEEN ON THE PHONE WHEN THE MESSAGE CAME through.

'Um, sir?' Jeffers asked. 'I think they're about to go.'

Hawthorne held a hand over the mouthpiece of his phone, looking out of the window. They were on the twenty-third floor now, waiting for the moment they could enter the boardroom and rescue the Board.

They'd expected there to be problems, but one of the security guards on the front desk pointed out that Mister Fenton, the man who'd placed the cameras in the elevators had an elevator he used for himself, the other end of the lobby, and on checking it, they realised this was a clean carriage. So, thanking the guard, they'd made their way up to the relevant floor, taking their time to move over to the main elevators, having bypassed the cameras.

And now, a minute later, both Jeffers and Peroni had their weapons out, but Hawthorne, still on the phone to his FBI superiors, hadn't removed his firearm yet.

'We go in when the power cuts and SWAT confirm they have the shooter,' he whispered. 'Not a moment before. I don't want anyone getting killed because we leapt in too early, and the sniper took a couple of final shots.'

'It's ESU here,' Peroni muttered.

'What?'

'We don't have a special weapons and tactics squad, or SWAT for short in New York,' Peroni repeated. 'It's an emergency services unit, instead. ESU.'

'Are they like SWAT?' Hawthorne asked.

'Oh, they're exactly the same,' Jeffers added. 'So much so people usually make the same mistake you did.'

Jeffers swallowed as he realised what he'd said.

'Not that you made a mistake or anything,' he added.

Hawthorne made a half smile, half "screw you" expression as he showed the call.

'Well, whatever they're called, you don't need to tell me,' he said. 'I've got your boss on the phone right now. I'll have a countdown given to me to prepare.'

He listened to whatever was being said.

'Actually, forget that, I think we're about to go,' he said. 'Remember, as far as we know, everyone in there is a hostage. So don't shoot at anyone unless they shoot at you first.'

———

Detective Koebel was watching the press conference set up from across the street, Kate Spencer standing beside her. After Kate had explained who she was, Koebel had immediately brought her away from the cordon and across the empty street, before any of the surrounding reporters could take control of the situation, and maybe get an advanced scoop before the others - although Stephanie Blake had tried several times over the last ten minutes to claim that as she was the one who'd brought Spencer in, she should be the one getting the story.

That, however, wasn't what the sniper had asked for, it

wasn't what McClusky had ordered, and currently the last thing Koebel wanted to do right now was rock any boats.

If the building goes up in flames, they're all going to get caught in the blast area anyway, she thought to herself. *The whole lot of them, dead in seconds.*

This gave her a little smile, as she remembered a joke she'd once been told, after her first, incredibly amateurish attempt at controlling the press.

What do you call a bus full of reporters going off a cliff?

A good start.

Sighing, she turned to face Spencer.

'Are you sure you want to do this?' she asked. 'I get the shooter wants the world to know things, but it's a hell of a risk, standing under there.'

Spencer shrugged.

'I don't really have much of a choice,' she said. 'And I don't mean like those people up there. I know they're having a terrible time, but I can't really bring myself to feel sorry for them, after what they did to my parents, my community. I mean, I've been trying for years to get someone to listen to me, and nobody gives a shit. The press won't talk about it, and you won't arrest them.'

'That's a little harsh,' Koebel replied. 'We arrest criminals—'

'Over three hundred people died at Protex, including kids,' Spencer snapped back. 'How much of a criminal do you need to be, to have the police knock on your door these days? How rich to make it all go away?'

'From what I hear, it was an accident,' Koebel said, holding up a hand to stop Spencer's response. 'I'm not saying it wasn't terrible, and I'm not saying I believe them, I'm just saying what I, as a consumer of news, hear from the media.'

She pointed across at the reporters, still setting up.

'If those people there change the story, and we learn of

things not known before, then of course the police and the FBI will look into it.'

'FBI don't give a shit, either.'

'There's an agent up on the twenty-third floor right now, who might think differently,' Koebel smiled. 'I'm sure after the – well, after whatever all of this is finished, he'll be happy to talk to you.'

She looked back down at Spencer.

'So, do you have a speech ready?'

'I've had a speech ready for years,' Spencer gave a small, nervous smile back to the detective. 'Never thought I'd be able to give it, though. All I know is that he's asked for a press conference, told Blake he wanted her to arrange for me to be on it, and he's promised them once I'm done, he'll arrange for one of the Wrentham Board of Directors to speak to the press directly afterwards.'

'How did he know you were here?' Koebel asked.

'How do you mean?' Spencer frowned at the question. 'On the street? Or in New York?'

'New York,' Koebel clarified. 'After all, you're an Arizona native. To have you here, just as he needs someone from Mercy to make a speech, seems mighty convenient.'

'Yeah, I can see that,' Spencer smiled again, but this time the expression was more relaxed, more genuine. 'I've been in New York all week at the Climate Change conference. It finished yesterday. He probably knew I was in town for that.'

'You could have flown home by now.'

'And then I guess he would have got someone else,' Spencer, tiring of this, snapped. 'Look, detective. Am I under suspicion or something? Because this is feeling remarkably like a police interview.'

'Sorry, force of habit,' Koebel replied. 'And this hasn't been the easiest of evenings so far.'

They watched the press for a moment, Koebel clicking at the roof of her mouth with her tongue.

'How do you know someone from the Board will come out?' she eventually asked.

At this, Spencer turned, surprised.

'Because that's the entire plan,' she said. 'What they've done, what they've admitted to … it's everywhere.'

She paused, reassessing the comment.

'Well, what I mean is it's everywhere, if you know what to look for,' she added.

Koebel looked blankly at her.

'What am I missing?' she asked.

Pulling out her phone, Spencer opened up a website on the browser.

'Let me show you,' she said. 'It'll explain everything, and explain why the press have turned up on a Sunday night, and are willing to risk a falling building for the story.'

In an abandoned corridor, in a glass-and-chrome building across the street from Wrentham Plaza, Sergeant Harrelson of the New York ESU, or Emergency Services Unit, stood against the wall, turning quietly to his right, looking at his three colleagues.

The original plan had been to cut all power on the entire right side of the street, so the sniper holding the Wrentham Board hostage wouldn't know for sure if he was being targeted, allowing the team to move in fast. But then, when hearing about this, Harrelson had pointed out the obvious flaw in the plan; the sniper was twenty floors above them, and in the time it would take them to run up twenty flights of stairs, the prey would likely be long gone.

Officer Montel, now standing at the end of the line,

checking his helmet, had claimed it was doable. He was an ultra-runner or something, did a lot of those "Spartan" races where people ran around deserts doing stupid assault course obstacles, and he reckoned he could make it up twenty flights in four minutes. However, this was based on times created in stupidly fancy lycra clothing and vests, and not while he was weighed down in a utility uniform and PASGT – or *personnel armour system for ground troops*, if you gave it the full name – vest and helmet, his Colt M4 assault rifle in his hand, and while also trying to keep as quiet as possible.

There was no way Montel was making it up there in less than *seven* right now. At best. And by then, the sniper would be gone, especially as Harrelson reckoned, even with their training and experience, that the other officers, including himself, wouldn't make it up there quietly within nine minutes.

And so, they had changed the plan; they knew which building he was now in, and as there was every chance the sniper knew they knew, they kept to the shadows, a small team, waiting for an opportunity to get into the building while the sniper was distracted. The press, arriving a little while back was exactly what they needed, and while the camera lights turned on, scanning the building for the sniper before the police stopped them, the ESU unit had breached the underground car park, and found their way into the stairwell.

It had been a slow journey up the twenty-three flights, but they didn't want to risk an elevator, in case these had been tampered with, and each turn of the stairs meant a pause, while they used tiny mirrors on extendable poles to see if there were CCTV cameras watching. Incredibly, they'd only found two, both turned off. This was likely because the sniper had used the same route to enter the building himself, or possibly even intended to use it as a way out, but what it meant was, although slow and careful, the team had been able to not only reach the target's floor but also enter the corridor without compromising themselves.

The plan, however, was still to cut the power; they hoped the sudden change in the situation would freeze the suspect long enough for them to neutralise him. Harrelson wasn't a dreamer, however, and he'd done enough of these to know the chances were this suspect wasn't going to raise hands and meekly be arrested, and would instead choose *death by police.*

Looking down at his rifle, he slowly and quietly checked it over. The last thing he wanted right now was some kind of weapon breach, as he aimed it at a potential terrorist's head.

'Going dark in ten,' Officer Lin said, moving her head from side to side, letting small clicks out of her neck as she loosened up.

Harrelson pressed on his neck microphone.

'About to enter the office,' he said, motioning for the others to follow him along the corridor, aiming at the office they knew the sniper to be in. They'd checked through maps of the building, and even virtually travelled through a three-dimensional mock-up on a laptop screen, but although these all led to the same location, to do it in real time was a completely different experience, as they slowly made their way through the open-plan office, the lights turned off because of the employees and staff not being in on a Sunday, rather than the power being cut just yet.

Not a sound was made as they walked towards the target office, the door closed.

Stopping outside it, Harrelson raised his hand in a fist. They knew it was a small office, and even if he was by the window and focusing across the street, a heavy footstep would surely be heard.

'In three,' Officer Lin mouthed a countdown, listening to her radio as the fingers, in the air, counted down.

'Two.'

'One.'

The lights further down the corridor winked out as the power to the building was cut, and Harrelson turned to the door, making a chopping motion with his hand.

It was "go" time.

Across the street, Hawthorne pulled away from the phone for a moment, nodding at the others.

'Get ready,' he mouthed.

Peroni shuddered, checking his weapon. This was the easier of the two jobs that night, all they were doing was running into the office and rescuing the hostages, but there was still that thought, that concerned moment where, as they ran in, the sniper wasn't yet contained, and they were shot entering the room.

'You should go first,' he said to Jeffers.

'Why me?' Jeffers growled.

'You're bigger,' Peroni explained like it was researched science. 'You have more padding—'

He stopped as they heard a sound from the stairway beside the elevators. Looking back at Hawthorne, he saw him still in contact with McClusky, likely arranging to move in, but the door to the side was opening …

He wanted to scream out *police, stay where you are*, but knew the moment he did this, the people in the boardroom would hear him, and their expressions and reactions would alert the sniper, and so he moved quickly to the door to the stairwell, yanking it open as he stared down at a terrified and sweaty Penny Martin, hands in the air as she crouched, looking up at the gun aimed at her face, having walked up the twenty-three flights of stairs.

'What the hell are you doing here?' he hissed, the voice no

more than a whisper as he pulled her into the room. Hawthorne, still on the call, looked over and shook his head in resignation, ignoring the PA.

'It's my boss!' Penny replied. 'I was the one who called this in! I should be the one—'

'That saves her,' Hawthorne shook his head, hand over the mouthpiece. 'Jesus Christ. You people.'

'Is that what you're doing here?' Jeffers walked back to Penny, leaning in close as he whispered. 'Looking for a goddamned raise?'

'Wouldn't you?' Penny pouted. 'I want Miss May to see I'm ready to risk my life for her.'

She was about to continue when Hawthorne nodded across the hallway at her.

'Your phone's buzzing,' he said. 'Make sure it's not on any kind of ringtone if you're staying.'

'I'm not an idiot,' she started back, but Hawthorne had already returned to his call. Pulling out the phone, she saw a file had been transferred to it.

Tamira_May_Quote.mp3

Turning the phone to the lowest audio setting, she opened the file, ear to the speaker, listening.

'And she's such a little suck-up drama queen, I knew she'd call the police the moment she got it. She's so eager to please, the thought of being able to claim credit for my life being saved. God, that's got to be giving her the tingles.'

'I thought you hated her? You said you've hated all your assistants since you've been here. You called them all insipid, ambitious backstabbers.'

'I don't think that when they actually save my life. Okay, maybe a little. She thinks she'll get a promotion for this, I'm sure. But I'll probably fire her for this.'

'Why?'

'She's supposed to fall on grenades for me, but I seem to be sitting on a pretty big fucking grenade right now, and she should have seen this coming.'

The recording cut off, and with tears in her eyes, Penny looked at the door.

'You okay?' Peroni asked.

Penny didn't reply, nodding at the opaque glass of the boardroom wall.

'Looks like something's on fire,' she said, turning and walking back out of the hallway, returning to the stairwell. 'You should do something about that.'

As she started the journey back to the ground floor, Hawthorne came out, looking down at her, his own phone call ended.

'You okay?' he asked. 'We're about to go in. You want to stay? Be a hero?'

'For Miss May?' Penny shook her head. 'I know every secret she has, and every body she's buried. Fuck her.'

And with that, Penny, tears streaming down her face, carried on around the stairwell and out of sight.

Hawthorne walked back into the hallway.

'Something's on fire,' Peroni said as he pointed at the glass.

'Get ready,' Hawthorne said, dialling a number. 'I'll call it in.'

The office was drenched in darkness as the NYPD ESU unit stormed through the door, almost taking it off its hinges as they moved in, guns at the ready.

There was furniture in the office, but none of it caused any kind of blockage between them and the kneeling, silent sniper, his weapon still aimed across the street.

There was a moment where Harrelson looked up, following the rifle's angle and saw into the boardroom, the members now standing around some kind of flaming box, but before he could be distracted, he turned back to the figure, the broken glass of the office window in front of him large enough to place his weapon through, but small enough to stop him pulling it out at speed to turn on them.

'New York PD!' he screamed. 'Put down the gun! *Get on the floor!'*

The figure by the window, silhouetted by the outside street, pulled the rifle back into the room, twirling it to gain a bead on them—

And the New York ESU team, having given fair warning, and with their lives now in danger, fired in response.

05:16

THE GUNSHOTS ACROSS THE STREET, THE BARKING SOUNDS OF automatic assault rifles could be heard in the boardroom, as Devin started cheering.

'Yeah!' he screamed out of the window. '*Fuck you,* you fuck!'

He would likely have said more, turning around to face the burning money, but at this point the locked boardroom door smashed open as two police officers and a man in an FBI windbreaker jacket and baseball cap burst into the room, guns raised.

'FBI!' the man in the cap shouted. 'Drop your weapons!'

Hayley, realising this was mainly aimed at her, dropped the kitchen blowtorch to the floor, the flame winking out as she released the ignition trigger.

Staring in confusion at the burning money, the man in the cap looked across at Jason Barnett, now slumped in a chair, weeping with relief.

'I'm Agent Hawthorne,' he said calmly. 'I'm here with NYPD Officers, Peroni and Jeffers. We're gonna get you out of here. Is anyone hurt? That guy looks a little worse for wear.'

'That's Jason,' Hayley said, suddenly eager to please. 'He was stabbed in the leg.'

'It was an accident,' Miles quickly clarified. 'I did it. Miles Fenton, CEO.'

'Yeah, he was trying to kill *me* at the time,' Devin glowered at Miles. 'Devin Macintosh. Asking you to arrest that man for attempted murder.'

'We can get to all that once we get you out,' Hawthorne replied. 'We need to exit the building quickly, there are—'

'Bombs strapped to the supports? Yeah, he told us,' Miko nodded. 'We're ready to go. But I wouldn't get close to the bitch in the mink. She's radioactive. Like, really.'

Hawthorne frowned at this, but nodded to Jeffers anyway.

'Call it in,' he said. 'We need paramedics at the main entrance, and …'

He looked at Victoria, still clutching the Geiger counter to her chest.

'And maybe the centre for disease control and prevention, if they're around?'

He looked back at Jason.

'Looks bad,' he said. 'Can you walk?'

'I'll help him,' Hayley, now super eager to please, was already beside him, helping Jason to his feet now. 'We'll be fine.'

'What happened?' Devin asked. 'We heard shooting. And the power went off, because he – the sniper, that is – stopped talking.'

'ESU neutralised the terrorist,' Jeffers said, a hint of pride in his voice.

'You mean killed?' Victoria asked.

'Whatever it took,' Hawthorne replied. 'Who's Tamira May?'

'I am,' Tamira was gathering her remaining things, slinging her bag over her shoulder. 'Why?'

'Your assistant was up here with us,' Hawthorne replied. 'She saved your lives. And before we went in, she was sent an audio recording. I think it was your voice.'

'Where is she now?' Tamira, looking worried, glanced through the door.

'She took the message personally,' Hawthorne replied. 'Once this is over, I'd suggest giving her some sort of promotion, because she seemed to be convinced she knew where your bodies are buried, and I got the feeling you don't want her as an enemy.'

'He's dead.'

Ignoring the conversation with Tamira, Victoria was walking towards the window. Stopping at the edge, she held out her arms as she screamed.

'*Fuck you!*' she shouted. '*Fuck you!*'

'Can we please get out of here?' Tamira, watching Victoria, asked.

'That's what I'm here for. Gather your things,' Hawthorne motioned for Jeffers to assist with getting Jason out of the boardroom, while the others quickly grabbed any personal items that weren't already destroyed.

'We have trauma teams downstairs, so once we get out we'll need to check you over and take statements,' he carried on as they gathered back together.

'We'll need our lawyers,' Miles interrupted. 'That's the first point of action here.'

'No, the first point is getting you the hell out, now the whole thing's over,' Hawthorne replied. 'Now, if you'll follow me, we'll get you to safety.'

As they exited the boardroom, it was Eddie that made the first comment.

'What the hell?'

Hawthorne, already pressing the button for the elevator, looked around at him, seeing that all the Board had now stopped, staring down at the carpet in front of the office. A carpet that, on the looped footage, had shown the head of a dead woman, a dead woman the Board members seem to have expected to see on the floor.

'What's the problem?' Hawthorne asked as he watched the elevator doors.

'The girl. The dead girl,' Eddie looked up at him.

'There was nobody there when we arrived,' Peroni replied.

'There was someone in the footage, though,' Jeffers added. 'The photo you had?'

Hawthorne nodded.

'It was looped, though,' he mused. 'They could have got up at any time.'

'There's no way she got up,' Eddie shook his head, looking around the sides of the door, in case she'd crawled away to die somehow. 'She went down right here. I'm telling you, I saw it. Saw her when I was told to lock the door.'

Hawthorne thought about this for a moment.

'This woman,' he said. 'Is this the "Donna" that you wrote about, Miss May?'

Looking at the others, Tamira nodded.

'Yeah,' she replied, her voice hoarse.

'Well, maybe she wasn't killed,' Hawthorne suggested optimistically. 'Maybe she managed to get somewhere safe? I'll have the police do a sweep. If she's injured, she can't have got far.'

'If she's injured?' Eddie was incredulous, looking back at the office as he continued. 'I saw it with my own eyes! He blew out most of her spine! She went flying forward, into the corridor!'

As the elevator *dinged* beside him, Hawthorne observed Eddie carefully.

'Did she, though?' he asked. 'We don't have anyone here, and only you as a witness.'

'We all saw her shot,' Miko added.

'Yeah, but not killed,' Devin shook his head now. 'Look around. No blood. Maybe he wanted you to think he finished her. The door shut right after, when the chickenshit there did what he asked.'

'I had a sniper target on me,' Eddie looked at Devin now. 'I seem to recall you had one on you tonight as well, and you were just as, what did you say? "Chickenshit" as I was.'

'Don't let it concern you. We'll get to the bottom of it,' Hawthorne waved at the elevator. 'Come on, we need to go now. It'll be a tight squeeze, but we can all get in.'

'Surely if the bombs go off, being in an elevator is fatal?' Miko asked.

'Miss – I'm sorry, I don't know your name?'

'Call me Miko.'

'Well, Miko,' Hawthorne explained. 'If we're on the staircase and the building goes up, we're dead anyway. So, let's try to get out faster than by foot, yeah?'

He checked his watch.

'Dammit, we're on just over three minutes,' he muttered. 'We need to—'

He stopped as he realised Eddie Purcell had re-entered the boardroom.

'Come on!' he cried out as the other members of the Board passed him, moving into the elevator.

'The glass is wrong,' Eddie was staring at the floor now. 'I should have picked up on it, but everything was happening so fast.'

'We know the glass is wrong!' Miles shouted from the elevator door. 'We already know the glass was swapped!'

'I mean the impact!' Eddie shouted back. 'If you throw a stone into a house, through a window, yeah? The glass breaks and falls inside, carried through by the force. It should have been the same with the bullet shattering this window, as it came through. All the window's glass should be on the floor, but there's not enough glass here for that. It's like it just shattered, and half fell in, and half fell out. The external force wasn't there, like the window wasn't smashed apart by a bullet, but instead was triggered to shatter--'

'Will you just give up on your Columbo shit, and get in here!' Miko shouted, looking warily at Victoria beside her. 'I don't want to be next to this glowing bitch any longer than I need to.'

'I don't know why you're all worrying,' Eddie grumbled as he walked over to the elevator, pushing his way into it. 'The prick's dead. He can't press the button. We're safe.'

'Unless it's on a timer,' Miles said ominously as the doors closed around them, and the elevator started hurtling towards the ground floor, and safety.

On the street, Koebel stared up at the Wrentham building, shaking her head.

'You dumb bastards,' she said, looking back at her phone, and the video she'd been watching, the video Kate Spencer, now preparing for the press conference, had shown her. 'You utter dumb bastards. You have no idea what you've got waiting for you.'

She spat on the floor.

'You should have let him shoot you,' she muttered, looking up at the entrance to the building. There was some kind of scuffle going on, with someone being targeted, holding their bag up to hide their face. Running across, Koebel saw it was the PA, Penny Martin, being escorted out of the crowd by an officer.

'Hey!' Koebel shouted. 'You'll get your pound of flesh in a moment! In the meantime, the next one of you who harasses an innocent girl not only gets kicked off this street but also arrested! Got it?'

Murmuring and complaining, the reporters returned to their positions in front of the entrance, as Koebel walked over to the tearful Penny, taking her by the arm and moving her away, past the officers watching the drama unfold, and over to an opposite office frontage.

'You okay?' she asked. 'The reporters throw you off kilter a little.'

'It wasn't them,' Penny sniffed, wiping her eyes on her sleeve. 'I knew she didn't rate me, but I didn't think she thought so little of me.'

'Who?' Koebel asked before nodding. 'Oh, wait, you mean Miss May?'

Penny nodded.

'I heard what she said about me,' she muttered, her voice barely above a whisper. 'It wasn't nice.'

'None of it's nice,' Koebel replied, placing a reassuring hand on Penny's shoulder.

At least that's what she thought she did, but the PA spun to face Koebel, her face now suspicious.

'None of what?' she asked, her face paling. 'God, don't tell me the clip went out?'

'What clip?' Koebel was confused now.

'The clip I was sent!' Penny pulled out her phone, showing the saved mp3 file. 'What were you talking about?'

Koebel swallowed, unsure how to move on here, looking across the street as the noise built. Once more the press were scrambling into position, already shouting out questions, but this time, rather than attacking some unaware bystander, they were now facing Kate Spencer, standing at the top of the steps that led into Wrentham's building, and preparing to start her press conference.

'Honey, that clip? It's from a much bigger thing,' she said eventually, looking back at Penny. 'Here, let me show you.'

'Room's clear,' Lin said as she finished securing the darkened office room. The lights still hadn't come back on and they'd had to use both their own torches, as well as the light from the buildings outside, which to be fair gave them more than enough to work with.

Harrelson nodded, moving close to the unconscious body now slumped, face down, in front of the window. They'd fired as one, but it had been a reaction shot; quickly taken but targeted at the torso, incapacitating rather than killing, as the shooter looked to be wearing some kind of Kevlar vest. But the power of the bullets hitting the torso would have broken a few ribs, and as far as he could see the shooter was down, but alive.

He was distracted by movement across the street – the FBI and police were now in the room, gathering up the hostages, while the metal box still burned.

Looking back, he saw a phone on a long, thin hard case, likely the case for the rifle; the screen was lit up, showing a countdown.

02:56

'Damn,' he muttered. 'The timer was almost done.'

'Is the building secured?' Lin asked, worried.

In response, Harrelson shone his torch over the case where the phone was; beside it, he saw a switch, wired to what looked like a receiver.

Slowly, he knelt, waving for one of the others to come over, shining their own torch onto it, so he could use both hands.

'This is the trigger,' he said. 'Looks like he went old school. Clock runs out, he gets an alarm, he flicks a switch, boom.'

With the torch now shining down on it, he pulled out a pair of clippers, checking the trigger switch for any surprises, before clipping one wire.

There was no beep, no click, no light switching off, and the phone timer, nothing more than a countdown app kept going, but Harrelson leant back with a smile.

'Bomb doesn't go boom anymore,' he smiled, glancing at the downed sniper. 'Ah, shit.'

'What is it?' Lin asked as Harrelson picked up his torch, aiming it at the unconscious shooter. He was slowly waking, groaning, his voice muffled somehow. And, looking closer, Harrelson could also see the jacket's front was secured by what looked to be a carabiner, to the window ledge.

'It's like he's attached to something,' he said, moving closer, carefully, making sure there weren't any other booby traps around. And, as he examined the vest, he swore again, straightening up as he looked down.

'Bring up a picture of Corey Gregson,' he said.

'Sir?'

'Just do it!' Harrelson snapped as he clicked on his own radio. 'Harrelson to Koebel. You there?'

There was a pause, and then Koebel's voice came on the line.

'Good shooting, guys.'

'Don't bring out the ticker tape parade yet,' Harrelson said, looking at Lin as she tapped his shoulder, showing him an image on her phone. 'Damn.'

'What's going on?' Koebel, only getting the audio, was concerned.

'We've examined the shooter, but I don't think it's the shooter,' Harrelson explained. 'It's Corey Gregson, the missing Board member.'

There was a pause down the line.

'He might still have been the shooter,' Koebel suggested. 'Maybe he was pissed at the—'

'Negative,' Harrelson cut her off. 'He's wearing a flak jacket that's secured to the window, stopping him from leaving.'

'Couldn't he just take it off?'

'Not really,' Harrelson was examining the rifle now. 'Someone taped his hands to the rifle. In particular, the trigger and the stock. His mouth was also taped over. He couldn't move, and when he turned to face us, the rifle came with him. It was dark … we didn't see …'

He knew Koebel understood and appreciated her not trying to say anything to lessen the situation.

'We almost killed him. He's down, but not dead, at least,' Harrelson looked around. 'And with the vest, it's like the sniper wanted him to stay alive. And there's something else. There's a laser pointer on the window sill next to it, aimed across the street. It's connected to a gimble, and a phone is attached to…'

He paused.

'Shit,' he muttered. 'The shooter was remote connected to the pointer. He was controlling the gimble, moving the laser wherever he needed it. Anyone in the room would have thought he was here, aiming at them, when he could have been anywhere with a connecting phone signal - and the poor bastard here couldn't stop it, as he was taped to the gun.'

'So, the shooter wasn't the shooter,' she said.

'No, he wasn't,' Harrelson stood up, looking around the office, as if looking for any kind of clue to tell him what was going on. 'We need to get it out there, all units. We were played. The sniper is still loose. I repeat, the sniper is still out there. And get us a medic fast, as Mister Gregson's about to wake up in a ton of pain.'

He looked up at the office across the street, seeing the last of the Board members getting into the elevator.

'Get a message to the FBI guy,' he said. 'Tell him that his day's just got harder …'

He looked down, out of the window, watching the press conference from a distance. He couldn't hear anything over the wind, but he could see the crowd.

'And it ain't over yet,' he whispered in horror.

02:09

To say the elevator was crowded would have been an understatement; currently there were eleven people in the carriage, including the two police officers and the FBI officer, and although it was only around twenty seconds in length, the journey down to the ground floor seemed to take minutes, if not hours, to Eddie Purcell.

'I need to piss,' he muttered.

'Hold it,' Devin grumbled. 'You've managed for two hours so far.'

Ignoring the argument, Peroni spoke now.

'Once we get out, you might want to call your loved ones, let them know you're okay,' he suggested.

'Yes, thanks,' Miles replied sarcastically. 'Like we hadn't thought of that.'

'You might want to go first, Devin,' Miko smiled darkly.

'Ha ha funny,' Devin replied, looking ahead at the door.

'You and Miles could both phone them,' Victoria said. 'They're probably kicking the shit out of each other in the hotel room by now. You could save the cost of a phone call.'

'You should think less about our problems and more about

your own,' Miles snapped back angrily. 'You feeling any super-powers yet? Glowing in the dark, maybe? How about rapid hair loss?'

Considering this, Victoria looked back at Peroni.

'Once this is done, I want to press charges against Jason Barnett,' she said.

'That Jason, the one being carried by my partner?' Peroni asked, nodding at Jeffers, in the elevator's corner.

'Yes.'

'Why?'

Victoria craned her head around to glare at the half-conscious sales director.

'Stalking, harassment, possible paedophilia.'

Peroni looked back at Jason, focusing on the bandaged, burned leg under tattered trousers.

'Is that why you stabbed him?' he asked.

'I didn't stab him,' Victoria looked horrified at the accusation. 'I cauterised the wound.'

'With a blowtorch,' Devin added. 'While taking way too much pleasure in the act.'

'Hold on, so if you didn't do that,' Peroni frowned. 'Then who did?'

'Miles did,' Eddie muttered.

'I was aiming for someone else,' Miles explained awkwardly at this.

Peroni looked at Hawthorne, who shrugged.

'I dunno what happens in one percenters meetings,' the FBI agent said. 'Maybe they're all like this.'

Peroni turned around in the carriage – not a minor feat, considering the crowding – and addressed the Board members.

'So, does this happen a lot in your meetings?' he asked.

Nobody answered.

Peroni went to continue, but there was a little shudder in

the carriage as the elevator came to a stop, and a ding as the doors behind him opened.

'This ain't over,' he said as he moved backwards, out of the elevators and into the back of the lobby. 'You shouldn't set fire or stab each other.'

The Board members moved out as well, but Hawthorne was staring down at his phone, a message having just appeared.

'Hold,' he said to Jeffers and Peroni. 'We wait here a moment.'

'But the bombs!' Hayley protested.

'Goddammit, I said *we stay here!*' Hawthorne looked around nervously. 'There's a door there. Where does it go?'

'It's a meeting room,' Miles frowned. 'It's for when we have visitors we don't want upstairs. We don't like it though, as it doesn't have windows.'

'Perfect,' Hawthorne motioned for Peroni and Jeffers to aim the Board members there. 'Nobody can get to you in there. We're going to take a little detour.'

'What's going on?' Miles asked.

'It's just a precaution,' Hawthorne tried to fake a smile, but he was too nervous, looking around as he did so.

'Don't lie to us, please,' Victoria said now. 'What's happening?'

Hawthorne stopped at the door to the downstairs meeting room.

'Fine,' he said reluctantly. 'I got a message as we came out of the elevator. The sniper across the street? It was Corey Gregson.'

There was an explosion of angry mutterings at this.

'I bloody knew it,' Tamira said smugly.

Hawthorne, however, held up his hand.

'But he wasn't the actual sniper,' he continued. 'He was a decoy. Hands tied to the rifle, mouth taped shut. Left there for the NYPD ESU team to shoot, thinking he was refusing to surrender, and was about to fire at them. Set up for *suicide by cop.*'

'Corey's really dead?' Victoria's eyes were wide now. 'Shit.'

'No, he was wearing a vest, but he's probably in a lot of pain right now, but this means that the sniper – the one that made your lives a misery for the last two hours – he ain't where he was,' Hawthorne opened the door, waving everyone into the room. 'He's still out there, and the game's still being played.'

The meeting room was simple in style. As Miles had pointed out, there were no windows, as it was effectively built with privacy in mind, in the middle of the building, and with no way for anyone outside to see what was happening.

Inside were three sofas and chairs, and a bank of flat screen televisions, nine in total in a three-by-three grid, currently turned off, along the wall.

'Overcompensating, much?' Hawthorne asked as he looked around the room quickly before allowing the Board members in.

'No light from windows,' Miles explained as he entered. 'We sometimes have a screensaver, like a beach, or a woodland setting on in the background. Lights up the room nicely. Helps people get comfortable.'

'Well, don't get too comfortable,' Hawthorne looked at his watch. 'I'm keeping you here for a minute or two, nothing longer.'

'Just let us out,' Victoria muttered. 'I need to see a doctor.'

'If I walk you out there, and the sniper's found another spot to shoot you from, I could lose two, maybe even three of you before he's taken down,' Hawthorne protested. 'You want to risk those odds? Stay the hell here until I can speak with the ESU team. Then we'll work out what's the next step. Yeah?'

'Still don't see why it has to be in here,' Miko complained.

'No window, no targets,' Hawthorne moved back to the door, facing the Board, motioning for Peroni and Jeffers to join him.

'But the bomb!' Devin exclaimed. 'It's about to go off!'

'There's just under a minute left on the clock, and ESU has their bomb squad in the car park right now,' Hawthorne reassured, checking his watch. 'And they cut the kill switch left in the sniper's nest. Only way the shooter could detonate now is to actually be in the car park itself. So, as you can understand, we're checking everything.'

'I feel so secure now,' Tamira mocked.

'They know what they're doing,' Hawthorne glared at the Board member. 'And it won't take them long to disconnect the detonators. Until then, sit. Stay.'

With that, he followed Peroni and Jeffers out of the meeting room, closing it behind him.

The televisions were still off, the only light in the room came from the side lamps, bathing the room in a relaxing golden glow.

'Shiiiiiiitttttt...' Devin exhaled slowly, stressing out his arms. 'This has not been the best day for us.'

'You think?' Miles was watching Victoria as he replied, her eyes darting around the room as she walked to the closest light. Using the Geiger counter on it, she jumped back as if bitten, screaming as the device beeped.

'The lights are radioactive!' she cried out to the others. 'They've left us in here to gain more toxic radiation!'

'Don't be an idiot,' Tamira walked over, snatching the Geiger counter from Victoria's hands. 'They wouldn't—'

She stopped as, now aimed at her, the Geiger counter squealed.

'That's the exact same number as I had!' Victoria exclaimed. 'Oh, Tamira, I'm so sorry ...'

But then she frowned.

'You didn't eat a tablet ...' she realised.

'No, I didn't,' Tamira aimed the Geiger counter at another light.

It squealed.

She aimed it at Miles.

It squealed.

'What the hell are you doing?' Miles exclaimed.

'She's proving it's nothing but a piece of shit,' Victoria, anger having replaced the fear she'd had a moment earlier, took the Geiger counter from Tamira and hurled it at the wall.

'*Cocksucker!*' she screamed. 'I hope they fucking kill him! He made me think I was dying!'

'So, you're not dying?' Miles was confused now.

'If she is, then so are you, because you both had the same numbers,' Tamira smiled. 'Christ, Eddie, You must be laughing—'

She stopped, looking around.

'Hey,' she said. 'Eddie's gone.'

'Bullshit,' Devin looked around. 'He's probably on a settee over ...'

He looked at the seats, seeing only a collapsed Jason sprawled on one, his leg held out straight. Performing a full circle of the room, Devin eventually stopped, facing Tamira once more.

'Oh, you're kidding me,' he whispered, as, from the door, they suddenly heard a click sound, as if the door had locked from the outside.

Hayley got to the door first, pulling at it.

'It's locked!' she shouted, hammering on the door. 'Hey! Let us out!'

'Motherfucker!' Miko shook her head in a mixture of anger and respect. 'It was Eddie all along!'

'Bullshit!' Miles exploded. 'He's been with us for years! And he's just as likely to be hanged by the press—'

'He didn't give anything up,' Jason whispered from across the room.

'What?'

'I said, he didn't give anything up,' Jason rose painfully, using the edge of the sofa to pull himself to his feet. 'Think about it. Even that bullshit with the zap ball, he said nothing. How do we even know he was electrocuted? It could have been an act.'

'What, so now you're going to comment on his ethics?' Miles shook his head. 'I won't hear—'

'*Think*, old man,' Miko interrupted. 'You me, all of us gave up a secret, no matter what it was. Eddie didn't.'

'Yes he did,' Hayley turned from the door to reply. 'He spoke of the beating of the intern. And Ryan being thrown off the roof.'

'No. *We* said about the beating. He said it was self-defence,' Miko was counting the answers off on her hand. 'And he denied pushing Ryan off, remember? Even went as far as to give us a big speech about how he was sorry, and how he actually sided with Ryan against us. And then the sniper said Corey threw Ryan off the roof.'

She looked at Devin now.

'All of us opened our souls, except for him.'

Devin stared at Miko for a long moment.

And then, sighing loudly, he walked over to where Jason stood and sat down on one of the sofas.

'What are you doing?' Hayley frowned.

'I'm sitting the fuck down. What does it look like?' Devin snapped back. 'We're in here until whenever Eddie decides, anyway, so I decided I'm going to grab a seat before you all realise we're stuck in here too, and there aren't enough chairs.'

At the back of the ground floor of the Wrentham building, away from the elevators and the main entrance – currently a reporter-led circus – were the visitors' washrooms.

They weren't as opulent or as exclusive as the executive ones, but as toilets and washrooms went, they weren't bad. And it was here, in a room of empty stalls and sinks, with mirrors behind them, that Eddie Purcell entered, checking behind to make sure he wasn't being followed.

Eddie moved into the washroom quietly and quickly, closing the door behind him. He walked over to the wall of sinks and mirrors now, finding an empty spot to stand.

For a long moment, Eddie stared at the reflection facing him; his clothes were bloody, his tie long gone, his shirt slightly torn, probably from the craziness in the room. His face, however, didn't seem to be too bad, all things considered.

He turned the tap on, taking some cold water into his hands and splashing it onto his face, staring at himself as he did this, before grabbing a wad of napkins from the side and wiping his face and hands down. This done, he took a deep breath before reaching into his inside jacket pocket and pulling out a thin black box about the size of a cigarette case.

It was a box nobody had seen before, a box he'd never shown before. And, with it now in his hands, he stared at it, turning the box over in his hands.

There was a noise outside, probably Hawthorne.

Were they looking for him?

He didn't think so, but if they were, he had to work fast.

Placing it on the counter beside the sink, he popped a catch and opened up the small black box.

With a smile, he looked into it, relaxing, his posture changing.

'Finally,' he whispered to himself, before reaching into the box and withdrawing the contents with great care.

Tamira was pacing, agitated as she spoke.

'He played us from the start!' she bemoaned. 'I bet that secretary was in on it, too. Smug little bitch.'

'How do you reckon that?' Victoria, now saved from toxic death, had relaxed into a kind of fatalistic torpor, slumped next to Devin on the settee.

At her words, Tamira walked over.

'Well, for a start, he was the one that claimed she was dead, the only one of us that properly "saw" the body, wasn't he?' she explained. 'They probably did this together. Some kind of massive, sick joke.'

'And how did he do the voice?' Devin asked.

'Voice box to disguise it,' Tamira replied knowledgeably.

'While he was in the room with us?' Devin laughed at this. 'Now that's a magic trick I could get behind.'

'I dunno!' Tamira exploded angrily, waving her arms as she continued to pace around the room. 'Do I have to think of everything here?'

'It could have been a recording ...' Jason whispered weakly. 'He knew what to say, because he'd given himself gaps ...'

'Oh, and you can shut the hell up,' Victoria said, rising to face Jason now. 'We still aren't through, me and you. I hope you have good lawyers, because mine are gonna eviscerate you. You're gonna go to prison and be adopted as the main chew toy of a big, bearded man named "Bubba".'

She leant in.

'I fucking guarantee it,' she hissed.

'On a plus side though, you'll get cuddles every night before bed,' Miko said from across the room. '*Special* cuddles.'

'Guys?' Hayley pointed at the televisions against the far wall; they were spluttering and crackling. 'Are they supposed to do that?'

'Christ, what now?' Devin moaned. 'Haven't we been through enough …'

He trailed off as the screens lit up.

10

'Oh, shit,' he whispered.

09

'No no no!' Victoria jumped up. 'The bombs! The fucking bombs!'

06

'Hey! Help us!' Miles hammered on the door, but there was no answer.

04

'I've always loved you,' Jason whispered while looking across the room at Victoria.

Who, probably luckily for him, heard nothing.

02

Victoria and Hayley, forgetting that they were enemies, grabbed hands as they watched the clock.

01

The number flicked on the screen briefly, before—

00:00

NOTHING HAPPENED FOR A LONG, TERRIFYING MOMENT, AS THE members of the Wrentham Board of Directors held a collective breath, waiting for whatever end was coming. If the building was about to collapse, the first they'd know of it would be the ground giving way, or perhaps the ceiling collapsing onto them, crushing them with the weight of thirty-plus floors of chrome, concrete and glass.

But the building didn't collapse on them.

In fact, nothing changed at all.

The screen, showing the 00:00, suddenly winked off once more, leaving them in a half-light.

'Well, that was pretty anti-climatic,' Devin muttered. 'I almost wish we had been killed, just to change the channel a little.'

'You just wanted to be killed so you didn't have to face your wife,' Miko said.

'If you want to change the channel, we can arrange that,' a voice spoke through the speakers. It was a familiar voice, a mocking voice.

It was the voice of Justice.

'You son of a bitch, Purcell!' Miles cried out. 'I vouched for you!'

Justice didn't reply to the accusation, but instead the screens crackled again, and then, one by one, all nine screens lit up, showing a news channel in the middle of a "breaking news" piece.

'Oh no,' Hayley whispered, as, on the screen, they saw the newsreader speaking, the sound not yet on, taking a couple of seconds to catch up with the video. But behind the newsreader was a stock image of the Protex Oil Refinery, and the bottom Chyron, the moving ticker of news along the base of the screen, read out a sobering message.

WRENTHAM INDUSTRIES BOARD MEETING VIDEO RELEASED

The screen changed now to a silent video of the Board, arguing in the boardroom, taken secretly from a top corner of the room, most likely Miles's secret CCTV camera.

'For Christ's sake, where's the remote?' Victoria rummaged on a coffee table, tossing some magazines before finding it, picking it up and aiming it at the screen as she turned up the volume.

'... Believed to be under the control of an anonymous hitman, the Board gave out their deepest secrets, including those relating to the Protex Refinery explosion, in Mercy, Arizona two years ago,' the newsreader spoke now, the voice loud and echoing around the room. 'What they didn't seem to be aware of, was that the whole meeting was broadcast live over the internet, with every revelation eventually now being seen by millions, after the anonymous hitman gave out the link to watch it just under twenty minutes ago.'

'Turn it off!' Devin shouted, rising from the chair. 'Turn it off right now!'

Tamira laughed at this, as Victoria turned down the volume instead.

'It's too late,' she said, walking over to Victoria and taking the remote from her stunned hand. 'It's out there. You can't put this genie back in the bottle, no matter how much money you throw at it.'

'Goddamned Eddie!' Devin snarled. 'I bet the money wasn't even real! I bet it was only ten grand or something, and the rest were dollar bills or even just newspaper!'

'You mean the money might exist still?' Hayley looked hopeful.

'I somehow don't think they'll let you have it while you rot in your jail cell,' Miko smiled.

'They might when they realise you're in the cell next to me,' Hayley snapped. 'They'll know you're fantastic at "persuading." Apparently, the whole bloody world now knows.'

'Christ, they'll know about Gina,' Miles muttered to himself.

'That's what you're worried about?' Miko was laughing now. 'Your wife? Not the fact that you told millions of people that not only did we kill those people, but you did it for some shadowy Uber-corporate Board? Christ, Miles, you won't even make the cell before they *Epstein* you!'

'Guys, something's happening,' Victoria pointed at the screen, turning the video up.

'—now go live to Wrentham Plaza, outside the very building this footage was taken from, where the daughter of one family killed in the disaster, Kate Spencer, is reading a statement.'

'How is there a press conference outside?' Jason mumbled wearily from the edge of the settee. 'Why weren't we told of a press conference?'

'Press probably turned up when Tamira called her idiot secretary,' Miles muttered.

'My idiot secretary is an idiot assistant, and she probably saved our lives,' Tamira replied before paling. 'Shit. Everything I said, she'd have heard.'

On the screen, camera footage of the press conference began, with a blonde woman facing the cameras.

'For years, my parents' death was ignored by Wrentham Industries, who claimed legal loopholes to keep them in the clear,' she said on the screen, looking straight into the camera.

'Wait a moment,' Victoria squinted, leaning closer. 'Isn't that the secretary?'

'What secretary?' Miles, not following, asked.

'How many secretaries have we talked about tonight?' Victoria exclaimed. '*The* secretary! Donna! The one shot! That Eddie claimed was lying in a pool of her own blood!'

'She faked her death?' Miles looked around in astonishment.

Devin sighed.

'How the fuck did you manage to become CEO?' he asked seriously, as, on the screen, Kate Spencer, better known as the recently deceased secretary "Donna" continued her speech to the cameras.

'But tonight I, as well as millions of others, heard the truth,' she stated calmly and clearly. 'The truth that not only did Wrentham cause the accident with their greed – caused by their own Board's personal needs – but they also lied about the repercussions of the event.'

'Shit,' Victoria looked at the door. 'This isn't a place of safety. This is a fucking holding cell.'

'And I implore our nation's police to arrest these criminals, to check through the footage of them, taken candidly, without realisation that their words had consequences, and to ensure that they cannot continue to lie their way out of yet another disaster,' Spencer continued.

Tamira went to continue the conversation when there was a

rattling of the door handle, and then a crash as the door splintered inwards, armed members of the NYPD's ESU team standing in the doorway, rifles aimed at the Board.

'Get down on the floor!' the team leader shouted, as the Board complied immediately.

'Fucking Eddie Purcell,' Devin muttered to himself as he lay down, hands now behind his head as he rested his face against the carpet.

Eddie Purcell wasn't expecting an armed response team either, as he carefully took the baggie of cocaine from the black case, placing it on the back of his hand in a long line as he snorted it deeply, before almost finishing the bag with another line for his right nostril.

I've had a shit day, he reasoned. *I need this before I get out of here. And even then, Devin will still be moaning.*

He hadn't been lying when he said he needed a piss, but his need to snort a line had taken precedent. It had been over two hours since he'd had a little tingle, and the stress of the whole damned thing had him gagging for a little piece.

And, when they'd emerged from the elevator, a force of chaos incarnate, revealed as eight Board members and three cops, Eddie had taken this opportunity to escape to the visitors' bathroom, to not only relieve himself but also *relieve* himself.

Besides, if there were press outside, he felt way happier letting the other pricks deal with them first.

He'd come out later once the pounds of flesh were taken. Yeah, that was a plan.

And so he'd pulled out his coke box, snorted down a couple of lines, and was about to put it away, when the door smashed in, and armed officers came blazing in, rifles at the ready.

'Get down!' One of them shouted. 'I said—*gun!*'

'No! No!' Eddie shouted, realising their mistake and holding the case up for them to see. 'It's cocaine! Not a weapon!'

He dropped it, allowing it to fall away as he clambered down to his knees, hands behind his head.

'Whaddaya think, Lin?' one officer asked, as a second, armed female officer stepped forward, staring down at him.

'He's no terrorist,' she smiled.

'How do you know?'

'Because he's just pissed himself in a three-thousand dollar suit,' Officer Lin smiled as she walked back to the door. 'Cuff the prick and get him out of here.'

———

In the lobby of the Wrentham building, the other members of the Board, hands cuffed behind their backs, were being removed from the meeting room as Detective Koebel, with Jeffers and Peroni following her, walked over to them, a vicious-looking smile on her face.

'I demand my phone call!' Miles shouted out to anyone listening. 'Do you know who I am? I'm the CEO here!'

'Oh, we know who you are, Mister Fenton,' Koebel turned to face him now. 'Unfortunately, so does most of the world by now.'

Turning back to the others she cleared her throat to grab their attention.

'Wrentham Board of Directors? I'm Detective Koebel,' she explained. 'You're under arrest for …'

She couldn't help it. She started to chuckle.

'Shit, man. You're under arrest for so many different things. Someone read them their rights.'

'We were set up!' Devin protested.

'That you were,' Koebel nodded. 'Didn't stop you talking, though, did it? Did any of you, at any point, think "hey, maybe telling this utter stranger our deepest corporate secrets might be a bad idea," or anything?'

'It was all lies!' Hayley exclaimed.

'Yeah, all lies, to save our lives,' Tamira, taking the comment and running with it, nodded in agreement. 'We were playing him. Trying to entrap him. In a way, we're heroes.'

'Did you trap him?' Koebel asked.

Nobody replied.

'Thought as much,' Koebel shook her head. 'Weirdest goddamned entrapment plea I've ever heard, though. But sure, you stick with that. We'll find out if it works soon enough.'

As they started being walked across the lobby, Miko struggled free.

'I'll tell you what you want if we can cut a deal,' she promised. 'I'll throw them all under the bus.'

'You goddamned Judas,' Victoria snarled.

'I'll do whatever it takes,' Miko, ignoring Victoria, continued. 'It was Eddie Purcell. He was the mastermind.'

'Really?' Koebel stopped, staring at Miko suspiciously. 'You're sure?'

'I am,' Miko nodded, sure she was getting somewhere.

'Well then, you're a shit judge of character,' Koebel nodded behind them, where, being walked by two armed officers, tears streaming down his face, his nose still covered in cocaine residue, and his trousers soaked with piss, was Eddie Purcell. 'Because he looks as far from the textbook image of "criminal mastermind" as you can possibly get.'

She looked back to Peroni and Jeffers.

'Get these shitbags out of here,' she ordered.

'What about Corey?' Devin asked suddenly, halting her.

Koebel mouth-shrugged as she considered this.

'He's had a shit night, and he's now being taken to ER for broken ribs, but when he's well enough, he'll be standing in the dock, right beside you.'

But, as the officers moved the Board towards the entrance, Victoria stopped, leaning closer.

'If you're going to do this, at least take us out through the back entrance?' she pleaded. 'Maybe the garage?'

Koebel smiled.

'Time to face your audience, Mrs Harvey,' she said.

'It's *Ms* Harvey,' Victoria couldn't help correcting, and her expression showed she regretted it the moment she spoke.

'I know,' Koebel grinned wider as she walked off. 'Time to reap your corporate rewards.'

Outside, Kate Spencer was finishing her speech, her voice cracking a little as she spoke.

'Perhaps now that the truth has come to light, we can stop other companies from repeating the horrible tragedy that took hundreds of lives in Mercy,' she said, before nodding. 'Thank you for listening.'

The reporters moved closer now, but before they could press in too quickly, the doors opened and FBI Agent Hawthorne came out, waving them back.

'Hey, hey, hey!' he cried out commandingly. 'Come on, give the girl some space!'

He looked back into the building, seeing the approaching crowd of people.

'We want answers!' a woman in her late fifties, short grey hair under a woollen beanie replied, holding a Dictaphone up.

'You'll get your real pound of flesh any moment now, Mrs

Blake,' Hawthorne replied, looking back and gently escorting Kate Spencer from the steps, walking her through the crowd, shifting a duffle bag over his shoulder as the reporters, realising the massive news scoop about to emerge, jostled for a better position.

A second later, the doors opened and the Wrentham Industries Board of Directors was brought out, handcuffed. The reporters surged around them, all asking questions, led by the jubilant Stephanie Blake. Koebel half-heartedly batted a couple of microphones away, but then decided better of it, and slipped away to the right of the crowd, walking across the street so she could watch the show from a distance.

Miles tried to hide his face as he walked past, the reporters asking him about his wife.

Victoria tried to grab at a camera as it snapped in her face, screaming obscenities as her mink coat was splattered with mud.

Everything they ever feared was happening right now.

And for Detective Koebel, it was glorious.

She couldn't help herself; she laughed. And she was still laughing when the officious-looking woman in the black suit walked over to her.

'You Koebel?' she asked.

'I am,' Koebel looked around to face the woman. Mid-thirties, hair pulled back, she looked like she could be a lawyer. 'You here for one of them?'

'I'm here for all of them,' the woman pulled an ID out, showing it to the detective. 'Whitney Miller. FBI, New York branch. You know this is our jurisdiction, right?'

'I don't understand,' Koebel said, as Jeffers, seeing the conversation, walked over.

'I'm saying it'd be nice if the FBI didn't find out about all of this from goddamned CNN,' Miller snapped.

'You didn't!' Koebel didn't appreciate the tone and squared

up to face the agent. 'So, before you kick off at anyone, check your facts! The FBI has been here all along!'

'We have?' Miller paused, uncertainty in the situation now running across her face. There was every chance she'd got the wrong end of the stick, and she was concerned she'd been misled somewhere down the line. 'Who?'

'Hawthorne!' Koebel replied. 'I think it was Michael, or Mike—'

'Mike Hawthorne,' Jeffers nodded. 'He was with us when we saved the Board. He's just escorting the woman who made the speech out of the police cordon.'

'Mike Hawthorne is doing that?' Miller's arrogance was returning. 'And he went up the stairs? When he saved the Board members?'

'A few,' Jeffers admitted, cautiously. 'But we used a back elevator.'

'Oh, that's all right then,' Miller growled. 'I had wondered how he got his *wheelchair* to the twenty-third floor.'

She looked back at Koebel.

'Mike Hawthorne took a bullet to the spine two years back,' she explained. 'He's been desk bound ever since. On account of him being paralysed and wheelchair bound.'

She looked around.

'So, please, show me FBI Agent Hawthorne, because if he's up and walking, it's a bona fide miracle! Praise Jesus!'

She nodded over to the press.

'And while we're talking about grade-A screw ups, what the hell was all *that* about?'

'One of the daughters of Protex victims, Kate Spencer,' Koebel, her mind spinning with the news about Hawthorne, replied. 'She's—'

'A *child*,' Miller sighed. 'Christ, Koebel. Didn't you even check her identity? Kate Spencer, the *real* one, is seven years old.'

'I didn't think to … Hawthorne vouched for her …' Koebel trailed off, groaning to herself as she looked towards the cordon – but Kate Spencer and FBI Agent Mike Hawthorne were gone.

It was as if they were never there.

Down the street, and away from the circus, Hawthorne looked across at Spencer.

'You okay?' he asked.

'I will be when the court cases start,' Spencer smiled, reaching up and pulling off the blonde wig, using her hand to run through her short black hair as she tossed the wig into a bin to the side. Turning down a side alley now, Hawthorne pulled off his own baseball cap, placing his shades into it, and pulling off his moustache in the process, tossing them into a waste bin against the wall. Then, quickly pulling off his FBI windbreaker jacket, he threw that in as well, pulling off and tossing in his latex gloves for good measure.

If Devin or Victoria had seen him right now, clean shaven and with nothing else on his face, they might have recognised the cleaner they walked past earlier that night.

But they weren't there to witness this, and the man and woman of many names so far that evening walked over to a black Mercedes, opening it with a key fob, throwing the duffle into the back of the car.

'How much?' the woman once known as Kate Spencer or Donna asked.

'Four hundred and fifty, give or take,' the onetime-Hawthorne smiled. 'The rest is still burning thanks to the accelerant we soaked it in. I left it up there. Nobody will work it out. And if they do, they'll just blame the Wrentham Board.'

The woman climbed into the driver's seat; the man clambering into the passenger's seat beside her, closing the door behind him.

'Call it extra commission for a job well done,' he said, as the woman started the engine. 'Where now?'

'Houston,' she replied with a smile. 'Got a call. There's a company trying to take a town from its inhabitants.'

'Then let's go,' the man said, looking out of the window at the buildings above them. 'I've had my fill of New York.'

And, as the Wrentham Board's nightmare began, the man, the woman, the money, and the car left Manhattan, their job finished.

For now.

ACKNOWLEDGEMENTS

When you write a series of books, you find that there are a ton of people out there who help you, and so I wanted to do a little acknowledgement to some of them. There are people I need to thank, and they know who they are. The people who patiently gave advice when I started this, the designers who gave advice on cover design and on book formatting, all the way to my friends and family, and their encouragement.

Editing wise, I owe a ton of thanks to my brother Chris Lee, as well as Jacqueline Beard MBE, who has copyedited all my books since the very beginning, and recent addition Sian Phillips, all of which have made my books way better than they have every right to be.

Also, I couldn't have done this without my growing army of ARC and beta readers, who not only show me where I falter, but also raise awareness of me in the social media world, ensuring that other people learn of my books.

But mainly, I tip my hat and thank you. *The reader.* Who took a chance on an unknown author in a pile of Kindle books, and thought you'd give them a go. I write these books for you. And with luck, I'll keep on writing them for a very long time.

Jack Gatland / Tony Lee,
London, January 2023

ABOUT THE AUTHOR

Jack Gatland is the pen name of *#1 New York Times Bestselling Author* Tony Lee, who has been writing in all media for thirty-five years, including comics, graphic novels, middle grade books, audio drama, TV and film for *DC Comics, Marvel, BBC, ITV, Random House, Penguin USA, Hachette* and a ton of other publishers and broadcasters.

These have included licenses such as *Doctor Who, Spider Man, X-Men, Star Trek, Battlestar Galactica, MacGyver,* BBC's *Doctors, Wallace and Gromit* and *Shrek*, as well as work created with musicians such as *Ozzy Osbourne, Joe Satriani, Beartooth* and *Megadeth.*

As Tony, he's toured the world talking to reluctant readers with his 'Change The Channel' school tours, and lectures on screen-writing and comic scripting for *Raindance* in London.

As Jack, he's written several book series now - a police procedural featuring *DI Declan Walsh and the officers of the Temple Inn Crime Unit*, a spinoff featuring "cop for criminals" *Ellie Reckless and her team,* an action adventure series featuring conman-turned-treasure hunter *Damian Lucas,* a spy thriller series featuring burnt MI5 agent *Tom Marlowe,* and is writing, under his own name, an urban fantasy series entitled *The Playing Card War.*

An introvert West Londoner by heart, he lives with his wife Tracy and dog Fosco, just outside London.

LETTER FROM THE DEAD

"BY THE TIME YOU READ THIS, I WILL BE DEAD..."

A TWENTY YEAR OLD MURDER...
A PRIME MINISTER LEADERSHIP BATTLE...
A PARANOID, HOMELESS EX-MINISTER...
AN EVANGELICAL PREACHER WITH A SECRET...

DI DECLAN WALSH HAS HAD BETTER FIRST DAYS...

AVAILABLE ON AMAZON / KINDLEUNLIMITED

THE THEFT OF A **PRICELESS** PAINTING...
A GANGSTER WITH A **CRIPPLING DEBT**...
A **BODY COUNT** RISING BY THE HOUR...

AND ELLIE RECKLESS IS CAUGHT IN THE MIDDLE.

JACK GATLAND

PAINT
—— THE ——
DEAD

A 'COP FOR CRIMINALS' ELLIE RECKLESS NOVEL

A NEW PROCEDURAL CRIME SERIES WITH
A TWIST - FROM THE CREATOR OF THE
BESTSELLING 'DI DECLAN WALSH' SERIES

AVAILABLE ON AMAZON / KINDLE UNLIMITED

THEY TRIED TO KILL HIM...
NOW HE'S OUT FOR **REVENGE.**

NEW YORK TIMES #1 BESTSELLER **TONY LEE** WRITING AS

JACK GATLAND

THE MURDER OF AN **MI5 AGENT**...
A BURNED SPY **ON THE RUN** FROM HIS OWN PEOPLE...
AN ENEMY OUT TO **STOP HIM** AT ANY COST...
AND A **PRESIDENT** ABOUT TO BE **ASSASSINATED**...

SLEEPING SOLDIERS

A **TOM MARLOWE** THRILLER

BOOK 1 IN A NEW SERIES OF THRILLERS IN THE STYLE OF
JASON BOURNE, JOHN MILTON OR **BURN NOTICE,** AND
SPINNING OUT OF THE **DECLAN WALSH** SERIES OF BOOKS

AVAILABLE ON AMAZON / KINDLE UNLIMITED

JACK GATLAND

THE LIONHEART CURSE

HUNT THE GREATEST TREASURES
PAY THE GREATEST PRICE

BOOK 1 IN A NEW SERIES OF ADVENTURES
IN THE STYLE OF 'THE DA VINCI CODE'
FROM THE CREATOR OF DECLAN WALSH

AVAILABLE ON AMAZON / KINDLEUNLIMITED

Printed in Great Britain
by Amazon

40974865R00169